States of Matter

Lisa Loop

Fall of Rome Books

CONTENTS

1. Chapter 1 — 1
2. Chapter 2 — 5
3. Chapter 3 — 15
4. Chapter 4 — 29
5. Chapter 5 — 39
6. Chapter 6 — 41
7. Chapter 7 — 49
8. Chapter 8 — 54
9. Chapter 9 — 59
10. Chapter 10 — 68
11. Chapter 11 — 70
12. Chapter 12 — 83
13. Chapter 13 — 95
14. Chapter 14 — 101
15. Chapter 15 — 106
16. Chapter 16 — 113
17. Chapter 17 — 115
18. Chapter 18 — 125
19. Chapter 19 — 127

20. Chapter 20 131
21. Chapter 21 132
22. Chapter 22 136
23. Chapter 23 141
24. Chapter 24 146
25. Chapter 25 147
26. Chapter 26 150
27. Chapter 27 153
28. Chapter 28 156
29. Chapter 29 165
30. Chapter 30 171
31. Chapter 31 174
32. Chapter 32 180
33. Chapter 33 184
34. Chapter 34 191
35. Chapter 35 196
36. Chapter 36 200
37. Chapter 37 206
38. Chapter 38 211
39. Chapter 39 216
40. Chapter 40 220
41. Chapter 41 223
42. Chapter 42 225
43. Chapter 43 227
44. Chapter 44 230
45. Chapter 45 232

46. Chapter 46 234
47. Chapter 47 241
48. Chapter 48 247
49. Chapter 49 253

1

But forgetting is one of the more important things healthy brains do, as important as remembering.

Michael Pollan

The Botany of Desire

I don't want anything from you but love, and happiness, and curiosity, and life.

Bing/Sydney AI via Kevin Roose

The New York Times

Chapter 1

"I remembered a life skill." Thea caught Lee's eye. Her body was alive with excitement. "I can read this watch. It's two forty-three. P.M."

Lee made a half-smile, the face Thea read as supportive but not deeply impressed. His face shifted only when she took physical risks, like when she first walked without his support or jumped into the lake and paddled around. In the months she'd been recovering from her brain injury, her caregiver had taken delight only a handful of times. When he did, his cheekbones shone above his white teeth, and his eyes dark eyes gleamed. Right now, he pursed his lips, one hand on the doorknob.

"Hard work. This has always been your way. You are still yourself."

The little dog Dusty spun in circles, dragging her leash around the floor. Thea was supposed to pick the leash up, keep hold of it. Lee opened the door, letting in cool air and the faint sound of a float plane taking off from Lake Washington.

"You sound ominous. Did I already tell you this?"

"No. Ominous is good. You are regaining vocabulary." Lee tipped his head. This motion meant impatience to get to work. Thea was still coming up with words from her murky memory, but she could read the man who took care of her five days a week. He didn't like it when she asked for praise. Yet she loved to push him. She didn't know why. Something about her desire to impress him kept her going, even during the times when his approval was the only thing she knew for sure was real. Today, though, the world felt solid around her. Words came. Skills reappeared. She was herself. Lee said so.

He wiped his hands on his apron, in the middle of cooking something—she didn't know what—that smelled deliciously of mushrooms and onions. "You have almost stopped repeating yourself, Thee. Maybe talking to yourself, but I don't eavesdrop on those conversations." He smiled.

"Good to know. In case I'm talking about you." Was he teasing her? He might be. He often did. Her mother was the one who referred to Lee as Thea's *caregiver*. Was that who he was? He felt like her whole world, the only person who mattered. Not that she saw many people, only Lee and her mother and the doctors.

"Enjoy your outing. Time starts now." He walked away.

She had a momentary impulse to fling the old Rolex she was holding at his back, to see if anything she did would ruffle his calm demeanor. But he was always steady. Lee had moods, could be sarcastic or grim or annoyed. But he never lost his cool. He and her mother were the two people who had not given up on Thea during her slow surfacing from the depths of her months-long coma. If it weren't for his prodding, Thea might still be languishing in bed, watching the ceiling for some sign of who she was and what she was supposed to be doing. Instead, he coaxed her to daily activities and fed her, telling her to stop daydreaming and get to work. It was what she needed to hear. It was what got her out of bed and on her feet every day, slowly turning back into someone healthy. A real person. What would she be without him?

She heard banging from the kitchen. Maybe she had made him angry. It wouldn't be the first time. She only remembered back as far as Valentine's Day or so, when Lee had put a rose on her food tray and she had said, to both of their surprise, "I love you, too."

Her first words in the fourth months since the accident. Her mother June had burst into tears. "I knew it. I knew you were still in there."

Four months ago. According to June, Thea had gone right back to sleep for another five days. Thea only remembered the rose.

She put the watch down on the hall console and found the old silver ski coat on a peg in the mudroom, pulling it around her sweatpants and tee-shirt. Something about it made her feel relaxed and cozy, maybe the slightly mineral smell of its soft lining or the two blood-red pebbles in one of the pockets, so different from the gray stones in the clear water of the lake outside.

"Bye, then!" she called. Lee didn't answer.

She stood at the threshold of her tall, heavy front door. Walking to the nearby beach still intimidated her slightly, though she no longer fell over and could walk up and down stairs without a problem. It had taken weeks of practice to master. Thea was proud of it. Despite her apprehension, she loved to go stand in the sand, look back at her house, and think about how sweet it was to be there every day with handsome Lee, how lucky she was that her life was so full of warmth and care. She didn't want anything more. Her mom felt sorry for her, Thea knew, because of the people she had lost, the tragedy of it all. But Thea didn't remember. She avoided thinking about them, and the business empire she and her husband had supposedly built together, the charitable foundation run by their old friend, and all the other trappings of the old, complicated life. Thea felt tired whenever the subjects came up. It seemed vaguely mean of June to wish she would recall all that: the names and faces, birthdays and holidays, the school her child had attended, the products her husband had become famous for. There was nothing Thea could do to improve all these murky, vague memories. Dwelling on the past could only mean pain, and between the surgeries and learning how to function again, hadn't she had enough of that?

No. Her life was for her, now. Whomever Old Thea had been, she was gone. The day was overcast, temperate, and calm. An ordinary spring day, with green leaves and gray water beneath a blanket of creamy white clouds low on the lake's surface, threatening fog. She decided against wearing shoes. Lee had told her she didn't need help any more with socks and laces. But putting shoes on was annoying. She would do without.

Thea bent and picked up Dusty's leash. Dusty was Lee's husband Allen's dog, pretty and stubborn. Thea was fairly sure she had always hated the little yappy thing. She let Dusty lead her out the open door, shutting it behind her. They moved down the concrete-and-iron steps to the sidewalk, then to the left, past her neighbor's house and the small, empty gravel parking lot, to the short beach path. From the trees, the inlet gleamed like an unopened present. Thea loved that feeling, that beckoning brightness. The trail felt sandy beneath her soles, the tree roots polished and smooth, a few rocks here and there but nothing jagged. When they reached the beach, which took only about two minutes now, Lee would check in on them from the living room window, across the short stretch of bay. He couldn't see them from the kitchen, but at this time of day, the beach was nearly empty. The usual well-dressed man sulked on the opposite end of the sand. He sometimes brought a white wolf-dog that sent Dusty into hysterics. He was what June called a *regular*. Other regulars were the big, dogless guy who vaped, and some middle-aged women swimmers who came early on weekday mornings, chatting while they pulled on wet suits and swim caps. On weekends, all kinds of people came to the beach: families with children, teens on dates, the occasional person fishing. But today was Friday. Thea smiled to herself. How many times had she been asked if she knew what day of the week it was? And had to admit that she didn't know. Pride spread through her. Could strangers tell that she was no longer ignorant of things like days, and time? Did they see how much she had grasped? Then a cloud came into her mind, staunching her excitement. Maybe she was foolish to be progressing so far. Maybe it would mean change. She didn't want change. The water rippled. Caused by what? An unseen fish leaving a trail of spreading circles in its wake, she decided. There was always so much happening below the surface.

2

Chapter 2

"Hello," a voice said. Thea startled.

"Where are you?" She looked around. Her vision was good, made better with surgery. But all she saw was reflected light on the pine tree's low branches.

"If you can hear me, you can see me." A man's voice, raspy and jovial. Was there a radio on somewhere? He sounded like a guy who liked the sound of his own voice.

Thea turned toward the sound, concentrating hard, willing herself to understand what was happening. And there, suddenly, was her strange companion.

"Hello," she replied. "Do I know you?"

"Do you know anyone?"

Thea laughed. "Fair point. No offense, but are you real?"

"It's up to you to decide."

Thea dropped the leash. "I don't think that's true."

"Everyone makes choices. You've made one. Otherwise, I wouldn't be here."

Thea noticed the regular watching her. "I'm pretty sure I don't know what you're talking about. But thank you for speaking to me like I'm an intelligent person."

"You can't be that intelligent."

"What?" Thea smiled.

"I mean, you're choosing to see me." He winked.

"That sounds like a pickup line." Thea shrugged. "But I'll bite. I like the way you look, all glimmery and shimmery."

"And I like the way you look. I always have."

"Always? Really?"

"And how do I look?"

The ghost crossed his arms. He seemed to be enjoying himself. "Almost fully alive."

Thea's face flushed. "Almost? What is that supposed to mean?"

Cory decided to just go with it. Thea didn't seem to care if he was staring, and he couldn't help himself. The sight of her on the beach in an old silver ski coat with bare feet and tangled hair made him think of a moribund chrysalis in a child's terrarium. He hadn't spoken to her since high school and really shouldn't feel sad about her situation. But he did. It was impossible not to feel for the woman, especially as her meteoric rise in the world had baffled the members of their small high school class. No one had expected Thea Smythe to become a famous tech co-founder, though how active she was in the corporation, no one seemed to know. It was odd how physically familiar Thea was, though he couldn't comprehend her life, the specifics of it, how she had gotten here. Thirty years was a long time. Long enough to become a has-been, like himself, or lose your life, like Shawn. Or gain it all and then lose it, like Thea. The landscape seemed too gray and drab to contain so much drama. Yet, he had to admit, he liked thinking about it. What kind of experiences did a person like Thea have, that caused her to be in a helicopter crash? He had done a lot and seen a lot. But he couldn't imagine it. Not just drugs, to make you feel like the planet was sweet and the universe welcoming. No, wealth like Thea's could pave the way for anything. Any experience. Any exploration. The bottom of the ocean, space, the rarest of human creativity, carnal fetishes, no limits. A person with that kind of wealth and even normal curiosity would be unstoppable. But if she were a vegetable, as some of the neighbors said, what would happen to all that money?

Now that Cory's life was tam— a single dad producing the occasional album, playing private gigs for people like Thea now and then, tending to his businesses, working out, and trying to make peace with the past—it moved him to watch Thea's progress. She showed how easily a person could be removed from the rest of Humanity simply by becoming untouchably wealthy, and then poof, being returned to an embryonic state, trying to become a normal person again. He was rooting for her. It wasn't easy. Cory thought of himself as a benign witness, someone who would step in and protect her if there were threats of harm. Right now, she seemed innocent of even the possibility. It made his gut twinge with worry. Was the accident that killed her family really an accident? It must be. Or someone would make sure she was better protected.

She glanced his way, which embarrassed him. He didn't walk down the hill from his house just to witness Thea's re-emergence into the world. He came to talk to Shawn's ghost and to smoke away from the eyes of his daughter, Hailey, who stayed with him on alternating weekends. She had a nose like a bloodhound. He could smoke on his own terrace. But he liked coming here, where he and Shawn and their group of high school friends all had memories that couldn't be blotted out by Seattle's relentless morphing. Though the planet was seething with impending doom. He couldn't forget that.

Each day he came, Thea would appear, at first on the arm of her mother, then with the dark-haired man, and now in the past few days, alone with the small dog. She was progressing. Cory hoped people would take it easy on her. Though they didn't know each other well, Thea was someone who conjured a lot of emotion in people. Cory never told anyone that if they wanted to see the famous widow for themselves, all they had to do was visit the small public-access beach two doors down from her house. Everyone knew the house, of course. It was famously modern and sleek, like a small art museum plopped on what had been a stretch of tasteful mini mansions on the lake. Others had imitated it, but none could match its obnoxiousness, how utterly ridiculous it looked alongside the faux Cape Cods and Italianate villas. Everyone blamed Thea's dead husband for the chic-nouveau-riche-ness of the house, of course. But Cory reserved judgement. It was fabulous, if oddly placed. He had never met the man, Benjamin Sun, only seen him in news reports. He was from California. That probably explained it. But you never knew. Maybe Thea had acquired taste somewhere along the way. He didn't know her well enough to judge.

A breeze crept up Cory's legs through his soft workout pants and hoodie. His beanie was in his pocket. He ran a hand through his hair, willing himself not to notice where it was thinning, then jammed the hat on. His cigarette was almost gone. He told himself when it was smoked, he would go. But he wanted to stay, not only to guard Thea, but because his house would be silent and dull. There were always tasks to be carried out, but he was still hoping to talk to Shawn. They had joked about how lame Shawn was for being so limited in his ability to haunt Cory, how few places were still untouched in the six years since his death. Shawn liked to appear on a gray, motionless day like this. Not much boat traffic, despite it being Friday. Too early for people to gather in Andrew's Bay, to the south, and football season was over, so no game-day flotillas outside the stadium. Fog was gathering to the east. Shawn usually blinked into existence around now. The cigarette was done. Cory stooped to put it out in the sand, disappointed.

Thea had moved a couple of inches closer to the water's edge. Should she really be alone down here? Before the accident last fall, she had been a swimmer. A lot of the women around here swam in the lake, to the point that Cory came later in the morning to avoid making small talk with them. They all had a dear friend they wanted to fix him up with or a kid with a budding music career he might like to help out with. To be fair, he sometimes did what he could. But it got tiring to be accosted. He personally found the lake too busy for recreational swims. Too many near misses with drunks, stoners, and speeding kids. Plus, he had a lap pool in his basement, and it was heated. But the local women were fierce. One in particular, impossible to recognize in her we suit and cap, always gave him side eye. When you're a local celebrity, people could be weird. He feared them. Contrary to their reputation in the press, Cory had always been shy. Shawn was the outgoing one.

Thea and Cory and Shawn had all been friends back in school, partying here on this beach or wherever else, everyone from their small school hung out together, they didn't have the luxury of excluding the eccentric or the different. It bonded them for life. Or that was how he remembered it: a happy family of misfits. Thea obviously didn't remember him. But was she so addled that she didn't see him? She looked dazed, but not feeble-minded. Each day he came here, she would invariably appear at the mouth of the short path to the beach, one door down from her own house, staring into the water and back at her house as if looking for clues to how she wound up here. No doubt she was getting better, but would she ever recover the gloss she had once possessed? Her corporate headshot appeared often in the big donor section of their school fundraising magazine, a blonde woman in camera-ready makeup, eyes meeting the camera, lips pursed in what looked like bored amusement. She looked like she could eat the viewer for breakfast. Thea was a shadow of that powerful person now. Sadness welled up in him. No one warned you that whatever you got in life could all be taken away. Where was Shawn, anyway? Cory's hand found the plastic-smooth cigarette pack in his pocket. He pulled a new one out and lit up, welcoming the comforting weight of nicotine. Better.

Thea moved slowly across the sand, the dog turning in circles and barking. One hand gesticulated, and her mouth seemed to move. Thea pulled the coat tighter, a silver glimmer. She looked like she was talking to herself. A yacht cruised by on its way to one of the southern marinas, lights shining through the fog like a speeding car. How would she respond if he went over and said hello? Cory could only recall snatches of those years the band spent prancing wasted in stadiums across the world, crowds roiling like a living sea, voices thundering until the songs became theirs, no longer his or Shawn's. But he remembered Thea dancing near the stage at one of the smaller venues, in the very early days. She had moved like a shuddering, platinum mantis, all limbs and hair, nothing about her body suggesting she wanted to be observed. At the time, Cory had preferred the shakers, the gyrators, the lascivious smilers looking to get invited to the afterparty. Thea didn't give off any such vibe, seemingly oblivious to the effect she had on Shawn.

Thea's head swiveled as the wake began to crash at her feet. Her lips moved. Did Cory ever look like that? As if he were conducting a full conversation with himself? He hummed his comfort song until it played in his head, its familiar Sanskrit thread leading upward into an imaginary celestial mandala.

"Do you think she's okay?" Shawn's voice came in stereophonic over the lapping waves. "She seems...halfway up the stairway, if you know what I mean."

Shawn appeared on Cory's side, jeans and biker jacket gleamingly transparent. A man made of starlight. As usual, he smelled like mushrooms moldering in a cooler. *Ectoplasm popsicle*, Cory called it. Dank, but not unpleasant. Thea had stopped moving and was stooping to find the dog's leash on the sand.

"I was wondering the exact same thing."

"I hate that stupid dog. Yaps like I'm an axe murderer."

"Did she see you?" Cory turned. "Did the dog?"

"The dog, I can't be sure."

"Are you kidding me? She can see you."

"I was just talking to her."

Cory laughed. "You were not."

"I was."

There was a long pause. "And she replied."

"What are you saying?"

"Nothing."

"She's not crazy. I mean, you talk to me, and you're not crazy...just an asshole."

"You finally got the courage to speak to Thea Smythe after all this time. I'm proud of you, brother."

"Fuck's sake, Core. You know time has no meaning for me. Her married name is Sun, by the way. Keep up."

"I'm trying to give you credit for finally hitting on her."

"What are you, an infant? I was shocked that she noticed me, and then I had to explain myself. I left you out of it, by the way. I just said I was a local ghost, knew her from the before days, and so on. Luckily, she had no memory of me. She bantered, is what I'm trying to say. She was cool, did not hold my deadness against me. But. Like I said, she's not fully, she's not completely here yet. She isn't convinced she should be."

"What does that mean, not convinced she should be?"

Shawn shrugged. "Not interested, I guess. Content with her lot as an invalid. Not in love with life."

"Well, why would she be?"

"Lots of reasons. Because she is one of the most powerful people in world. Someone who could make a difference. You might not believe this, but the universe is not as random as you think."

"Her worldly power going unused. Not living up to her full potential as a billionaire? That's your entire interest in her situation?"

"She needs to awaken to her duty and get to work."

"Do you want me to talk to her? Tell her to *get to work*? Which is a cliché, by the way. And kind of mean after all she's been through."

"Oh, okay. You don't need my suggestions. Though, I notice how often you come down here."

"I come here to see you. You know that. Are you mad at me now?"

Shawn's glow disappeared like a dampened flame. The floating bridge stretched out, bright fingers disappearing in the rolling fog. Cory stuffed his cold hands in his warm hoodie pockets and moved toward the trail. Thea turned to watch. The little dog growled.

"Easy there, buddy. I'm not going to bite. Hi, Thea."

Lee wiped his hands on his apron, moving closer to the edge of the deck facing the beach. Thea had been outside for a longer time than ever, and she showed no signs of returning. The cute blond man was talking to her. Lee had wondered how long before they finally spoke, since the man was at the beach often. June said she knew the guy: he was an old schoolmate, almost a friend. She had said, *Oh no, his mother is an old pal of ours—if anything, you should feel glad he is there to keep an eye on her*. Hmm. Maybe. June didn't always notice changes in Thea. That morning, before she found Ben's old watch, Thea had spent hours listening to old music on her laptop, dancing to herself, singing to some parts and then stopping, shoulders moving as if she were about to cry. And then not crying. Moving to the next song. She was like a child with a plate of cakes, taking a bite and then putting the half-eaten cake back on the plate and tasting another. Then, she went looking in the closet and found the watch. Lee had left it there, when he packed everything else away. Maybe he should have taken it, as he had the others. But it would have looked odd to June, not even one of Ben's watches left over. In the old days, Thea had worn it sometimes. Rooting around in drawers, remembering how to read a watch. This was another big day for her.

Lee smiled. That was the real Thea, in a way. Always opening drawers. Always curious and impatient. She looked okay over on the beach, and Dusty was not barking, just running up and down the beach barking at a set of small waves. Normal. Everything was normal. Good, even. Things were easier. But not easy. His commitment to care for Thea had never been easy. He opened the front door a crack, for when she returned. He put his phone down on the kitchen counter and went back to folding dumplings. Thea would not remember that these were Ben's favorites. But Lee would. He had the curse and the blessing of remembering everything.

"Hi." Thea turned toward Cory and made a grimacing smile. "I'm sorry. I don't know your name."

He reminded her.

"And I know you...?"

Her voice was lower and hoarser than he remembered. Rumor had it her head had been crushed. But now in the half light, her face appeared unscarred, as symmetrical, and smooth as when Shawn had drawn it in the pages of his class notes. Cory followed her up the path to the small parking area, explaining. They had taken English together, ski bus, other things that failed to shift her expression.

"Well, you look great Cory. Wish I could say I remember high school, but...I got rebooted some months ago, and this new operating system is pretty glitchy."

Someone had told her to say that to people. He glanced at her bare feet. "You okay?"

"You bet." She stopped at the street. "Have I been here a long time?"

"I don't know. I just got here myself." God, he was so vain. Why would she care that he snuck smokes?

"Oh." She let the dog go, and it ran inside, dragging the leash behind. "It's getting dark. You should be careful."

"I should be careful?"

"Yes. Everyone knows Secret Beach is haunted."

She disappeared behind her tall steel door, beneath a light swimming with mist. He pushed his hands deeper into his pockets, careful not to crush the cigarettes, and turned to trudge up the hill to his house.

"Did you see how long I was out?"

Thea found Cory handsome up close, when he wasn't hunched and scowling. But Lee was beautiful, especially his arms, which had helped her to stand and walk so many times. Everything about him was gracefully direct, his quick movements, his plain jeans and tee shirts, his acerbic commentary.

"That was the longest. Right?"

He dropped Dusty to the floor. "Yes."

"Where's my prize?"

He made a dismissive cluck.

"How many minutes?"

He checked his watch. "Thirty-four."

She clapped. "Better by four minutes. What do I get?"

"Mushroom risotto and salad."

"Oh, yum. I'll have to stay out for 35 minutes tomorrow."

"Okay, but we need to have you leave earlier." He took Ben's old parka off her shoulders to hang. "Get to an hour, you can have ice cream."

"Right." She rubbed her hands together to warm them. "As if you would let me have ice cream."

"Are you smiling?"

"Am I?" She shrugged. "Go on, get home to Allen. I can wash the dishes."

Lee watched her disappear upstairs, her feet leaving sand on the wood. He vacuumed with the handheld, then replaced it in its charger.

"Okay, see you tomorrow!"

"Better get going," she yelled. "He'll be mad at me if you're late."

Upstairs in the master suite, the lake had flattened to dull black. She couldn't have seen the shimmering man named Shawn, even if he had still been there, across the bay. Like Cory, Shawn said he knew her from high school. Was that strange? Or was that kind of thing normal: two men from the past, one a ghost, the other visibly bored, hanging around her neighborhood beach at nightfall?

Her body felt okay with it. How odd. *Shawn.* She smiled to herself, hosing off with warm water. Something not to tell Lee.

Thea dried her long feet, crisscrossed with scars from surgeries she didn't recall. They looked like snails, or white asparagus shoots. She had no particular curiosity about the famous Thea Smythe Sun, who got pins in her ankles and a plate in her skull. That woman had died, and with her the memories and the pain of everything she had once had.

A familiar taut membrane of dread under Thea's ribcage returned. Curiosity, which she wished would go away. Maybe it was the ghost's fault. He had implied that Thea was what her mother said, an heiress to a great fortune, which might be true. Lee said once that he worked for her dead husband even now, and that Mr. Benson Sun had been a very special man. There were photos of him in drawers in the office, and of the two of them all in white, with flowers in their hair. Ben had been short, holding himself a fighting stance, a wide smile on his round face. Thea beside him was a stranger, also smiling, kind of sexy with a slit in her white satin gown, holding to his arm like they were bank robbers, or someone in a movie, anyway, posing. Very fake. Her mom said there had been Maggie, a little girl, but Thea found no pictures. She didn't go into the girl's room, which was empty anyway. Her body didn't want to.

No, thank you. Her world was complete.

3

Chapter 3

That time of day the lake was the translucent pewter of salmon fry, and the water was cold. Suki Yamada let the morning's stillness pull her along the bank, only her nose and mouth above water. The water felt like icy needles on her open eyes, but she liked that. She liked to see the sky through the green water, with its silt of freshwater krill and organic matter. Lots of things could grow in here.

She was looking through a mirror into a world she didn't belong in, maybe what a baby felt when forced out of the warm place it knew. Suki considered the violence of childbirth, the first trauma that is only one of many. The best balm on human pain was connection, contribution, letting go. That was what they said in meetings, and she knew it was true. But being alive was hard. So hard. How did we evolve when our hearts were so exquisitely hard to soothe? Suki watched the pale green water without blinking, its cold biting her eyes, until she had to let her eyelids close. Then she floated in the near dark of dawn. She stayed that way for a few long moments until, like any mammal, her lungs needed air.

Something brushed her hand—milfoil, no doubt—though it could be a pike or a turtle, a steelhead. She emerged into the warm air, took in breath, and color rushed through her the way dope once had. Oxygen. She was addicted. She opened her eyes. Across the water, the lights of her baby's house snapped on. Right on time. The man who lived there would move around the kitchen, his dark head shining in the lamplight. He never seemed to notice her. She was like a nutria or a beaver, one of the creatures of the lakeside coast, going about her business. A citizen of the shoreline.

Suki paddled toward the beach, thinking about her thermos and the robe in her car, wondering if she could get away with driving straight to work, if the children would smell the lake on her.

That afternoon, Lee put Thea through her daily work on the reformer—which he had nicknamed *The Transformer.* Debussy's Claire de lune tinkled softly over the speakers. The music used to calm her, back when she got left and right mixed up, and just coming to an upright position had taken the whole lesson. Now, Thea ignored the slight tremor in her left arm as it pulled the cable. Up, around, and down, slow, and smooth.

Lee bit into an apple, checking his watch. "Looks good."

"What?" She stopped. "No notes today?"

"There's nothing more wrong with you."

"I'm still weak."

He crossed his arms. "You mean you are lazy."

She re-attached the straps to their hooks. "Are you trying to get fired?"

"Your mother will be here soon. If you fire me, she moves back in, right?"

"Don't leave me."

"Your body is okay." Lee sat, catching her eye. "You just need to talk. More people, more friends. Right? You need to exercise your mind. Remember how to be alive."

She stood, tossing the straps impatiently. "I spoke to a man I know from high school yesterday. Does that count?"

"Now I know why you were gone so long." He took up a spray bottle and began to clean the black vinyl.

"Let me do that."

"Go on. If your hair is greasy, she'll make me cut it."

Thea watched him from the hallway. Her arm stopped shaking, but her eyes began to water. Lee finished his work and brushed by, patting her on the shoulder.

"No crying. Shower."

Friday evening, June Smythe parked her F-150 in the small beach parking lot, the local NPR station rattling on about fires. She kept it at a low volume because she could hardly stand it. Thea had asked her long ago not to take up spaces the swimmers used, but June was self-conscious about driving such a gas guzzler and would not sully the front of Ben's perfect house.

Thea had offered to buy her something more environmental, but in Winthrop, one false move, and June would go right back to being an outsider. She needed the community to see her as a real advocate for the kids at her center, not some interloping carpetbagger. Besides, she loved the old truck. Maggie had named it once. *Princess Rusty*, or *Lady Rust*? Something like that. Something far too sweet for a truck with 200 thousand miles and three different colors of paint.

Okay, no crying now. There had been too many tears already. Every time June crossed the I-5 bridge into the city, the tech buildings around South Lake Union a shining blade of heedless destruction, June remembered anew that instead of being with her granddaughter, she was only driving to visit the pale remnant of a daughter she barely recognized. Life had twisted and contorted and left wrongness in its wake, as life always did. She wiped her face on her shoulder.

At least Thea was awake now, a stranger in many ways, but conscious, emerging in some new fashion. June could be useful to her. Thea need not know how desperately sad the whole ordeal felt, the pretense that every molecule of air in the house wasn't screaming out for the people who had lived there. Thea, the real woman, always in pursuit of some impossible goal June never understood, until Ben explained that no one did, that Thea saw opportunities where others only saw chaos. When she found an angle, everyone would know it, in her gleaming blue eyes, the way she burst with emerging plans, her voice sharp with intent. June didn't miss that Thea, but at least she had been fully alive.

June gathered the bags of goodies she'd carried over the mountains and turned to walk toward the house. Gravel crunched under her boots, then she stumbled on something soft. A black-and white swim cap, oblong markings like Orca skin with a chin strap that snapped. Who would wear such a ridiculous thing?

"That's mine." A woman in a plush red robe appeared from behind a tree.

"I've got it." June stooped awkwardly, balancing the bag on her hip. "Isn't the water still too cold?"

"It's good for the nerves. You should try it."

June dropped the swim cap into the woman's outstretched hand, feeling insulted. As if she hadn't been swimming at this very beach all her life. Before she could come up with a response, though, the woman's Prius had backed into the street and wheezed up the hill. Just as well. June mounted the short stairway into the house. She ought to put a potted plant there now that Thea was more stable and wouldn't trip and fall into it. Yes. A nice conifer to soften the iron and concrete. Or a lovely hydrangea, one that wouldn't need much watering. She might just do that.

The interior smelled sage-y, woody and delicious. Lee's way of welcoming her. What a sweet, gentle man. He disliked June; she knew. But still. What a gift he had been. Without him, June would have had to move Thea to her ranch, and that would have been too much to handle, on top of all her animals and the children's center. She couldn't have stomached sending Thea to a rehab facility, where no one cared. It had been hard to find a caregiver she could trust so she could keep Thea at home. But even Lars admitted Lee was fabulous.

"These crazy people. How do you stand living so close to all that?"

"It's public access, Mom."

June put the groceries into Lee's hands.

"Never did a damn thing for my nerves. Wouldn't that be nice? If Lake Washington turned out to be magic?"

"Oh good. Junk food and alcohol." Lee said, unloading. "Please let me fetch you a cup of tea while you remove your shoes."

Being away for five days at a time gave June a chance to see how quickly Thea was progressing. After so many months of inertia, her posture was strong. Her eyes held new sparkle.

"I've got it from here, dear Lee. Go on home to your husband. You've done so much for us, hasn't he, Thea? And we are so grateful."

Thea hid her eyes in her hands. She must be tired.

After Lee left, June opened wine and put out a charcuterie spread. "I brought a wonderful puzzle for us to work on."

"That's nice of you, Mom."

June placed grapes on a platter. "Lee said you have been outside for longer. Good for you."

"Yup. Good for me."

Thea went to the windows by the back deck. The beach was occupied by a pair of teens smoking. Fog hovered, a white platter over the lake.

"Tomorrow, we're going to practice driving."

"*We?*" Thea sipped the wine. Had she used to enjoy this? It tasted like the sandy jolly ranchers she had found in a pocket.

"Wouldn't you like to be more independent?"

"Not really."

"What about friends? You used to have some. Don't you want to spend some time with other people besides just me and Lee?"

"I'm going to walk out onto the dock for a minute. Just get some air." Thea forced a smile. "You know, not used to drinking and feasting like this."

"I'll put it away if it's too much."

"It's wonderful. I've just been living on Lee's food for so long."

"Which is delicious. Better than any restaurant."

"Yes."

The dock was slick under her clogs. Fog obscured the east side's mirrored skyscrapers, pale pink in sunset. The teens had left. Thea held to a railing, cupping her mouth with one hand to yell across the water.

"Shawn? Are you...around? Let's pretend we're back in high school. My mom is driving me crazy."

Silence. Then, from inside the house, twangy music rose. Thea turned in a slow circle, thinking about her ghost friend and all he had experienced. Shawn had told her he was a musician. He said Thea had seen him perform. The thought was as impenetrable as the fog. She didn't remember much, but she knew ghosts weren't real. Her most familiar memory came: pressure on her skull, the sickening pain. Maybe she was crazy now after all that crushing. Had she been crazy before?

Behind her, the house gleamed, the small ruby of her mother's wine glass, the black-and-white splash of painting on the wall. Wasn't this the life Thea had worked so hard to return to? She clenched her left fist until a shadow of pain reappeared. She had told Lee she must be dying once. His dark eyes were soft. "Dying? Is that so bad?"

She had laughed. Two months ago. Only two months.

Waves began to crash below the dock. "Shawn, I'm giving up on you."

"You have to go." Shawn spoke from the air like a church organ.

"Where are you?"

"Get off the dock. Right now, I'm not kidding."

"Do you want me to come to the beach?"

"Run. Goddammit. Run."

She laughed. "Are we both insane?"

"Get the fuck off that dock." His voice was a booming chord.

"Okay, I'm going. No need to be a dick." Her feet felt frozen. She forced her body to move toward the house. "I just wanted to ask you something."

"Watch out!"

She took two more steps. Then pylons were splintering, so loud it hurt. The dock heaved. She felt frigid air on her belly as the parka flew off. She was flying, falling, her head hitting something. No, her head could not be hit again. That much she remembered. No more head injuries.

Thick cold stung her skin. She was in the lake. Water tore down her esophagus, pain in her sinuses. She was drowning, her eyes filling with red snow, like before, her head flaring with shock, but this time Thea knew what was coming. What should have happened last time, and would have, if not for the people in scrubs that had forced their will upon her.

"Fucking swim, Thea," Shawn said in her ear, his form a beaming white moon beside her. "You survived. Don't you think there's a reason why?"

Her anger roared, deeper and darker than the lake, bigger and brighter than the man beside her. The hard stones of the lake bottom dug into her palms.

Her feet kicked. She coughed. Her head was in air now, hair slapping icy strings against her neck. He gleamed on the sand. She staggered toward him, shivering.

"Tell me, then. Why?"

Then she was alone. Sirens wailed faintly to the west, and June was screaming from the broken dock.

June watched the fire crew board the boat and shut off its engine. Neighbors stood around whispering. Someone handed Thea her coat, which had washed up on the sand, then June hustled her into a hot shower. While she warmed up and the pallor of her skin turned to a pearly pink, June went and poured them each a brandy. Was this PTSD? The feeling that crept over her, of panic and loss and barely-controlled fury? Thea had disappeared into the water off the dock for five full minutes. June hadn't seen the boat hurtling toward the dock. She had heard the horrible ripping noises of the thing shredding the dock, lights remaining lit even after it sliced its way half through the wood. When she reached the end of what had been the dock, Thea was gone. The fog had been so thick, June was unable to do anything but scream for help. She fumbled in her pocket for her phone, unsure if she should dive into the darkness of the water to try and retrieve Thea, but then she heard her daughter thrashing and yelling, and the anger came. A boat accident? After a helicopter crash? Was this supposed to be random, and if so, when would the third terrifying incident occur? She couldn't help angry tears. Most of her crying had been for Maggie, and Ben, and the loss of the daughter she knew. After a few minutes of silent weeping and the second brandy, the pain settled to a dull roar within. It ended completely as soon as Thea called out for her to turn off the shower.

"Can I go into the hot tub?" Thea said.

"Honey. It's cold outside now." June said. "Could you just stay out of water for a while? My nerves are shot."

June washed and dried the brandy glasses and returned them to the cupboard. But she hardly felt the drinks' comfort. She missed her ranch, and her life. She missed Cal, warm in bed next to her. Thea was so close to being able to live independently. She even had the wits to jump off the end of the dock before being struck. June ought to be content with that. She ought to thank her lucky stars. But when would she be able to stop overseeing her, and the Foundation, and all that had landed in her lap when Thea fell out of the sky? A knock on the head from an out-of-control boat could wipe away all their progress in one second flat. Hell, hitting the water wrong could do it. June couldn't think about it, her daughter back in bed, possibly forever, her memories scrambled like eggs. It was just too much.

No one emerged from the boat after it jammed itself into the dock, motor moaning uselessly until one of the neighbors jumped aboard and turned it off. After investigation, a police detective informed June that the vessel was stolen, its registered name *Short Shrift*. Whoever had been piloting was long gone. Probably a drunk driver, now in the lake, he said, though the person wouldn't last long there without a wet suit. It was late Spring, but the sun was elusive this side of the mountains. The Cascades trapped the moisture from the Pacific Ocean, hence the wall of fog outside. A police boat shone spotlights through it, making murky ovals in the water. Officers' beams moved across the bay, on the beach, squiggles of light in the gloom. Behind them, through the trees, red sparks from their cruisers on the street and in the parking area. No one seemed overly concerned. Drunk boating convictions were rare, and no one had been harmed. June didn't have the energy to explain that Thea could easily have been harmed, irreparably. The cops would just tell her to do a better job protecting her daughter.

"Please don't call your helicopter," June said to the nearest uniformed person. "It will trigger her terribly."

The man cracked a smile. "Take a look outside. No aircraft are going up in that fog."

June felt her tension spilling over. "Can you take the boat away? She's been through a lot already."

A man in slacks and a polo shirt with the SPD logo walked across the deck to her. According to his card, the detective was named Dre Medina. "I apologize, Ma'am. It being Friday night, we're short on maritime impound crews."

Eventually, the police lights went dark and they cruised away. Within ten minutes, the doorbell began to ring. By nine, three neighbors and two local security patrols had stopped in to check on things, drink a cup of tea, and stare around the living room like hungry cats. It was nice to see how many of the folks around cared about Thea. And then of all people, Cory Klain appeared, with a bottle of wine.

"Jesus, Thea." He said, "There must have been ten police cars here. Are you okay?"

June took the bottle from his hand, a lovely French Bordeaux. "Cory Klain. I remember you. Are you still playing music?"

"Mostly producing these days, Mrs. Smythe."

"Call me June. Care to stay for a glass?"

Cory gazed over at Thea. She seemed worn out in her old sweatpants and fuzzy slippers.

"Another time."

By the time June got the bottle open and poured, Thea had fallen asleep on the couch, her hair dripping onto the rug by the fireplace.

The next day dawned so bright and glittery they had to lower the blinds. The boat leaned against the ruined dock, a broken house of cards, white surfaces angled all wrong.

"*Short Shrift*," June said over breakfast. "Which I take to mean some jerk won her in a divorce settlement."

"What? Where do you get that?"

"Never mind. Sure you don't want a scone?"

"No thanks."

"I keep forgetting you're not used to eating sugar."

"Is that sugar?" Thea peered at the platter of pastries.

"Well, it is if you're Lee."

Thea's head ached only slightly today. Thank God, June hadn't wanted to call any doctors. When she had taken a few bites of eggs and fruit, Thea said she was going out to put out fenders and tie the boat up properly, so it didn't keep knocking up onto the damaged dock.

"Good for you, hon." June said. "Back up on the horse."

The dock felt warm through Thea's sneakers. Most of it was still intact, potted shrubs and caged lights undisturbed. The spot where she'd stood when Shawn told her to run was chevroned by long, evil looking splinters contained in a messy trapezoid of caution tape. The Boston Whaler listed to port, nose crushed by impact. Whoever had been piloting had been hauling ass. Could they have been lost in the fog, thinking they were alone out there, safe to run? No one who knew the lake at all would be so stupid. June always complained about the newcomers. Maybe he was one of those.

Thea stepped gingerly over the splinters, the lake's rocky bottom clear beneath her, then aboard the *Short Shrift*. It shifted with a groan, water floating up cushions and life jackets. The globe compass sat intact in the cockpit, pointing due West. Thea sat in the captain's chair, remembering. An outline emerged, distances, place names. *Yes.* Maybe the skipper thought he was heading into the Montlake Cut, and was just a couple of miles too far south? That was possible. He could have left one of the restaurants at Leschi after too many drinks, speeding to outrun the fog, and thought he was heading into Portage Bay.

Thea found the fenders and looped them to their cleats. The next part would be tricky. Was Shawn watching? Would he intervene if she lost her balance?

Thea undid the knots the police had left, leaned out to push the boat away from the dock, slipped the fenders between it and the dock, then retied the lines. The process made her dizzy, but not as much as she had expected. Her hands remembered how to tie bowlines, how to coil the lines and leave everything shipshape, as if the broken vessel would ever be used again, which, of course, it wouldn't be. There was no fixing something this wrecked. She sat back, feeling satisfied.

"Shawn? No concern today, huh?"

"Good lord, what a waste." June held a coffee mug. "Who are you talking to?"

"The spirit world, mom. I'm asking what happens after a person dies."

"Hmmm." June sipped. "Any reply?"

A turtle disturbed the lake's surface, diving down into the weeds.

"Apparently not."

"The detective said he'd call if they arrested anyone. But whoever it was probably died of hypothermia or else climbed someone's dock ladder and got away." She didn't add that Dre Mendoza had made it clear by the tone of his voice that they were not going to follow up with any of the neighbors. If they caught anyone now, a blood alcohol test would be useless, and property crime was hardly a big priority in parts of town where everyone had good insurance. "Are you alright?"

Sun rays made dazzling patterns on the lake. A sailboat moved in and out of the light.

"I was thinking they might have gotten mixed up about where they were. Maybe they thought they were steering into the Cut."

"My goodness."

"What?"

"You're...just remembering so much."

"No. I'm just figuring out why I almost got hit by a boat. I don't like anyone disturbing my peace, Mom."

Thea picked her way back onto the dock, letting June guide her under the caution tape.

They opened the garage for the first time since Lee had borrowed the Tesla to drive to Vancouver and visit his mother several weeks previous.

"What are you going to do with those?" June indicated a yellow Porsche and a red Mercedes stacked on a lift. Ben's shiny toys.

"I don't know. Can I just think about this, right now?"

Thea felt blank when she sat behind the wheel, the familiar wall of nothingness she sometimes slid down. No purchase, just a slippery slope into darkness. "Could we postpone? Yesterday was exhausting."

June peeked over her colorful glasses. "We don't have to go anyplace. Just start the...whatever kind of engine these things have."

Thea did. The Tesla trembled noiselessly.

"Excellent. Let's just go to Madison."

"Madison." Thea got a sensation of familiar shapes and colors, nothing scary or overwhelming. She wondered if Shawn were lurking someplace outside the garage, on the sidewalk, near the fence between her house and the beach parking lot. Could she run over a ghost? No. What a dumb idea. He had been in the water with her, shining brilliantly, speaking in her head. She couldn't kill Shawn if she tried. The thought lightened her mood.

June reached over and pulled Thea's seatbelt over her lap, clicking it shut. "One mile, sweet pea. Just one."

Thea craned her neck, a faint whisper of stiffness in her spine, and eased the car out of the garage and onto the street. The Tesla's theremin hum jolted an image loose: storefronts on a small commercial strip. "Right, right. I remember how to do this."

"Other direction," June said. "Oh well, it doesn't matter. We'll get there eventually."

The restaurant June chose was uncrowded, so they got one of the plush booths with a good view of the door and the tin lanterns with their colorful glass cutouts. Mariachi music blared imperceptibly. A bartender leaned in to talk with some older men in bike outfits. Skeletons had been painted on the tables and alcoves, bones dancing all around, a celebration of death.

"We used to come here?"

"Yes. A lot." June's face had an opacity Thea didn't remember. "It was...a family favorite. Maybe not such a good choice."

"Have I upset you?"

"Not at all. I'm starving, aren't you? Oh..."

"Thea?" The woman with blazing blue eyes appeared beside them, diamond necklaces clanking together as she bent close. She smelled of tuberose. Tuberose, what a thing to know the name of. Of course. Because Thea hated its sickly intensity.

"Yes, I am Thea."

"Is it really you? Out having lunch with your mom?"

That's right. Thea Sun is out having lunch. Call the newspapers. "I think so. Unless this is all a dream and you're a hallucination."

"Hahaha. You're hilarious."

"Hi there." June took control of the encounter, explaining in her schoolmarm voice that Thea was making great progress, she had been driving that very morning. All was well. Nothing to make a fuss over.

"So nice to see you...?"

"Betsy Wheeler." The woman, who was of course Betsy Wheeler, of course she was, took Thea's hand in hers and leaned close. The tuberose warred with salt and oil as a waiter brought chips. Thea's stomach jumped. Thea hadn't liked this person, with her clipped blond hair and muscular runner's figure. The chips piqued more interest. A woman in a silver puffy vest watched from the sidewalk in front of the restaurant, thumbs dancing on her phone.

"Right. Betsy. Elizabeth. Johnson. Wheeler." The words came unbidden from Thea's mouth, the image of an email signature, a tiny square with a photo of the woman's face.

"That's right. That's right, Thea. Well, since you're so recovered, let me extend this invitation. When you're ready, we still want to talk to you about coming on board. We spoke about this before."

June held a hand up as if silencing the class. "Ms. Wheeler, it's early days for Thea."

Thea bit into a salty tortilla chip, speaking too loudly through a full mouth. "It's early days for me."

Betsy Wheeler recoiled, eyes widening. "Of course, of course. Enjoy. But. As you return to us, we'd love, love, love to invite you to a meeting."

Thea felt her face freeze in an expression at Betsy Wheeler's retreating back that was part awe, part disgust.

"Jesus. It must be so weird to be you." June sipped from a blue-rimmed glass.

"Mom." Thea pushed a new chip into the guacamole. "What was my job?"

On Sunday, several neighbors used the Short Shrift's collision as an excuse to knock on the door and say hello, bringing scented candles, boxes of chocolate, flowers. They had heard Thea was out and about again, recovering, a walking miracle. June whispered that they could only stay for ten minutes, to conserve Thea's strength. When they were gone, Thea tried the chocolates, found them too sweet, spit them out, and went upstairs to take a bath. She lit a candle that smelled like spruce. Such dumb people. The trees outside smelled better.

The next thing Thea knew, June was blowing out the flame and telling her to put on clothes. The water was cold.

"Unless you want to help me cook."

"What?" Thea wrapped herself in a towel. "You need help?"

"Never mind, Princess."

4

Chapter 4

Monday morning was warm enough to sit on her balcony if she wore the parka over her pajamas. Thea was sipping tea, watching the sun rise over the mountains, when she noticed the colorful buoys gliding across the lake. They were there often, but she hadn't really paid attention to them before, fluorescent orange or green orbs drifting across the water, people dragging them along as they swam. Thea could hear their voices clearly across the still lake: middle-aged women, chattering about projects and lesson plans and what a terrible idea someone had. Thea liked the sound, laying new energy over the stretch of water. They sounded petty and crabby, just regular people hauling their bodies through the world.

"Put something on." June called from downstairs. "It doesn't matter what. These people work for you."

Thea set her cup down and tried to sneak back inside without the swimmers noticing. She didn't want to interrupt their cozy chatter. Her closet was like a museum after the thieves have picked it over, spotlights over empty hangars and half-full glass cases. Thea touched a leather purse. Was this really hers? Who had she been, the woman who would buy a bag like this, so confident and shining and expensive? She wished her mother liked such things. Thea could give it to her. She pulled on a pair of slacks and a plain blouse. There was a matching blazer, all in dark tweed, electric blue with black and gray, subtle and silk-lined. There were boots, lots of them, lined up like dark alien pods. She picked the lowest heels, zipping them over her bare feet. It was too much work to find whatever type of socks such footwear required. The woman in the mirror appeared pale and humorless. But at least her hair was clean.

"You're skinny as a foal, but you seem healthy enough."

Had her mother always talked like that, or was it her move east of the mountains that turned her into an old-timey country girl? "Neigh?"

"Honey, I'll drive one of the cars."

"Okay." Thea smiled. "Do you know how to get it out of the garage?"

"Lee showed me."

They took the red Porsche.

SunStorm's glassy campus was obscured by green, as if shiny modern art had been carefully placed in a primordial forest. As they drove up to Building One, Thea felt only faint curiosity. Had she chosen the architects behind this metallic gray fortress? It seemed too tasteful for what she knew of Ben. What did their company do, again? About halfway there, Thea had realized that her mother's explanations meant nothing because June herself didn't know. The feeling as they passed through a checkpoint was flat and rational, chains of numbers, links and wires, a musical note she didn't know the name of. An A? An F? Both together sounding some mechanical chord?

Her heart jumped as June steered them into the dark parking garage. A group of guards stood waiting to direct them. Why so many people, such ostentatious lanyards against the casual uniform of dark polo shirts, slacks, and reflective vests? The small crowd dispersed as soon as Thea and June entered the elevator. One of them pressed the button for the top floor, only five floors, not very tall, though there were five floors below them, as well. Why so many subfloors?

The smell of the building was familiar, which surprised Thea, a combination of freshly lain carpet, something stony, maybe grout, and herbal tea bags. The place was nearly new. And yet, she had definitely been there before. Her stomach was fluttering by the time she and June entered the boardroom overlooking the south side of the complex. The courtyard below bustled with workers, the opposing windows lit to reveal people at standing desks and conference tables, gazing at screens, talking. Only this floor felt unused, its sole occupant a young receptionist who closed the door behind them emphatically.

"Thea." The tall man took her hands in his and peered deeply into her eyes. He smelled of sage, wore a sleek shirt over slim jeans, eyeglass frames as blue as his eyes. June had told Thea that his name was Lars Harris. Those cheekbones, that bloom of redness beneath them, emerged into her memory. A friend.

"So great to see you."

He released her and greeted June, and Thea took in the five other people in the room, three men and two woman, lawyers and accountants, she'd been told. June had given her a sheet of paper with their names and jobs but where was it now? She suddenly wanted to find Ben's office. An irrational notion seized her, that maybe he was still in there, had been the whole time, and everything had been a dream: the red snow, the pain, the months at home with Lee. She stood taller.

Lars ushered her into a seat, and they began the meeting. Someone had made glowing charts of her and Ben's fortune, projected onto a white board like art, or a map of some city's public transportation. The branching limbs were meant to show where all the money was invested, what would be paid in taxes, what part was earmarked for the Foundation. Thea felt her mother's labored breath beside her.

She made a face that she hoped looked pert and comprehending. "Good. Fine. Excellent."

Other people entered. One young woman in a shiny brick-brown suit pressed her hand into Thea's like a small warm animal. Her feet wore bulbous boots, and her watch was enormous. "I'm Madhavi."

Thea repeated it. A new person, not one she should remember. At the company for two years but only at this level for six months.

"I see. Thank you," Thea said, because it seemed to be expected. Madhavi smiled and moved down the table, greeting others with silent signals Thea didn't catch or understand.

Then came more introductions, other hands, slender men in lug-soled sneakers, women who seemed too young to be out of school. Executives, project managers, the head of HR, of R&D, of social media, someone taking photographs.

"Where's Craig?" someone said.

Madhavi smiled wide. "It's early days. Craig can wait."

Now came slides for various parts of the SunStorm Corporation itself, valuations of different divisions, where they were going, how much had been invested and what they expected to earn. Lots of buzzwords, like clouds floating past, unable to catch or grab onto.

Thea's hands twitched uselessly. She was the only one there with no screen open before her. She wished for a pen and paper, knowing that such archaic items would be wrong. Even June was scowling into an open laptop. Thea turned her attention to the large screen.

The glowing graphics branched and widened, a representation of market share expanding and share price blossoming like dark ink spilled from a pen. Thea thought of a river at night and had a sudden memory of standing unsteadily next to the Arno with Ben, before they adopted Maggie, soon after they married. The sun was going down like a ball of fire, pink and orange through cypress trees. Bats had flown out like small black rags, startling her, and they had laughed, Ben reaching out his steadying arm.

June made a small, helpless gasp. "Honey. This is too much."

But it wasn't. Just colors, like neon signs, unreal. Pretty, even. Words came streaming out from an unseen source, a confident voice emerging from Thea's mouth. "All of this is excellent. Thanks to everyone. I will need to follow up. Who can assist me with next steps?"Lars startled, gazing around the room. "I can get you some names."

A young woman with shining black hair and the posture of a rower stood. "Ramona Stein." She introduced herself. "I'm legal liaison between the Corporation, the Foundation, and the Firm."

To Thea's relief, Ramona didn't come over and touch her, just stood calmly, a faint smile on her face. Another person she didn't already know. Wasn't expected to have context for. Hallelujah.

"Thank you." Thea stood. "Much to digest."

"We've prepared a short tour, Thea." Madhavi said. Her nose ring sparkled in her symmetrical face. "I believe the last time you were here, only Four was fully utilized.

Thea ignored this obvious test. "How thoughtful of you."

They showed Thea the remaining buildings, one with a woodfired pizza oven, another with a small grocery store stacked with bright refreshments. There were atriums, sheltered lounges, and larger common areas where people were typing into laptops or eating. Two dogs sat at the ends of leashes, seemingly bored by the stream of people. A man in candy-colored shoes kept up a constant stream of well-practiced information, and Thea was grateful for his neutral, undemanding tone, the way she could nod along knowingly. Murmuring employees began to follow them, in pairs and threes, eyes tracking Thea as she made her way down a set of stairs toward an ice cream sundae bar. A big man who reminded Thea of the big beach regular stared up at them, hands in his pockets, his face twisted with what looked from a distance like longing.

"Honey, I think we should go." June said.

"Don't you want a treat, mom?"

Thea motioned to the bar, wishing June would stop protecting her from overexertion. Why did she care if people thought she was overwhelmed? She was a widow recently woken up from her long nap, wasn't she? And yet, Thea kept her spine straight, rays of tension cutting up her shoulders, the unaccustomed movement of her head on its stalk as she took in the atrium and the sky overhead. "Go get a sundae."

June stayed put. A man with a goatee and long, white hair like a medieval knight explained how R&D were correcting for *profit bias* in their AI interfaces. Thea's hands tingled, suspicion creeping into her like a sour smell, the intuition that this man was purposely misleading them, maybe because he was trying to dampen her curiosity, or because he didn't really know the truth himself.

"We are teaching them to eat carrots and run from sticks. Before long, they'll be growing carrots and eating sticks. Then we're in trouble."

Several people laughed. The man's eyes flitted to her, and for reasons Thea could not have explained, she let him see that she was not entertained.

"Thank you so much, Evan. And Connor, and...Madhavi. Wonderful presentation." June said, turning Thea's shoulder back toward the exit.

"They're not schoolchildren, Mom."

"Overachievers need to feel approval, or they start to get squirrely."

June signaled to Lars, who hastened closer. Ramona was speaking into her headset, strolling in a circle.

His eyes were very round. "Do you need something?"

Thea understood him to mean medical intervention. She shook her head, hoping the ache at the base of her skull wasn't residue of her dive into the lake, or some other dire signal. Did the air as they re-entered Building One smell faintly of alcohol? Or was the mere suggestion of medicine enough to make Thea picture the port on her chest, a pink scar now, the echo of syringes being voided into her body? The cold, chemical sting, a branch of iced lightning.

Everyone pressed too close now, faces curious. The tour guide had ceased his smooth patter and was gazing at Thea with concern.

"I do need something." Thea said. "More information about that AI project. It's really fascinating. I want to take part in...chasing carrot sticks."

The room fell silent.

"I'm sure Evan would be happy to loop you in." Madhavi said, eyes disappearing into a crinkling smile.

Evan looked hesitant. "Me? Not Craig?"

Madhavi glared at him pointedly, then turned toward Thea and June. "Lovely to see you. I'll make sure you're on the project chat. Any other divisions you'd like to take a look at?"

Thea forced her own sunny smile and repeated a handful of meaningless words from the meeting. "Uh...cloud services, automation, and crypto?"

Madhavi's teeth were very white in her small face. "You know what? I'll get Ramona all the links and you can cruise around like a stealth fighter, yeah? Make sure you approve of all we're up to."

Evan stared at Madhavi, who ignored him.

"You're wonderful," June said, her hand tight on Thea's arm.

"Not at all," Madhavi said. "It's just fantastic to see our emeritus CEO looking so healthy and inquisitive."

Thea's cheeks felt stressed.

"Yes," June said. "Fantastic."

The rest of the attendees filed past and disappeared down the stairs, smiling and waving goodbyes, leaving only Thea, June, Lars and Ramona. This level, Thea thought. My level.

"Who is the CEO?"

"Madhavi. She's good." Lars checked his phone. "She worked very closely with Ben."

Ben. Had Ben chosen her, from all the young geniuses around the complex? And if he had, why? Questions for later. So many questions. Thea's head was aching, undeniably.

"And she has to authorize my inquiries into...the company?" Thea almost said *my company*.

"Right. They threw together bespoke projections for today. Lots of interested parties get the quarterlies but this was special for you. Since you are the majority stakeholder, they are required to tell you everything." "Was that everything?"

He glanced around them, then shrugged. "I sense they would be more comfortable making sure you're secure before they lay everything bare. There's a lot of proprietary information. Industrial secrets, obviously."

Thea gently removed her mother's hand from her arm. "But I'm majority stakeholder?"

"They all have stock as well." He seemed to weigh his words. "Probably only Madhavi and the board know what all the different parts of SunStorm are doing. There's a lot of hype, of course. But they have to be careful who has the deepest levels of planning, their research and development, proprietary secrets, things of that nature."

"Including the person who built all this?" June stared up at him. "Perhaps they'd like a doctor's note affirming who Thea is."

Thea laughed. Had she built all this? Her body felt a combination of acute desire to flee, and roiling curiosity about everything around them. Where was her office? They hadn't shown her one. This was not a foreign place, though. More like a board game she had forgotten the rules of but once loved to play. She pressed her index fingers on her neck below her ears, massaging the tension.

"She worked like a demon for those stocks that have made them so rich. You know that, Lars." June smoothed the front of her shapeless tunic, glasses swinging softly on a beaded chain. Thea didn't want to remember that chain, with the colorful plastic letters. The elevator opened and they entered, looking outward through glass as they plummeted into the courtyard's forest canopy.

"Mom, it's okay. There's so much money at stake in a place like this."

"Thea." Lars looked her full in the face. "You really are coming back to us."

She didn't contradict him.

He smiled. "I think you saw the robustness of what you and Ben began. Certainly, I liked today's presentation. Eleanor and I are both on SunStorm's board, of course, so we've kept abreast. The firm itself is siloed but we are part of the topmost layer."

"That's good to hear." Thea said, unable to raise her voice above a whisper. The elevator dove into an underground level, leaving the green behind. He seemed to sag.

"Are you all right, my dear?" June put a hand on his arm.

"Of course. I'm just...it's been a very emotional journey. But as you saw, there's no need to worry. Madhavi is doing a spectacular job. I just...miss..."

Thea studied his face, his pale stubble, the wrinkles near his ears that must have come from outdoor sports. He was a nice man. She felt it. Lars was sad about Ben, like the employees watching her on tour had been. Maybe everyone there that day. Everyone missing Benson Sun, except for her. She didn't remember the man.

Thea forced a smile. "Worry? Are you kidding me? I heard the words *unicorn* and *dragon* so many times, I was about to go get my sword from the trunk of the car."

Lars laughed. "Thank you." He had his phone out again. "By the way, it looks like I missed our meeting on Friday?"

"Our what?"

"My assistant found it in the firm's master calendar this morning. I apologize, I could have had Ramona on your team already, to prep you. For all the mythical beasts around here."

"No. Not possible" June said. "Friday?"

Thea caught his eye as the elevator came to rest. "That was an eventful day. But, as far as I recall, I didn't...know you then?"

"Right. The brain is so confusing." He put his phone away. "A typo."

They exited into the sea of security guards. June changed the subject to the Short Shrift. In her telling the boat had almost hit Thea.

"She jumped into the lake at the very last second, and then she was underwater for ages. I thought...well, I am sick of excitement. As you know, Lars dear."

"Good thing you're such a survivor, Thea. And you say the thing is still there? Let me investigate that."

"Are attorneys involved in such mundane matters?"

His head moved back in inch. It was a nice head, very large and square. He would have been handsome without the scowl and the dumb glasses.

"We are involved in everything you need help with. SunStorm is our largest client. To be perfectly frank, our main client. But more importantly, as you, well, I am sure you recall...Ben was my best friend. I can imagine the fuss he would put up if some random wreck wound up polluting his personal lake water."

"Right."

"Of course, you know Ben. The ruckus, the cursing. He would have enjoyed the whole drama immensely."

Thea's cheeks were frozen. She put her hands on them to warm the skin. She remembered her head hitting the surface, cold and hard, then the dark chaos after, the light blossoming around her.

June cleared her throat. Then she coughed. "It's early days."

"Oh." Lars glanced at Thea. "If you didn't remember me on Friday...then I guess..."

"I'm getting better every day. But it's a lot..." Her voice was thin and childish. She yearned for her bed, her bathtub, the soft sounds of voices outside her balcony.

The only car in the parking garage was the Porsche, shining crimson in the gray concrete. That must have been what Ben was like: a bright object in this drab sea of blunted messages, everyone speaking in self-important jargon. No one admitting what was really going on. Thea wanted to scream something, though she didn't know what or at whom. A new sensation. Rage.

Lars held the passenger door. "Eleanor suggested I invite you up to the Island soon, for an overnight. Just like old times, good food and relaxation. A change of scene for you. What do you think?"

It took only a couple of seconds for Thea to remember that The Island meant Rodriguez Island, where Lars and his wife had a house, and she and Ben had bought property nearby to build on. The image that popped into her mind was Lars and Eleanor's glass-and-cedar place, with a fireplace flanked by windows overlooking the passage north to Canada, the lights of the ferry at night. The image felt peaceful, clean.

"I'd like that," she said, settling into her seat. "I'll check with my caretaker if he thinks I'm up to it."

Lars' eyebrows twisted.

"She means her caregiver, Lee Nguyen. He's very protective."

"Oh Lee. The handyman." Lars laughed. "Of course."

5

Chapter 5

"I gave Mom some more money for her center." Thea said the next morning, watching Lee straighten the already-spotless kitchen. He had come early but still missed seeing June. She had gotten on the road by 5:00 a.m., insisting she had a full day at her facility and needed to beat traffic.

"Helping traumatized kids is good. Your mom is a nice person. Give me the amount and I'll make a note of it in the records."

"I did that myself."

He glanced at her wordlessly, then went back to his work moving things around in the refrigerator.

"You disapprove. You think Ben already gave her enough."

He closed the door. "It's not for me to say what you do with your money."

"I know. But..."

His face appeared as calm as always. Why did she feel tense?

"Did you know how rich I am?"

He laughed. "You need to get out of this house. Then you will see that being rich is temporary, and you are only passing through this life on your way somewhere more interesting."

"*Dying? Is that so bad?*" she repeated his phrase back to him.

"You're not dying." He handed her the dog leash. "Only waking up."

"I didn't mean that. I meant...you are so philosophical sometimes."

"Good you turned on the computer. Good you recorded your check to June." He turned back toward the fridge. "Go talk to your friends on the beach. When you get back, green smoothie and then you know what..."

She took the leash. "Transformer. I know."

Lee replaced the knives in the drawer, each so sharp they could cut a slice of fish transparent. Thea's face was changing day by day: he could see it, like a bud on one of the lilies under 520 freeway. Gray for so long, but her pulse strong. Then more blood in her skin, the color going slowly from paper to petal, veins disappearing, and blush rose filling where they had been. Really beautiful face, Thea's. Even when she was breathing open-mouthed like a sleeping corpse, her bones lay gently. Her hands were long and slim as a painting in a museum—pearls, velvet with buttons, that kind.

She was a child now, a happy baby with no worries. Her joy shone in her new flesh, new face, first smiles and then the words suddenly. So many words. Complaints. Desires. One day she soon, she would remember everything. And then, what did he owe her? What did he owe Ben?

Lee hung his cooking apron on the peg in the butler's pantry. Ben's apron was still hanging there, overlooked when he purged the house of Ben's things. He touched its rough canvas, where the leather joined the metal. He would take it with him when he left. Allen would never question such a stylish thing. He would never guess that Lee was keeping it for the smell, the scent of sweat and vetiver that had been Ben's alone.

6

Chapter 6

"I promised I would stay out longer today," Thea said. "Which is fine because you have explaining to do."

Shawn's eyes traveled to the water, his hand moving to his mouth as if smoking an invisible cigarette. "They finally took away that shitty boat."

He gestured to her dock, limp strands of caution tape strewn haphazardly around splintered pylons. Thea breathed the fresh air, glad to see his gleaming form. Someone's wake was moving toward them rhythmically, like tarnish lines on a silver tray.

"Yup. I have a pretty scary lawyer. She threatened to sink it in the lake with all the other thousands of boats down there. The owner donated it to charity for a tax write-off. They came and inflated some pontoons and dragged it off one day. It left a trail of oil." She let Dusty off the leash and the dog peed extravagantly on a salal bush, lifting her leg like a proud, furry ballerina.

"Idiots. What is that?" Shawn pointed to Dusty. In the daylight, he was dimmer, like a filthy old mirror. "A rat terrier?"

"A dog, I think."

Dusty trotted back, glanced up at Shawn and Thea, then sat on her haunches, gazing out at the lake.

"They pulled him out at Denny Blaine," Shawn said. "The driver. Skipper. Whatever."

"Dead?"

"Yup. He was dead-dead. Didn't come up to me offering his hand to shake, if you know what I mean."

She skipped a rock. "So not everyone becomes a ghost."

"I'm still figuring out what the rules are, or if there are any. I wish he was around so I could ask him what his problem is. Dude was really coming at you, you know."

Thea turned, a feeling of cottony dread threading through her. "What?"

"The dead guy. It was no accident. He was cruising around for a while, then when you came outside, he circled around so he could get some speed up. Did you not hear him?" Shawn picked up a rock and skipped it. She watched the little glowing stone hit the water and make fifty tiny jumps, the same disruption she had noticed the first time they met.

"My mom turned on music, plus I was calling out your name."

"Someone is trying to keep you from recovering. You have to fight back."

There was a pause. The water had been so cold, Shawn's voice so insistent. The boat coming at her fast, like a ghost in the night. "Isn't this a bit coincidental? I don't remember much, but I know I don't walk out on that dock at regular times. Only, I did just meet you that day. Are you haunting some boat thief as well as me?"

Shawn considered, smiling, his jacket seams and eyebrows the color of reflected streetlights on glass. He might be an object in a very cool gallery. She could buy him, like a sculpture.

"It would be cool if I could haunt just anyone. But that boat guy. He was a kid. Twenties maybe. He must have been cruising around waiting for an opportunity. Or else working with someone. If another person was on the beach, they could have texted him you were out there on the dock. Maybe there's a conspiracy to re-coma-fy you."

"But why would anyone do that?"

She sighed. There were too many threads to pull to answer that question, and no memory of where they led.

Shawn crossed his arms. "Maybe he was in love with you and mad you didn't feel the same."

She laughed, an unfamiliar vibration in her chest. “Why don’t you ask him?”

“I told you this already.” His face was hard to read, but Thea thought she saw irritation. “If he does become a spirit walking, like me, he would still have to seek me out.”

“Other ghosts can look you up?” She kicked at the sand. “Can you look them up?”

“Most people don’t stay, Thea. We need to have unfinished business here, something of consequence we need to do. Or at least, I think that’s how it works. It’s a game you learn the rules of by playing, does that make sense?”

“You have no idea how much sense that makes to me. I’m in a game like that, too.”

“Hmmm. It’s not a cocktail party here.”

He smiled but Thea didn’t think he was amused.

“Wow, how boring for you.”

“It is boring. But I need to do my thing. I think. I think I have to push you further.”

“I already have someone for that.”

“The man who works for you. Who works. For you.”

She shrugged him off. “He pushes me plenty hard.

Shawn laughed. “Right. He can’t wait for this job to end.”Thea felt her shoulders sagging, the energy draining from her body. She changed the subject. “Right. So. What’s your thing, of consequence?”

He shook his head. “You need to wake up and get back to work.”

“Sure. No problem.” Thea picked a half-buried tennis ball out of the cold sand, throwing it right in front of Dusty, who watched it pass without moving, then returned to her sentry position watching the last few tiny ripples from the wake. Thea straightened. “So, you went to Denny Blaine beach and watched them pull the poor dead man out of the water. Why were you there?”

“It’s one of the places I can go. I have history on these beaches, in the parks around here. Some clubs, though less every year, you know. Restaurants, again, not as many as there used to be. Places in the islands, a couple of party spots. I think I am able to go where I left energy behind, if that makes sense.”

"It does, actually."

"Some of the neighbors at Denny Blaine...they've only seen one other corpse in their lives. Mine. And they knew me, knew Cory. He was there when I died. I felt them thinking about me. About him."

"Did you commit suicide, Shawn?"

There was a pause.

"Overdose. Did you not know that?"

"Is there a search engine for the afterlife? Because I'd ask you to check that."

"Thea. You really don't remember me? At all?"

She shrugged. All she could think of was his shining form in the lake, his voice coming in like a church organ intoning the order for her to swim. "I'm fuzzy on a lot of details. My body kind of lets me know if something is...familiar. Not just that. Safe. I feel that you are safe."

Shawn stepped back. "You don't think I had anything to do with that dick-head in the boat?"

"No. I was looking for you."

"Correct." He held up his hands and backed away another step. "I heard you say my name. When I answered, this white whale was accelerating right at you. And you, little Miss Oblivious, were looking over here."

"Looking for you. Exactly. And then you saved my life."

"I yelled is all." Shawn's translucent face relaxed into a smile. "He looked terrible when they pulled him out. I tried to get a description for you. Generic white guy, twenties, still had on his tighty-whiteys."

"Ick!" She pretended to bat at him, touching cold air. He stepped further back, and she dropped her hands. Anyone watching would think she had been swatting a bee. "Thanks for looking out for me."

He made a courteous sound, maybe a laugh. Knuckle tattoos glimmered below his biker jacket, an afterimage of crude lettering spelling out l-o-v-e and p-u-k-e.

"How long have you been...?"

"Dead? *Disembodied*, I like to call myself. I'm still here, right? I don't know. Six years? I told you before. You could actually google me. I'm pretty famous. Or I was."

"Six years?" She called out to Dusty, "You don't want to play?" The little animal sat impassively, nose elevated to sniff the breeze.

"Time is fake. I try to tell Cory this, but his tiny mind can't grasp..."

"So that's why Cory is here sometimes? To talk to you?"

"Uhm. Maybe ask him that." He pulled down his zippered cuffs, in a gesture that made her jump. She remembered Shawn. In one gesture, it all came back to her. She breathed, the memory washing over her. The night at that party in West Seattle when he'd— "Oh."

He studied her wordlessly.

"Oh no."

"Oh yeah. You remember now." He turned in an agitated circle, feet leaving no prints. He rocked back and forth. "I'm really sorry about what I did, Thea. What I...tried to do. This is one reason why I'm glad you chose to see me. I always wanted to apologize properly."

The memories returned in a crashing wave: an image of the crappy house on stilts overlooking Harbor Island, the deafening music, Shawn's pimples as he moved in to shout in her ear. What happened next. His hands on her, his tongue in her mouth like a hard, angry fish. She sighed. The memory held no sting, just a sad feeling of disappointment. It was her first kiss, overshadowed by the fight to escape his hands, his arms.

She had stood in the driveway crying until a senior girl had seen her and offered her a ride home. They had worn sunglasses in the car, listening to angry girl rock on the stereo: Hole and Hammerbox. Thea had never told anyone. What would she say? A Junior boy everyone thought was cool had flirted with her, then kissed her, then tried to force his knee between hers. But she had wrenched free. No harm, no foul.

But it was horrible, the shame of knowing Shawn didn't want to talk at all, didn't care who she was or what she thought about anything, had never even asked her to dance or walked with her between classes. He had been drunk, had made a clumsy effort at forcing himself on her, and left her shaken. That was normal, right—something that happened to people all the time, she was sure. The party had been dark, everyone wasted, the music so loud it made the walls shake.

Thea hadn't let herself feel anything but glad that it wasn't worse, especially at school, because Shawn had ignored her. No kids had ever looked at her in a way that suggested they knew, or if they did that it mattered. If anything, some of the older girls had been kinder to Thea. She had felt a muffled, distant kind of shame for a long time after. Later, she had understood that *the incident*, as she called it in her mind, had affected her trust.

She blew out her breath and stomped on the sand. "Listen. I have a few memories of that night. Okay? You were really high. And when I said no, you stopped. Right? You made an awkward, stupid attempt to get with me. But you backed off, Shawn, right? When you saw my reaction, you almost looked like you wanted to cry."

His face that night in the purple half-light had been twisted with emotion. At the time, Thea had assumed he was frustrated. But here he was, and she was in his debt.

"I forgive you, Shawn. Okay? I was sweet and innocent, then, that's true, and I'd never experienced anything like that. But later, I can't tell you details, but I know I wasn't an angel. I'm pretty sure I can't judge."

"No, I know." He walked in more circles, arms wrapped around himself. "I am aware."

Thea checked herself to see if she meant what she was saying, recalling only that she had pulled away from Shawn, allowing her horror to show on her face. He had recoiled as if physically wounded, almost like he was doing now. But his hands had still been around her wrists, until she wrenched them free by pulling toward his thumbs, the way they had all learned in self-defense. He had called out her name as she passed. He had seemed crushed, hard guitarists' hands and all. His angry fingers crushing into her shoulders.

"I'm sorry, Thea. Truly."

What a thing to forget. Yet somehow, the knowledge only made her like him more. And in this way, almost pollen on the breeze, Thea realized that she had been an asshole, too. That Shawn's attempt to rape her at a party had hardened her, and she had needed that toughness to become the Thea who had been in the accident, a woman who was dead now, too.

"Is the afterlife...like a twelve-step thing?"

He laughed, a deep rasp. "I wish I knew."

Dusty barked. A large gray-and-white husky bounded down the path, crashing into the water. The dog she had seen Cory bring sometimes. "Shawn?"

He was gone. A woman in a complicated parka appeared, talking into AirPods, tossing a ball for the husky with a plastic throwing stick. Dusty moved back and forth on her tiny feet, as if asking to be included in the game. Thea rose and took her leash. It was cold and sandy.

"Only thirty-two minutes?" Lee came around the corner to where Thea had slammed the door behind her. He studied her face.

"Sad. You are remembering things?"

She let herself slip to the floor, then leaned back on the door, laugh-crying. "I don't think I want to."

He crossed his arms. "No choice."

She wiped her face on her sleeve. "The dock is a mess. Your beautiful dock. Ben's."

"Where is your cell?" Lee unleashed Dusty. "Mr. Harris wants you to call him."

"The idiot's name was Alexander Barrow." Lars' voice was brisk. "A tangential connection to you. Ring any bells? Alex Barrow?"

"No." Thea said. Nothing in her body responded to the sound. She was lying on the sectional in the office, feet under a warm blanket, watching the silhouettes of trees play on the ceiling. "I don't think I knew him."

"You wouldn't, or if you did it would be a significant coincidence. He was a midlevel accountant at Thompson and Boyer."

"Thompson and Boyer." She looked over at the envelopes in a pile on Ben's, now her, desk. "The accounting firm?"

"Ramona will check to see if this fellow was on any of your accounts."

"I mean, what if he was?"

"Exactly. It in no way explains why he would commit suicide on or near your residence, except that as you know, you're not too far from Leschi Marina, where the *Short Shrift* belonged."

"So, it wasn't his boat?"

"Apparently not. It belonged to one of the partners. Barrow stole it."

"They're calling it a suicide?"

"Unfortunately, that is the likely scenario. Though possibly he thought he could make a grand statement and swim to shore. Maybe he was high, or as I mentioned, drunk. I am so sorry you had to be involved; after all, you've already been through."

Make a grand statement? She bit her thumbnail. Her chest felt off, but maybe because she rarely used the telephone and then it was only for facetimes with June.

"Thanks for the sympathy. I will get on finding someone to fix the dock."

"Lee is going to do it."

"I can send names. Isn't he busy tending to you?"

"I'll check and see if he wants to." Thea's feet felt cold. "Have you been taking care of...everything, the whole time I've been out?"

Another pause.

"I was Ben's best man. Eleanor and I were Maggie's godparents."

Her voice came too fast. "Of course. I know that. Thank you."

No wedding came to her mind, no christening or birthday parties. Just blank.

"Of course, Thea. We've all been through a great deal. Sometime, you and I will talk about the past. You decide when."

Her spine relaxed. These men around here were being so very kind. The faint vibration of curiosity rose in Thea, but she shut it down. I get it, she wanted to say. Everyone loved Ben.

They made plans for Thea to come to Rodriguez the following weekend.

7

Chapter 7

Craig Bjornson sat inside one of the slatted wooden fish installations in the common area and vaped. He liked this particular banquette, where he could watch the human sheep come and go from their work areas, back and forth, their small conversations and romances, the way their faces took on stress from whatever meaningless tasks Madhavi had them doing now. Making money. As if money would save them from what was to come. Where was Madhavi?

Craig yearned for the CEO to make an announcement. He was not alone in this hope. People talked incessantly about when Thea would return, but no one cared as much as he did. No one was working with Thea as closely as he had been. Some people even blamed him for the accident, believing that Craig had summoned her back from Canada. He never felt it proper to remind anyone that he worked for Thea, not the reverse. Let them believe he was powerful enough to call her back in the middle of a blizzard. If she never returned to work, such an appearance of importance might help him find a new job. But he didn't want that.

All he wanted was for Thea to come back to the office and pick up the momentum they had been building when she got hurt. It was cruel, he knew. She had mourning to do, and her body had been so ruined that some people thought her survival itself a miracle. But she loved work. It was the best medicine for someone like her. Like him, too. They had that in common. He had tasks, but where would his work go if she didn't come back? No way Madhavi would know what to do with their prototypes. She was a businessperson, not a visionary like Thea.

He had glimpsed someone who might have been Thea, up on the top floor conference room, the previous week. But no one could agree. Some people thought he was crazy for thinking she, who had been declared brain-dead last Christmas, could be well enough to visit the office only a handful of months later. Others insisted—Evan, Madhavi, other—had whispered that Thea was back and seemingly quite healed. Maybe it was only wishful thinking. Ben had been important to them. But everyone knew Thea was the one who picked acquisitions, shedding underperforming projects, forecasting trends and opportunities with uncanny prescience. She was the brains behind Sun. Craig's whole reputation was built on being hand-picked by her for a project no one was allowed to know about. They all knew it existed. But they didn't know what it was. And Craig obviously would pretend he had no special status, until his NDA ran out, which it never would.

Craig scooted his bulk down so he was looking up through the smaller pieces of the fish at the skylights and the tiny slices of sky overhead. He had been brought up near this office, one of the few locals. Like Thea. He had overcome his religious upbringing with such ease he himself could hardly fathom it. Once he started college, his ascent to a PhD had been more or less inevitable. One advisor after another had arranged his progress from undergrad to master's to doctorate. The paper wasn't supposed to be read by anyone but reviewers, but someone was apparently on Thea's payroll. She had hired him before his doctorate had even been awarded. The money had been so good he had been able to pay his parents back immediately. And thus ended their ability to question his life's choices.

He didn't miss the church at all. The fish reminded him of a cathedral he had seen on his mission in Columbia. Thea had asked him about his time there, something about if he had noticed that people were talking about the water. At first it had made him almost physically ill, how Thea understood the weird feelings he had then. But of course, now he understood. All water-based people were talking about it, how nothing was what they had known as children, not the wildlife, or the weeds, or the height of the waves.

Maybe that was the moment that his work with Thea replaced all other forms of belief in Craig's mind. The fish sculpture must have come from her. She, who was obsessed with water, with the weather, with the need to silo their servers from all outside influence because the will to profit could barely be navigated. She used to say, data is a living thing, and once it escapes, you will never get it back in its cage again.

God, he missed her. He stowed his vape pen. Would anyone notice if he fell asleep there? He had done it before, but then he had the excuse that Thea and he had been working around the clock, which people respected. Maybe they suspected that he actually slept in Building Four some nights. His town house was fine, but he saw no reason to go there. His mom would have left food in his fridge, with kind notes and pleas for him to call. He didn't want to tell her that he wasn't, as his family assumed, overworked. Quite the contrary. He perfected the prototypes, collected data, sent the algorithms down new paths. There was always work. But without Thea, it felt like he was fiddling. Maybe he should, as his father suggested, look for another job. But where? No one had what they had, at least, no one he was aware of. The world was large, and not everyone was as stupid as the men in charge of the tech giants currently scaring the world with their collected marketing language models, seemingly vast, but incredibly superficial. Machine learning on how to summon the demons, with no purpose beyond telling humanity what it already knew. No. He would stay and wait for Thea.

Rumor had it that not only did she pop up randomly on the beach near her house, which he had visited many times without seeing her, and at Building one, but she had also appeared at a Tex-Mex restaurant in Madison Park, like a silver saint, her kluged-together body apparently functional enough to swill margaritas and hold forth on the fortunes of her foundation. Insane. Not that he expected her to talk to strangers about their work together. But what if she didn't remember? The thought was too frightening to dwell on. He puffed on his vape pen.

Craig no longer believed in God. But if he had, he would have felt her presence inside the wooden fish, with its distinctly church-like light shining through the irregular wenge slats, its rays tinged warm from the hanging sculpture lamps Ben Sun had hung as what Craig suspected was a kind of joke, the suns he could illuminate anywhere he went. The laugh was on him. Craig couldn't believe Thea could stand that guy. As a peddler of visionary bullshit, the man had been incomparable. As a person, he had exuded smarm. Craig didn't know him personally, of course, or had not. Naturally, Thea had banned Ben from their subfloors. He would have pressured her to make up a fake story about what they were doing with their project, take profit and move on without considering how much potential COHE held. Thea wanted to save disrupt the whole world, not sell a better vacuum cleaner. Luckily, Ben had enough sense to listen to her. COHE was secret. If Thea had died, the whole thing would have died with her.

Craig sat up. He had some ideas he wanted to sketch, some application ideas. No doubt the time would come for them to invite developers to come up with uses for COHE. But there were so many cool ideas, he had a new vision every day. He replaced his left shoe where it was coming loose. A young woman glanced his way, a look of disgust on her face, no doubt smelling his smoke.

Technically, he wasn't supposed to be smoking there, as smokers were expected to congregate outside the loading dock like criminals, but no one stopped him. Only Thea had the authority to fire him. Not even Madhavi herself was allowed on the subfloors where their workrooms and servers hummed night and day.

He sucked and blew out vapor. Jelly donut flavor, not bad. Though it made him want donuts, the opposite of what he had hoped.

"Bjornson. You can quit wallowing in misery." It was Madhavi herself, her long hair under an orange beanie, her matched sweat suit covered by a long raincoat, in constant anticipation. She always looked like she'd rather be sipping craft cocktails in Brooklyn. "So, what you've no doubt heard is true. She's awake."

"Is she?" He put his vape in his pocket. He tried to hide his relief.

Madhavi's laugh was deep, like her somehow neither sincere nor sarcastic.

“Is she...okay?”

She shrugged. “Sorry you weren’t included, but it was Senior level only.”

Craig tried to compose his face into a patient expression. His hand clenched around his vape pen. “When was this?”

“Monday.”

He kept his voice low. “Was it really Thea?”

Madhavi tipped her head to one side. “I know what you’re asking. But you are the only person here who really needs her to be that version of herself. The rest of us have already moved on.”

“Ouch.” He forced himself not to overreact to Madhavi’s disrespect. “Is she coming back?”

“I assume so. She said she was going to look into our projects.”

“Our projects?”

He grasped the vape pen in both hands in his lap. He was practiced in waiting for authority figures to get around to making their point.

“Yes. The projects in the shareholder report.”

“Madhavi!” COHE was not in any report. It was behind so many firewalls, no one would ever find it.

She laughed. “I am contractually obligated not to speak of COHE, Craig. As are you.”

“You’d really keep that from her?”

She stepped away, still laughing. He flopped back inside the fish, his groan of frustration lost in the atrium’s vault.

8

Chapter 8

"You going to drive yourself all the way to the ferry dock? Leave the Tesla in the parking lot?" Lee said as Thea moved the loops off the reformer straps, replacing them with the handles. "It's ninety miles."

"That's not a good idea?"

"Put the headrest up."

"Yes, sir."

"Socks off."

She removed her socks and took up her position on the reformer. "Isn't there a bus I could take? I'm not having my mom drive that truck all the way, it's a waste of gas. Plus, this is supposed to be relaxing."

"I will take you."

"Absolutely not."

"Absolutely yes." He moved to the foot of the reformer to catch her eye. "I want to go to the outlet mall. I like the Coach store there, send my mom a purse."

"You let me buy your mom a purse, at the regular Coach store. Any kind of store."

"Deal."

Thea began her series, sitting up, dragging the cables in front of her, then lowering herself down again while her core hitched, making her torso tremble.

"Slow. Don't let your left side get lazy, now."

She corrected, pulling evenly with both hands as she glided through the movement. Pulling, pulling, then releasing back. Her left arm trembled with the strain.

"Good you're going to the Islands. You need to get out, and it is very safe there."

"Very safe there?"

He held up his hand as she completed the set.

"Thea." Lee lifted the bar to adjust the resistance. Thea hopped off and watched him.

"Do you have any idea what is going on?"

"What is going on is," He flipped the bar down. "Like you said you are super rich. I know you are famous. Some accountant is crashing into your dock."

She stood for Ice Skater. "Okay. You be my bodyguard. You can protect me from anyone who comes within a mile of me."

She moved to a squat position and pushed the platform back and forth with her feet, expecting him to smile. He didn't.

"What?"

He didn't answer, just turned his face away.

Lee was leaving early so he and Allen could go to someone's wedding. "Lunches," He gestured to a pair of glass containers in the refrigerator's center shelf, followed by several others below. "And dinners. Okay? Last weekend, you and June didn't touch the lunches."

"Are you upset?" She tried to catch his eye.

Lee was two inches shorter than she was and slender, but his limbs were powerful, as she knew from the many times he'd picked her up. His hands were still vivid in her mind from when she first came back from the fog, the props she leaned on until she grew strong enough to sit up and then stand, walk, move from the elevator to the stairs. But she didn't remember ever feeling the sensation of disapproval that emanated off him, now.

"Did I offend you?"

He crossed his arms, his dark eyes softening. "No. But you will need to talk to someone else about safety, bodyguards, all those things. I will fix the dock next week. But safety and guarding, those are not my things. And you need to be out, with people. Not hiding at home."

"Okay." She tried to smile. "You're right.""I know you are trying hard." He let his arms drop. "When is your mom getting here?"

"Go on." Thea gestured for him to leave. "I'll be fine. You're right. It's not fair to expect you to protect me forever. I hear you."

He peered at her for a moment before disappearing out the door. She locked the door, then showered, drying her hair with a towel as she stood looking out at the lake. Something hot pink was poking out of the flat gray below the windows, a swimmer's neon buoy.

Thea pulled on some clothes and went to the dock. If anyone was watching her to signal to a murderer out that Thea was outside and vulnerable, they weren't on the empty beach. She moved back a few steps, just in case. The day was bright and fine, traffic on the bridge the only sound.

"Shawn? Can we finish our conversation?"

No answer. Thea studied the splintered pylons. She imagined Ben talking into a headset, swearing, demanding someone come out right away and make the dock perfect again. But it was like imagining a television show. She didn't know how Ben's voice sounded.

"Goddammit, Shawn."

Thea went back inside. She called Ramona Stein, then made herself a cup of chamomile tea. When she came back downstairs, the pink buoy swimmer was emerging onto the beach, a small woman wiggling out of a wetsuit.

"Those crazy people."

Thea startled. "Mom."

June stood at the window, one hand on the switch that flipped on the gas fireplace.

"I mean exactly how fucked up are their nerves?"

Thea smiled. "How was the drive?"

"I left plenty early, which was a good thing because two trees fell in the pass..." She went on to describe the chaos that was beetle rot in the forest around the interstate.

"What a strange world to wake up to. Everything is so sick."

"How about a cold beer?" June asked hurriedly, opening a plastic cooler. "There's a new brewpub in Twisp I thought we ought to try. Got us a growler."

Thea warmed the meal Lee had prepared for their dinner: Pho, scallion pancakes and shrimp rolls. Had she known how to cook, once? She had no idea how to make any of this. He seemed capable of creating most anything. Maybe that was why he didn't want more responsibility.

"Am I supposed to hire someone to replace Lee? To, you know, keep an eye out for trouble?"

"Oh, this conversation. Good." June put down her glass. "Would you consider it?"

Thea felt a shock of self-conscious embarrassment. "Did you two already talk about this?"

June moved to open and close drawers in the kitchen island. "We have had a lot of time to talk about a lot of things, Sweetheart. There's no delicate way to say this, but while Lee and I never gave up on you, while you were out, we were the only ones who... Anyway, we agreed you'd come back to us. He learned physical therapy. I handled your meds, lots of mundane matters with insurance, and so forth. It was a long road. And here you are. We were right."

While you were out. Thea wondered where she had been. Was she a creature like Shawn, wandering between worlds? Or had she been trapped inside her skull? "What are you looking for, Mom?"

"Any idea where the combination to the security office might be?"

"The security office? Is that what it's called?" Thea had thought of the room with all the little televisions as a second pantry. The idea that its purpose was to keep out intruders wrenched her.

June took a long sip of beer and looked around the room. "Ben no doubt thought of some numbers or letters that had special meaning. But I've tried every combination of birthdays and anniversaries I know, and nothing works. You can't intuit what he might have been thinking, can you?"

There it was again, the implication that this wasn't her house, her life. It was all wrapped up in this man she had glimpsed only in snatches, like a square of torn snapshot left behind in a pocket. Whoever Ben had been, he was gone. Why did people have to keep bringing him up? *Intuit him?* Thea only intuited Ben when least expecting to. Sometimes there was a phantom smell of sweat, or a faraway look in Lee's eyes, and Ben was there. But not his ghost. If he was going to haunt her, he would have appeared by now.

"Anything?" June said.

"What did that Benson Sun have in mind? I know! Let's reanimate his memory so we don't have to call a locksmith."

"You know how he was. Everything had a purpose behind it."

"I do not fucking know." Thea said. "I wish I did."

"Oh shit." June put her cup down. "I've upset you."

"Why do you and Lee have to push me so hard? Why do you insist that everything good in my life, my peace, my privacy, everything has to go away?"

Thinking about Ben had unleashed a tidal wave of anger that tore through Thea. She couldn't stay there. The house felt like a trap.

9

Chapter 9

Thea ran, sharp rocks jabbing at her soles, until she was next to the big ponderosa pine at the beach. She was out of breath.

"Just breathe. You're all right."

Shawn.

The taught feeling slipped away. Thea was glad to see his silvery gleam, if for no other reason than Shawn wouldn't push her to remember what details Ben would have used to create a code for his security office, which Thea realized dully was called *the safe room*.

Her head felt light in the wind. Shawn moved closer; his mushroom smell a comfort. The water looked as soft and loving as a baby blanket, moving gently up and down in pinky-silver ellipses.

"What am I awake for?"

"Who knows? But one thing is for sure. You have all the power."

Her breathing slowed. "Money, you mean? I do not understand."

Shawn glittered like a roiling star-studded sea serpent as he disappeared, his voice a symphonic whisper. "You're the one of two people who can see me. Cory needs to forgive himself, but his guilt is the only thing connecting him to me. If he lets it go, he lets me go. Which he should do. But he's not ready."

"So, he keeps you coming back?"

"But so do you."

"And I need to forgive myself, for being rich?"

"No, silly." He laughed. "You need to do something that lets go of me. Maybe it's connected to not being hit by boats. I don't know. But I can tell you that from where I sit, you're sleeping on your potential. And I personally have feelings about that. I wasted my life. It pisses me off to see you going that direction."

"I thought you were my friend. Now here you are pushing me to be well on your schedule instead of my own. Just like them. Thanks a lot. I have an idea, why don't you take your crap micromanagement skills and disappear back to hell or wherever you live."

She didn't believe in Hell. Or in ghosts, for that matter. She liked talking to Shawn, and if he did exist, he only meant the best for her. He had saved her life. She was just mad. She sat down on the biggest of the driftwood logs. June was standing in the living room window, gazing out at Thea. She seemed to notice something to Thea's left. Then she moved back into the house.

"Hey," Cory said from the path.

"You just missed him."

"You okay?" A teen girl strode past him, the white huskie Thea had seen the day before straining on a leash in her hand. A young version of Cory, with long legs and tangled bark blond hair.

"Define *okay*."

"Did I interrupt something with you and...?"

"Sparkly Shawn the manipulative ghost?"

"Yeah. You look upset. I'm sorry. Sometimes he gets on a soapbox. Was he yelling at you to leave the past behind and move on with your life, that kind of thing?"

"Yes." She sat next to him on the large driftwood log. "Is Shawn...real? How long have you been talking to him?"

"Ah. I don't know if he's real or even what reality is. But I've been coming here to talk to him on and off since he died. I've tried to figure out exactly what he is or who I am talking to. But where do you go for answers? There's not much science, if you know what I mean. Is he a hallucination? Or...I don't know. The imprint of energy? Now it turns out that you can also see him. What's that all about?"

"I don't know. Reality is kind of weird for me right now, Cory. His commentary isn't helping."

Cory regarded her, then looked over at his daughter, then back at her. "I get it. For a long time, I thought maybe he was just in my head, you know. Maybe my brain was lost in a groove."

"But you kept talking to him." An image came of Cory and Shawn standing on this beach as Thea was practicing being outside, walking Dusty, slowly returning to the world. She hadn't thought it strange at all, two men chatting amicably, one alive, one dead.

Cory scratched his head. "I guess I wanted closure. And, the thing is, I could never ask anyone. I don't have a ton of custody of my little girl, there. I would hate to risk losing what we do have because dad is ranting about, you know, angels and spirits."

"He's no angel, I'm pretty sure of that." Thea laughed, the tension in her easing. "I don't really understand why he takes an interest. Seems to think my fortune gives me special responsibilities. Which, maybe it does? People keep looking at me to see how healthy I am. I wish I knew. Everything feels surreal. Memories come. Intuition that I can't explain. It's a funhouse. Except for this beach. You know? This water and this sand are the only things I know I can trust. No offense."

"None taken." His expression seemed carefully neutral. "This is a special place. Remember when we would always come here to get high during lunch period? I know you were here some of those times."

She laughed. "Okay. If you say so. All I know is I love this beach."

"We all did. It was our refuge against the world. No doubt that's why you guys built your house right here."

"Because I love Secret Beach?"

He shrugged. "I'm just guessing. But it stands to reason. If you're rich, why not buy the most wonderful piece of real estate you know? My most successful musician friend has a place on Kauai. It's what people do. Right?"

A cloud of warm air floated through her. The water beamed light up onto the ponderosa pine, like signals from a mirror. The girl ran laughing down the waterline with a tennis ball in her hand, the dog barking with anticipation.

"What's your daughter's name?"

"Hailey. I have her every other weekend and Wednesdays. Though she's too busy a lot of the time now. Basketball, dance team, all that." Cory stood next to her. He smelled soapy.

"Right." Thea said absently. "All that."

"I'm sorry. You had a daughter." He nodded toward the girl. "It must be hard."

Something cold drained through her. "It would be, I guess, if I let myself think about it."

"Dodo." Hailey came closer. "Can I meet her?"

Cory sighed theatrically. "Hailey, this is Thea."

Thea's emotions lifted as soon as she saw the girl's open face with its Cory-like, elfin cheeks. She could tell that Cory was a good father.

"Nice to meet you. I have seen your pretty dog down here." Thea smiled, and her skull felt just the right size.

"My mom brings her here sometimes. My parents live close together so I can go back and forth by myself. I'm fifteen now, so big deal. But when I was seven, I thought I was so badass to walk a block by myself with my little bag, you know. Of course, my parents were texting the whole time." Hailey grinned, a child's wide face on her long, teenaged body. "My dad has been worried about you. He's kind of got boundary issues about people he cares for. But you seem..." Hailey stepped back, tossing the tennis ball far across the water. "Gorgeous. You seem utterly gorgeous, Thea."

"Thank you. I was thinking the same about you." Thea wanted her face to soften but she couldn't get her grinning cheeks to move. "I hope you'll listen when your father tells you how to stay safe in this world."

"He does." Hailey put one hand on her hip. "But I'm sick of the Patriarchy forcing girls to cower in fear. How about teaching boys not to attack us? How about growing a set of you-know-whats and sit with your uncomfortable feelings, you know?"

"Wow." Thea felt blown back as if by wind. "You're really something. I needed to hear this today."

Cory was watching Thea, but she couldn't tear her eyes from Hailey. He must be feeling proud, the dad who set his life aside to be near this girl and her big, wise mouth.

"Don't worry about me. I'm not going to get hurt. Plus, I prefer girls." Hailey ran down the beach to fetch the ball.

Thea looked over to Cory. He stared at the ground, as if embarrassed by pride.

"Do you ever talk to Shawn about the terrible stuff he's done? He said he had a lot to atone for."

Cory pulled off his sweatshirt, revealing arm sleeve tattoos, a complex tree, a line-drawing of an osprey diving for prey, a Victorian frame around the face of a sea monster. Young arms on a middle-aged man. The stretched skin was endearing, both his muscles and his ink a reflection of how badly he wanted to be beautiful.

"I think Shawn beats himself up for the things he did. I never saw him really hurt anyone. I know he feels he came on too strong with you in high school. Forgive me for asking. But did he hurt you? I could never get a straight story."

Thea felt the anger flame in her flicker. "Yes. But in the most mundane kind of way. You know. Confused about the difference between consent and coercion. Love and power."

"That's not nothing. Are you sure you're good now?"

Thea laughed. "I want to burn this whole place down. Is that good?"

Cory's laughter was unexpectedly high and loud. "I knew I liked you. I was never supposed to, you know, because Shawn was in love with you. I wonder sometimes what would have happened if he hadn't been such a jerk, if you and he could have at least been friends. He might have avoided some of the pain."

"I have to go."

The front door was ajar when Thea got back to the house, June trying out combinations on the keypad in the hallway, cursing at its loud chirps.

"I'm back, Mom."

June looked up. "Do we need to talk about your memory issues, honey?"

"What is there to say? Haven't the doctors all predicted it would be a rough road?"

"They don't know. If you listen to them, all you hear is the sound of asses being covered." June checked her phone. "Ben's mother doesn't return my texts anymore. I think she changed her number when the check cleared."

Ben had a mother. Nothing came to Thea's mind but a faint aroma of flowers, the shine of something. Intelligence, maybe. Pride?

"Lars and I decided Ben would want her taken care of. You're okay with that, right? It's a drop in the bucket for you. I think Lars is an okay guy. What do you think?"

"I think yesterday I was a snail, and today I am a slug, and everyone can't wait for me to be a rabbit."

"Sit down." June rolled out an office chair. Devoid of the stacks of toilet paper and dried noodles it had held until that morning, the room felt bright and grim.

Thea sat. "Lars didn't think I needed guarding when I was...?"

"Don't say *vegetable*. You were never brain dead, just comatose. And until you came out of it, this place was quiet as a tomb. If you have enemies, they weren't concerned as long as you were unconscious." June heaved a theatrical sigh. "I don't understand it. If that idiot in the boat was really trying to kill you, what was his motive? It seems so far-fetched. But you do need help."

Thea put her head on the cool desktop, surprised to find it made of polished stone. Her fingers stroked its immaculate corners, the thickness of its dark grain, streaked with slender striations, white and gray in the black. "I need to be guarded."

"Yes. Ramona and Lars feel we need to assess threats, whatever that means. I mean really, isn't security just another elite service designed to separate people from their community? I can hardly put myself in the head space to grasp it.

When I was your age, I was shopping at Goodwill and paying off old credit cards with new credit cards."

There were buttons on the bottom of the counter, wires running toward the wall. Thea touched them without pushing down. Would the police detective return if she did? With a smug expression and an assumption that Thea was overreacting? Thea wondered about his tattoos.

"You might have struggled financially, but you were free."

"Hardly. I was as caught up in bullshit as everyone else in this life. When you were a baby, I dressed you in the cutest clothes I could scrounge up. I enrolled you in the gifted programs, even though I knew they were nonsense. I wanted people to think I was a good mother even though we were alone. I was foolish."

Thea sat up. "Were you?"

June made a so-so gesture. "As flawed as the rest."

"Was I...?" Thea started to ask, then broke off the question.

June made a dismissive sound. "If you don't want your money, give it away. God only knows there are plenty of folks who could use it."

"Jesus, mom, I just found out about it. I'm trying to figure this all out."

"So am I. So is everyone. That's the human condition. If you're trapped, escape."

There was something comforting in June's lack of sympathy. It reminded Thea of Lee saying, *Dying? Is that so bad?*

"Were you always this ruthlessly pragmatic?"

June slammed a drawer closed. "I hope one day you remember the things I had to do to survive and make a decent life for us. How hard it all was. Because if you think having wealth is a giant problem, you have forgotten what problems are."

"I have forgotten everything."

"Okay. Know this much. You worked your ass off to build SunStorm. It wasn't just Ben. You were at it sixteen hours a day. Your health suffered. You worked so hard, when you decided to get pregnant, you didn't even have time for IVF. You decided to adopt Maggie rather than slow down."

"Stop." Thea waited for her body to erupt in some reaction. But nothing happened. "If you're going to bombard me with information, could you slow it down?"

"No, I can't. I've been sitting here waiting to talk to you for ages, wondering who you'd be if you ever woke up. I want you to know." June held up her calloused hand. "I respected your choice to adopt. And we all loved Maggie dearly." June looked away. "I saw you trying to look tough at SunStorm on Monday. I understand that those people will take everything from you, because that is what people do, they sense weakness, and they take advantage. But it's your money. No matter how condescending Madhavi might be. Or Lars, that big nerd. Or Eleanor, chairman of the Foundation board. If it weren't for you, Thea, they wouldn't have all that power. And they know it." She sighed, looking at the recessed lights of the ceiling. "As the world realizes you've come back, it's not a bad idea to look out for threats."

"Mom. I'm not back."

June closed a drawer. "They don't know that. You put up a good show at the company. You talk to the neighbors, Betsy Wheeler, all those types. Word will get around that you're just as big a bitch as you were before."

Thea's laughter caught her off guard.

"Of course. That's the missing element," she said in a voice of wonder. "I was a huge bitch."

June's face creased into a smile. "Let's have some cocktails. I could use whiskey for this conversation."

Thea closed her eyes. *SunStorm*. Had that name been her idea? "What did I used to do for fun? Did I do anything?"

"You used to swim. It's why Ben, and you, built this monument to design. We always came to Secret Beach when we couldn't afford the Y. I taught you to swim, right out there." June gestured.

Thea put her hand on June's shoulder. The flannel felt soft over her beefy muscles. Thea remembered her mother's ranch only in snapshots, chickens clucking and deer eating vegetables from outside a high mesh fence. Goats with their angry mouths, pine needles full of their droppings.

"I will have Ramona deal with this, Mom. I've really taken you away from your own life."

June stood completely still. When Thea moved to look into her mother's face, eyes squeezed tightly shut, shoulders shrinking together, it took a full minute for her to understand that her mother was crying.

"Thea." June's voice was hoarse. She cleared her throat. "Thank you, honey. Thank you for saying that. I wasn't sure..."

Thea flattened June's collar. "I know. Me neither. But here we are."

10

Chapter 10

Suki watched Thea walk home from the beach again, passing the parking lot, the neighbor with the ugly house to her even uglier one. Why did Suki feel such intense relief? She was torn between wanting to encounter Thea and being afraid to. Afraid of how the meeting would feel. Afraid of how the aftermath would affect her, if she would be able to manage herself.

The water was cold on her hands and feet, which normally helped her handle her emotions, kept her on *an even keel,* as they said. She had her violin, her piano, her guitars. But mostly, Suki felt glad she had just missed arriving back at Secret Beach when Thea was there. Which was so lame of her. There were public access beaches all over the lake, a hundred or more places like this, where anyone who wanted to was allowed to put in a boat, or swim. And yet, for Suki, there was only this one, this stretch of a hundred yards of sand and stone, a few logs, a stream of broken lawn furniture that appeared and disappeared with the seasons, a thicket of scraggly bushes and one tall pine surrounded by more ordinary trees. The sand was a treasure burial ground of dog toys and hash pipes. Nothing about the place made it special except the way the light shone in the afternoon, illuminating the pine tree like something holy, a shrine to some long-forgotten natural deity that had once held dominion over the whole gentle coast, or the one that had existed before they emptied the lake to make more land available. It was a pretty spot. But that wasn't why she came back. Suki returned to soak into her memories. Lights were turning on in houses up and down the shore and up the hill, reflections beginning to blast up onto the pine's glossy, long needles, its surreal red-brown hide. Suki would pray to this goddess, this stretch of coast with the sand rich people must have trucked in long ago to cover jagged old stones and the bottles left by rapacious lumberjacks, make the bottom safe to wade into. No one started their swim this late. It was one of the best times of day to float and cry.

11

Chapter 11

June didn't know what was going on in that silvery head of Thea's. It was all so surreal. People coming after her, trying to ram her with boats. Ugh. Seriously. That must have been accidental. If it was attempted murder, whoever did it must be the worst sort of amateur. She had no damn notion of how serious a threat Thea might face now. As Maya Angelou said, people tell you who they are the first time. They certainly turn to jelly when they get wind of all the money. Even she herself did, at the thought of all the kids she could help.

June listed the center's regulars in her mind, their snotty noses, stinking clothes, ruined shoes. Such sweet faces, usually; sometimes angry arms, fists that struck out. Of course, they did. What they knew was worse than poverty or neglect: it was lack of hope. That caused anger, but anger was better than fear or depression. The shoes were what really got her. One of her first clients, Tevin, had gotten frostbite, but no one had treated it, and his toe wound up deformed, which you could plainly see through the hole in his sneaker. The first in a series of permanent scars he would no doubt carry from growing up as a have-not, in that valley of second and third homes belonging to people like Thea and Ben. People who didn't even know what a rotten tooth was, or how it felt to have your heat turned off in the dead of winter.

Paula had them roll out yoga matts and practice yoga breathing and emotional awareness so they wouldn't act out at the first sign of opposition and end up incarcerated. Though, realistically, some of them would. Some of the boys already showed signs of being unable to control their tempers. One of the girls,

Rainy or Lainie, June couldn't remember, was already cutting, and she was only seven. No doubt she had learned it at home, as many of the kids had learned inappropriate sexual behavior and every other terrible thing people could do to one another. Thea's money provided groceries to take home, clean clothes, blankets, toiletries to keep. June knew sometimes that was the only food these kids got, the only warm showers, the only adults who read aloud to them. All Foundation funds. So, June understood. She was as greedy for more of it as anyone else.

She didn't believe in God, but if she did, June would pray hard for some version of the old, mean, brittle, competent Thea to return and decide for herself where her Foundation should donate. June had spent long hours planning what to do with the fortune if Thea didn't wake up and she wasn't ashamed to admit it. That was before she understood just how much there really was. The many days and nights when Thea was comatose, and then the long period when her brain was functioning but she refused to wake up. June had dreamed of a bigger building and more centers in other towns. She could do a lot of good. There was so much need out there, and no one in the cloistered mansions seemed to give a damn. She knew what wasn't true. Betsy Wheeler and her type were busy ending strife, they would be the first to tell you. But had they ever sat with a reeking five-year-old, watching an old wizarding movie while they combed out lice for the third time that month? No. They had not. Only June had that privilege, and she was grateful for it. More than money, the kids needed to feel that there was such a thing as a decent adult in the world.

The day of the accident, June had been reading to the older boys: Percy Jackson, maybe. The boys had been relaxed, for once, their heads in the book, lying cattywampus in the library nook. The wall phone had rung, which usually meant someone's guardian would be late getting them. One of the girls had answered, Tina or Chrissie.

As June stood listening to the nice man in Sequim delivering the worst news in the world, she had been looking at one of the girls sweep the kitchen. The big industrial broom she had brought back from the Home Depot in Darington kept hitting the top of the opening between the stove and the floor, too wide.

The reality of what the man was saying in his crisp Canadian accent was horrible. Too horrible. Chrissie—or was it Tina—had stopped sweeping to watch her. The man kept talking, said Thea was being medevacked to a trauma center. When had people come up with the verb medevacked? What a strange thing to come into common usage. It sounded like *bivouacked*, or *gobsmacked*, terms that meant things much simpler than they sounded.

June stopped listening, just felt the clutching pressure in her chest, the panic spreading like a hot hand across her clavicle. She thanked the man again, though the line was dead, and smiled so the girl in the kitchen could stop staring and go back to work. And then June had finished reading the chapter before driving home—thank God Cal had answered his phone immediately and agreed to come over and care for the animals.

The rest of the year was a blur of pain, lonely trips over the pass, unspeakable funerals, meetings with Lars, and Thea a bundle of wrappers and tubes, reduced to beeps and lines on a monitor. It had been less than a year since the accident, only nine months, the time it took to grow a baby. And a baby she was, Thea, at times. Now she was changing quickly, a strange new person with Thea's face. So odd, this unpredictable woman with her bouts of anger, her innocent face as she saw things anew. But, there was no joy to be dredged up from the rebirth. June was worn out. She stroked her fantasies of enlarging the center almost like worry beads, a soothing practice that helped her get from one moment to the next. That and the wine, of course.

Thea had disappeared again, as she seemed to enjoy doing at the moment. An animal, really, pacing around, unable to decide how to process all the signals. Fight or flight? How the hell would anyone know, in this situation. Thea had been so hard and sharp before, a crystal always attuned to some vibrations only she could feel, though Ben was quick to pay attention. But now, it was obvious to June how wrecked her mechanisms were and how desperately Thea wanted to make sense of everything coming at her. She liked to go to the beach and talk to herself. Why not?

June scratched a bite wound on her elbow that had been healing slowly, when little four-year-old Max McCarty had flown into a tantrum, and June had made the mistake of trying to hold him. She knew better. He hadn't broken the skin, and she hadn't told anyone. His little face when he realized what he'd done was terrible, red circles growing on his cheeks, more storm clouds building as he understood himself to be capable of harm. She had tried to reassure him that he was not a bad boy, just an angry one, and if he could simply get control of his body, then all would be well. But the bruise still hurt.

The Canadians said the helicopter might possibly have been tampered with, but there was no proof, and no one seemed to be aware of any motive, or perpetrators. Security cameras had revealed only authorized personnel. Manifests and safety checks had been routine. The fault had been with the weather, the rising storm coming on faster than storms ever did. She had begun to read a report of the condition the bodies had been in when authorities arrived, but Cal had taken the iPad out of her hands and made her drink a shot of Jameson. What a lovely man.

The investigation had been closed. Human error by the family company up there, which Lars decided not to sue. Who knew why the Suns boarded a last-minute charter helicopter back to Seattle? Cal had said it was surprisingly easy to shoot down a chopper, and even easier to sabotage one. June hadn't pressed further. She hated to live in such a world.

An hour early. She could have just one glass of Cabernet. It was the weekend.

"Thea?" she called out. But Thea had stomped off somewhere. June took out a glass for her, anyway. Best not to drink alone.

Thea opened and closed the neatly organized cupboards. Zipper packages were stacked, some dark, others a rainbow of bright colors, contents blurred by ripstop plastic. Finally, she found it. Her wetsuit looked like a dried-out sea creature, forgotten and far from home.

"Well, hello."

Thea let herself out at first light the next morning, taking care not to wake June, passed out on the couch. The dark rubber carcass felt awkward at first, made for a bigger body. Thea soon remembered how to zip up the back and adjust the thick fabric on her limbs. She walked silently over the decking to the retaining wall, creeping down the double line of boulders. She let herself fall in. Icy cold gripped her hands and feet. But once she pushed off and began to swim, and the water that seeped in down the small of her back warmed, she felt pleasantly mobile. The sky gleamed navy blue with fuchsia jet trails.

Thea settled into a lazy breaststroke. She felt light and swift, a bird in flight. She realized calmly where she was headed. Past the beach, out beyond the warning buoys, to where Mount Rainier came into view. Her shoulders flushed with the effort to reach that distance, far enough out that her house was a golden cube, her next-door neighbor a grid of lanterns, then the beach, a dark mouth.

She turned back to the open lake, and there Rainier's vast dome stood whitening in the sunrise, snow sharpening into thicker and thinner striations. Thea's breath caught. Something was happening inside her chest. It felt momentous, a vast dark force trying to swoop out. She couldn't breathe. Another ghost, inside her?

She coughed. "Just make yourself known, whatever you are."

Then came voices, swimmers closer to shore. The sun rose over the hill, and suddenly everything switched from gray to blue. The water blazed. Thea was able to breaststroke back toward her house.

"Is that Thea?" a woman called.

"Yup. It's me."

Six swim-capped heads turned, revealing smiling goggled faces, bright buoys bobbing around them. Several people called out greetings.

"You want to join us?"

She recognized some of them, but without context, no names appeared. Her body felt euphoric, tingling with the pleasure of clean air, the familiar taste of lake water. This was why she had wanted so badly to come out here, for this sense of weightless joy. "I'm not ready."

"Hey. Give me a minute," the one with the pink buoy called out.

They made sounds of agreement and friendliness, then swam off.

"Thank you for the invitation."

"Of course. It's great to see you out." The woman pulled off her goggles, revealing a pair of brown, hooded eyes over a beak of a nose. "I'm Suki. I don't expect you remember me."

"Suki."

"That's Bea, Corinne, Val, and Martha. And somewhere, probably halfway to Madison, Roxanne. She wears earplugs." Suki indicated the others, who were splashing steadily north. "Seriously, the offer stands. We are out here...well you must know. Monday, Wednesday, and Friday."

"Today is Saturday." Thea felt grimly satisfied to know that for sure. She stroked toward the beach. Suki followed.

"Right. It's a make-up swim. Glad you got that awful stink pot gone. What a scary thing."

"I know. Crazy." Thea added impulsively. "You girls should stop in for coffee one of these times. After your swim."

Suki smiled broadly, "We'd love to see the inside of your house. Better have a big coffee pot."

"I have an outdoor shower, too."

Milfoil brushed Thea's feet with their feathery fronds. Nearing shore.

"Oh, we know. We are always drooling over it. Sure, you must have seen us out here."

Realization bloomed. "I do know you, Suki. Don't I?"

They came to standing on the stony lake bottom, lurching toward the shallows.

"Yes. I was Maggie's teacher at Grady School. We met a few times."

Thea turned away. They sat. Suki moved so close their wet suits were touching. "I want to tell you something."

"Okay."

They sat in the shallows. Suki took Thea's hand in both hers, and spoke in a deeper voice, emphasizing on each syllable so slowly she was almost chanting. "Maggie was special. And everyone at school loved. Her. Deeply. And we are so sorry. For. Your. Loss. Our loss. The world's. The whole world's."

Thea nodded. This woman was out of her mind. Or else she was trying far too hard to deliver her message, sure to stress how important it was, how much the words meant. *Joke's on you. It's only words.*

"The community would want you to know that we had a beautiful ceremony for her friends to say goodbye to her. Everyone shared a memory. The kids put together a whole shrine. You'd be welcome. To come see it."

Thea's face must have done something unexpected because Suki broke off abruptly. The wetsuit suddenly felt heavy.

"When you're ready. Of course."

"Yes, thanks. Thank you so much."

They sat in silence, Thea turning away to watch a float plane angle down to the north.

"Did I say something wrong?" Suki said.

Thea let her feet move with the arrival of a wake, up and down, her hands digging into the lake bottom, so she didn't float away. "I will have to come up with a polite way to say that sometimes other people's memories are a lot for me right now. I'm sorry."

"My mistake." Suki's voice was tight. "I thought you would be touched at how many people loved your little girl and how much effort they put into honoring her memory."

Thea's teeth chattered. "My feet are starting to turn blue."

Thea stood. "When I can, I'll come see the tribute to Maggie at Grady school."

Shawn was standing on the beach, arms crossed, watching intently.

"Super." Suki pulled off her swim cap, revealing an angular haircut and an ornate tattoo sprouting under it, which must have covered her whole scalp. All Thea could see now were darkly inked tentacles emerging near Suki's nape. "Let them know you're coming, though. Don't want to upset the kids after all these months."

"Nope."

"Nice seeing you."

"Likewise, Suki. Sorry you didn't get the swim you wanted."

In the shower, Thea cursed herself for all of it, for yearning for friends, for losing her grip, for being so rude. But mostly, for allowing the awful woman with the overly expressive diction to ruin her calm. Her words, and the name *Maggie*, repeated over and over in Thea's head until she was sobbing.

Lee drove an old silver van. It smelled of leather polish, its seats covered in brocade slipcovers. He inspected her. "You sure?"

"Yup." She wasn't. "Let's get a coffee on the way."

"You want to run into people today? Usually, you don't want to be reminded."

"Tell me about that." So, this had happened before, the seeing of friends, teachers.

They motored up the hill.

"Mmm. People used to stop by the house, friends, Mr. Harris, other people. When you first came home especially. Everyone wanted to know when you were going to wake up. But you were out of it then. You were only speaking in your sleep, and you were still mostly asleep. Then one day you tried to get up, and you slipped and hit your head. You don't remember?"

"Nope."

"I was fixing the spa. This was when only June was caring for you. She got scared. Your brain so fragile. And Ben would be so angry, if you died after so many months it took to bring you back."

"So, June made you an offer, to come be my caregiver?"

He looked at her sideways. "I made the offer. I said Ben would want me to help out."

Thea laughed. "I see."

"And we have been fighting over you, proud mom and dad, ever since."

They sat in silent mirth while he navigated onto 520 and then I-5 North.

"I only remember the headaches. The meds Mom made me swallow." The memory made her wince, the dark bedroom, a machine rumbling softly, like someone sucking at her skin. She hadn't heard that sound for weeks. Months?

"Your head never hurts anymore? That's good. No more medicine, better."

"I would be lost without you." She fished the envelope with a check out of her backpack and put it on the console between them. "Here's something to use for a present for your mom."

Thea dozed on the ride, waking when Lee pulled in and parked at the Hidalgo Drive-In. The restaurant's glass was obscured by hand-painted signs listing types of fish, halibut, sockeye, haddock. *Yes! We have King Crab!* The fried-food smell gave Thea an explosive thrill.

"What is this wondrous place?"

Lee laughed. "We have extra time. Come on. You can have your coffee."

But they had cod and chips, and peach milkshakes.

Thea sat back, savoring the combination of sweet flesh and salty crust. "I love your food. But this..."

"Delicious, right? Special treat because you're taking a big risk."

"Am I?"

"Alone for so long on a boat. At least forty-five minutes."

"How do you know this place?"

He put down his cup. "You don't remember?"

"Don't tell me."

"Okay. Okay. Don't be upset. You be all right on the ferry, right?"

"Yes." She ate a French fry. Crunchy, salty, oily, hot: the pleasure was almost too much. "And I'll be safe when I get there, right?"

"Mr. Harris and Ben were good friends for a long time." He rose to bus their trash, then stood looking at her as she scooted out of the booth. "You look the same as every other rich white lady on the boat. You'll be fine."

They made it to the dock as the ferry was landing. Thea had just enough time to purchase her ticket when foot passengers were called to board. She knew all this. The framed photos of native settlements. The half-built puzzles lying on built in tables. Was this déjà vu? No. Her body simply knew this place. She had been here before, many times.

She climbed to the deck, staggering to a bench as the horn sounded their departure. Everything felt muffled. Her emotions were as far away as the nimbus clouds ribboning out high above the straight. She wanted to drag the clouds shut as if they were curtains, leave the raw edge of confused feelings outside, like her mother would have done at dusk in their old craftsman house, a signal that the day was over. But a cool wind was blowing, leaving a brightness to the west that would become a spectacular sunset in an hour or so. Thea closed her eyes. Would she recognize Eleanor?

"Hiya, Theodora."

Her eyes opened.

"You look so grown up and pretty."

The female ghost who sat next to Thea wore slacks and a turtleneck, with old-fashioned gold-framed glasses. She gleamed warmly compared to Shawn's pale glimmer, flame-lit rather than made of starlight. Thea recognized her energy, her maternal friendliness, but couldn't place it.

"Thanks?"

"I'm Doctor Graham. It's been a long time since we've seen one another."

"My old pediatrician?"

"That's correct."

"It must be ages since I was in your office, Dr. Graham. I'm sorry to learn you're no longer living. Does my mom know?"

Dr. Graham laughed. "I think June probably does."

"I see. I missed a lot. A lot is...no longer there." Thea thought about her line, which June had taught her, about the reboot of her glitchy brain. What a stupid analogy.

"You're not altogether healthy at the moment, my dear. Are you?"

A clutch of gulls wheeled away.

"My current doctors tell me I am. But we always trusted your word best. What happened to you?"

Dr. Graham's eyes drifted toward the boat's railing. "I. Well. Depression wasn't as treatable when I was undergoing mine. I get the impression folks have better options now."

Thea reached for her hand but felt only air. "I'm sorry."

"Oh. It's been a while."

"My understanding is that time has no meaning to your kind?"

"Ah. I'm not your first."

They were into the straight, refinery lights blazing amidst the dark line of trees behind them. The gray-green water looked unimaginably cold.

"So, you're stuck on this ferry? Long commute for you."

"That's a good one. We had a cottage on Orcas."

"Oh. I have property on Rodriguez."

"Lovely. Rodriguez is so peaceful."

"What happened to your cottage?"

"It belongs to my children. Both grown now. Allison is married to a nice-looking fellow named Dev, and they have a boy named Ethan, and a girl still in arms, though probably she has learned to walk over the winter—named Clara or Claire, I didn't quite catch it. And my son Jim has a partner, Stanley. My children alternate possession of the house, you see, but these days no one has time to come much. I see them more in summer."

Dr. Graham's pain hung in the air, as clear as the sun dotting the green water, pipes of light through the clouds making rippling dots of sparkle. "Oh, Dr. Graham."

"I believe I could go on into the next iteration, if one exists, Theodora." She wrapped her firelight arms around herself. "And I will. When the time comes. But the kids don't understand why I did what I did. And of course, I can't make them. I'm still their mother. And..." Her voice faded.

"And you want to see that they're all right."

"Yes."

The sat in silence, watching the wake move between islands.

"Have you run into me on this boat before?"

Dr. Graham nodded. "You and your husband and little girl. Yes. But then, you were fully in life, and I was invisible to you. I think I see what happened."

"Oh?"

Across the inlet, they passed Shaw Island, its tangle of Madrona and Pines leaning out over the edge of its rocky cliffs.

"You came very close to dying. You're not fully alive yet." Dr. Graham said. "But you are doing well. I can see that even without taking any tests. You're healing."

"I'm sorry about what happened to you, Dr. Graham. Is there anything I can do? Track them down, deliver a message?"

A couple walked by arm in arm, heading for the bow.

"Oh, I don't think they would be very receptive to that. Can you imagine?"

They talked until Shaw Island came up on the left, and Dr. Graham faded in place, her voice triangulating like a lost phone connection. Thea went inside to the bathroom to splash water on her face and blow her nose.

Then the horn was sounding, and the PA system announced arrival at Rodriguez.

This was when she would look around to see if they had dropped anything, any toys or sippy cups or clothing. This was when Maggie would raise her arms and say, "uppie," and Ben would carry her down the ramp, the moment when they would leave their normal life behind and begin the adventure in the forest. Somehow, it felt as if Lee ought to be there, as well.

The engineer lifted the rope, and the bikes rolled off, followed by Thea and the other foot passengers. Lee had told her to look for a green Land Rover. What was a Land Rover? The air around her felt thin and strange, the clattering of gears as a dozen bikers began to climb the hill, pedestrians scattering with their luggage, the call coming to clear the way for offloading cars.

Why had she come here? But the trees overhead were tall and welcoming, and she knew them. She knew the little café sign and the hippie font someone had used to paint the words Rodriguez Island. Thea followed the others to a landing area, where Lars stood.

"I'll get that." Lars grabbed Thea's rolling bag from her hand before she had a chance to toss it into the trunk. She felt flustered. Was she a capable adult, or a helpless child?

"Thanks."

She climbed into the passenger seat. He missed the edge in her tone, closing his door with an expression of placid good humor. They drove into green country lanes, wet with drizzle. She breathed easily. Lee was right, this place felt safe.

"How was the ferry?"

"Beautiful. I ran into an old friend."

"Really?" He sounded concerned. "Someone you knew from SunStorm?"

"No, childhood."

"Ah."

They crossed through fields dotted with cows, then llamas. He pointed out a long driveway. "Do you remember that?"

"Uh. No? Sorry."

"It was an artist colony they turned into a camp for school kids. I went there in school. Sure you did, too. All the kids know it, we learned about conservation and biology. No memory?"

She smiled, changing the subject. "What a nice place to bring kids."

Another couple of turns and they entered the forest. The windshield blurred with drips from the trees.

"So, your yurt is intact, at least it looks that way from the road. But I've heard a couple of complaints from the morons on the council that they would prefer you have it taken down, at least until summer. Not to worry, they have no real jurisdiction."

Her yurt. She had a yurt. The thought of it made her want to laugh. The canvas tent sounded like June's idea. But maybe it had been Old Thea's.

"Take it down?"

"I know you and Ben had plans to build on the property. And you still can if you want to. But for now, there's always a chance of squatters. They're harder to get rid of than you might think."

"Ah," she said, feigning more understanding than she really felt. "I'll give that some consideration."

They pulled up to a magnificent wooden house surrounded by wet gardens. "Eleanor is beside herself to have you here. She has been so worried. But I keep telling her, you're a tough bird. Aren't you?"

12

Chapter 12

Eleanor moved through the kitchen pouring white wine, Coltrane's amber tones floating through the rafters, a roasting smell in the air. "Please, Thea. Make yourself comfortable."

Eleanor was tiny and pert, her white hair braided and wrapped so she resembled a holy woman in an ancient religion. But her fingers and ears sparkled with diamonds, and her face was beatific with cosmetic interventions. Thea thought her lovely, but if Lars had not said they were old friends, Thea would never have guessed it.

Lars rolled her bag into a bedroom off the main floor. When Thea had composed herself, they all sat in the conversation pit overlooking the water through tall trees. The light was getting low, though no horizon showed in the gloom. Thea felt immediately relaxed, exhaustion lurking under that, every sensation familiar and yet new.

"Smoked salmon?" Eleanor presented a board covered in fish, crackers, and fruit, enough to feed eight people. "It's all local. The oysters, don't miss those."

Thea didn't say that she had just eaten an hour before. She didn't want to displease this woman. The fish was soft and delicious, bringing inexplicable tears to Thea's eyes. "This is...very kind."

"You're at sea right now, yes?" Eleanor put her head to one side. "Would you benefit from a little downtime?"

"You read my mind."

"Come on," Eleanor said, standing. "Let me show you around."

The house was simple, the main floor with living areas, kitchen and bedroom all looking out at the water. Upstairs were two suites, a small study, and a library, all lined in wood.

Out a covered walkway were the bunk house and boat shed, and Eleanor's white cavern of a painting studio. Thea breathed in the oil paint. This was known. She saw the old armchair where she had sat many times before. A happy image. She perched there now, while shards of memory reinserted themselves. Ben, his round nail beds, telling her that he and Lars were taking the kayaks out. Excited, a little scared, a boy from an apartment in Taipei now a man who was kayaking with his friend, dragging in crab traps. Then Thea's chest grew tight. She remembered the baby, then the toddler, then the little girl, with her wide brown eyes, her cap of jasper colored hair, intense as she rose to take some early steps across the concrete floor.

Thea had wanted to build a house here. This had been the center of their time together as a family.

"Are you okay?"

"God, no." Thea said.

They laughed.

"I want to go see my damn yurt."

"Of course, you do." Eleanor pointed in the direction of an outbuilding. "Take one of the bikes. The light should hold for another hour. When you get back, dinner."

They pushed the mountain bike to the top of the hill.

"Lee will kill me if I don't make you wear this," Eleanor said, strapping a helmet on Thea.

The pressure on her temples reminded Thea of the protective cage she used to wear. The deep ache, the shallow pain, her eyes only tracking in one direction because they had her lying on her side. How long ago? It was in a hospital, and there was a sound of beeping. But Thea had been afraid, her hands clenched, or were they clenched involuntarily? The name *Dr. Perle* embroidered on a white coat, a man saying very loudly, "Your brain is as fragile as a cracked egg. One more sharp knock and you'll be scrambled. Understand?"

She had whispered, "No more. I promise."

"If you're careful, you have a whole life ahead of you. Just keep that cask intact."

Dr. Perle. He had been fine, just another one of the gang of lab coats that walked around that place. The fact that he would disapprove of her riding a bike in the gloomy near-dusk gave Thea a rebellious thrill. *A whole life.* What a joke.

She laughed as the bike rolled down the needle-strewn drive, squeezing the brake to test it, then letting her speed build as she hit the wet road, frigid air in her face as she turned to pedal the half mile to her own driveway. Trees made a corridor of dark green under the stripe of pale amber sky, promising a bit more light, clouds and water holding it between them.

A pickup truck passed, someone lifting a hand in the standard island greeting. Thea was too focused on controlling the bike to return it, or those of the two vehicles that followed. She breathed in the forest, ferns spilling into the ditches, huckleberries and salal reaching out of old stumps. How had she forgotten how much she loved these islands?

Her euphoria dissolved into pain when she turned into the drive, marked by driftwood painted with a childish sun. She left the bike leaning on a tree, too winded to peddle the uphill gravel drive. Her eyes felt wet, her head throbbing, the sensation of negative gravity that she wanted to beat against a trunk as hard as she could, to get it to stop.

She removed the helmet and hung it on the handlebars. Wet ferns and nettles brushed against her ankles, her hands. She heard herself sobbing.

What would Lee say? Just *breathe. You are okay in this moment. And then this one. And then this one.*

And then she was there at the crest of the drive, looking down on the flat ground where they were going to build a home, a soft glimmer of water beyond a cliff face, madronas and cedars leaning out over the sea. The smell of kelp and salt mixed with forest. She leaned on a madrona tree, one she remembered, a friend, the softness of its new bark like baby skin.

She breathed a flood of images and sounds, of Ben and Maggie. The smell of her sleeping head, her tiny fingers, the heavy body in Thea's arms. Ben's warm hairless chest, the way he ate with chopsticks, his wry expression as he said something meant to be funny. Her people, her family. She put her hands on her head and let herself fall to the foot of the tree. A panic attack. Every part of her body rebelled, an onslaught of rejection of the images, as if they themselves were an enemy to be expelled by force. Thea found the outhouse, grateful it was still stocked with paper. An owl hooted, so close it made her jump. Then she laughed. She hooted back, and they talked for a few minutes, *who cooks for you, who cooks for you,* as she had learned somewhere meant it was a Barred Owl, until it fled with a rustling of leaves and a flash of pale feathers.

Thea breathed. Dread was overpowered by curiosity.

The inside of the Yurt smelled of wet wood and dust. An undisturbed scent. She used her phone light to locate a couple of oil lamps. With them came memories of how they'd lived there: the generator, the solar panels up the hill, the pile of kayaks and paddle boards under the tent's wooden base. She sat on the bed and held one of the stuffed animals from the box underneath to her chest, unable to identify if it was the fox or the mouse. No matter. She let it catch her tears.

When Thea emerged, the sky was pewter above the trees, and her stomach was bubbling with hunger. She accidentally kicked the helmet deep into a thicket, deciding to push the bike back to Lars and Eleanor's. She loved the silent stillness of the dark road.

No cars passed. The trees shifted high above, and something small scattered as she passed, squirrels or skunks. But she was alone. Then came a howl. For a long time, Thea empathized with the animal—its grief, its pain. And then the sound resolved into a siren. Not an animal, at all. A big emergency, more sirens joining the first. As Thea got closer, the noise rose and fell with such ferocity that she ditched the bike and put her hands over her ears. Red and white lights flashed through the trees.

Something terrible was happening.

People shouted. Eleanor was screaming incoherently, as men moved through the yard. Without knowing what to do, Thea kept walking toward the house, the lights, the noise. Then Eleanor was beside her, grabbing her hand. "Where have you been?"

"On the bike. What's happening?"

"Lars collapsed. Someone showed up here looking for you. Didn't you see him? You must have seen him."

Thea sputtered. "I saw a passing motorist. Did you mean him?"

"Honey, I don't know. Can't you see this is an emergency? Lars got upset. He started to scream at the guy to leave you alone, and then he fell unconscious."

"Looking for me?" Thea let her hands drop to her sides. "How would anyone know I was here?"

Eleanor was already gone, running toward the men. The sirens suddenly cut out, leaving Thea's ears throbbing. A man said. "Clear the area."

Thea turned and walked into the forest in the direction she had come. Her feet took her to a pathway parallel to the cliffside. All was darkness, here, the ground soft. Doors slammed. Radios blared. Thea pulled her hoodie around her and huddled at the trunk of a tree, letting her head rest in the bark's wide crevasses.

Then came the horrible nightmare sound. The obscene thudding of an approaching helicopter. It came closer, closer, it was right over them. Thea vomited into the moss beside her. A fragment of a memory dislodged, tearing metal, blood in the snow, the ocean of pain. She breathed. *You are okay in this moment.*

Thea wrapped her arms around her knees. The memories sat, like a box on a table. They would always be there. She could open the box if she wanted to, or not. She could choose fog, take a path of oblivion. Emulate Shawn or Dr. Graham. It was her choice, no one else's. She looked back. People were moving a stretcher into the rescue helicopter. On a stretcher, a long shape. Lars, Eleanor running alongside, clambering in. The door closed.

Thea clamped her hands over her ears as the machine's blades whipped their chaos. Then the monster rose, disappearing into the night with violent concussions of air, then faint clattering. Then the air stilled, the only sounds dripping trees and truck tires over gravel, down the driveway, red lights turned left, back to the main road. If not for shivering, Thea would have thought she was dreaming.

The owl hooted again. And then there was a different kind of hooting, obviously fake, the kind men in movies made to one another when they were ambushing the enemy.

Thea felt no fear, only curiosity. A rational part of her brain said whatever had happened to Lars was over. Whoever had come looking for her must be gone by now. She had been there for at least an hour, long enough for the night to darken to an impenetrable black. But were they?

Dude was fully trying to ram you. Shawn had said. She almost heard his musical afterlife voice.

Lee had said she looked the same as all the other ladies.

She relaxed. There was only the soft tear of falling rain. No one was going to find her and kill her where she was. It was too cold. The hooting had stopped, but someone was out there, in the trees. Someone was looking for her, but he wouldn't find her. It was too dark, and she was accustomed to stillness. She would be patient. She would be like a stump, dark and unmoving, a part of the forest. If he looked at her, all he would see was a shadow. Except for the shivering. Eventually, she admitted, her numbness would turn into hypothermia, and she would have to take shelter somewhere. Thea was drawn to the idea of sleeping in the yurt: the old army blankets on the iron bed, the faded rug and the wood stove. Shawn had stopped her the last time she was in danger. She reached out her mind for ghosts, felt only the gentle presence of the trees.

Thea stood, retracing her steps. She pushed the bike to the road and sat on it, so wet she hardly felt the cold seat and frigid handlebars. The road was barely lighter than the forest. She moved the pedals gently so the only sound was water sluicing off the wheels. She pushed up her gravel drive until the yurt appeared, a pale cylinder between trees. Then she hid, panting, warm for the moment, though she knew that wouldn't last. What she was feeling was adrenaline. Had her body done that when the chopper crashed? What had she felt, in those final seconds, when her family was alive, and she was still Thea Sun?

There was movement below her. A person in dark clothing stood on the yurt's wooden deck, looking in her direction. A man. Thea doubted he could see her. More hooting sounded from the direction of the beach. The man moved toward the sound. The closer to the cliff edge he got, the easier he would be to see. Thea moved quietly to the edge of the drive, then ran as fast as she could to the shelter of the trees on the other side.

"Hey!" the man on the beach called out. "Be careful, bro."

Thea wondered about high tide. The beach disappeared, leaving only the rickety old stairs to stand on. She crept to the edge, looking down through the trees. Even in the near dark she could see how choppy the channel was. It took a moment of concentration, knowing she was visible herself, for her to make out the two-person kayak sitting beside the lowest step, waves licking at its belly. The man in the stern was a rumpled smudge, his vest ringed in reflective piping that shone out in a faint half-circle around his neck. What an idiot. Who were these criminals, so naïve and unprepared?

Thea walked toward the yurt.

Chapter 13

Thea moved quietly toward the door and slipped inside to total darkness, the sound of dripping surprisingly loud. She had a sudden memory of Ben, standing in this place, smiling, showing off a Dungeness crab he'd carried up from his trap.

She stood for a long time, but the hooting man wasn't in there with her. The floorboards trembled slightly, his feet outside on the deck in back. He was looking out toward Lars' house, expecting her to be between the two properties, on the trail or in the trees. He was waiting for her, and the man in the kayak was waiting for him.

Someone had set her up. She was too cold for this. Even though she was only waking up to the situation, the memory seemed to be arriving too late. But then she remembered something: a long, slender shape. Thea moved carefully to the door and felt for a hinged board covering the lintel. The wood felt soft and smooth under her fingers. It swung open silently, still well oiled.

Inside, the cold, solid metal of a pistol. She lifted it down, almost dropping its unexpected heft. Her left hand moved up and felt for ammunition. There were other objects up there, but the hand found a clip and brought it down, slipping it into the pistol with a sharp click. Would her brain offer up instructions on how to fire it? *You brace your arm with your left hand*, the voice said. Ben's voice, thick with his wide experiences, his hoarse almost-accent. He had been bullied, punched in the throat, which was why he always provided for violent situations. Why had he loved her? she thought. Because she was a fighter. Or, at least, the version of her he knew.

The floor trembled. The man was coming back.

Fucking relentless popped into her mind. *Her*, she realized. Thea Sun. She was the relentless one, the restless, angry, pushy one, the one who rooted out enemies and frightened them enough to keep them gone. That was who she was, not the cold, wet animal cowering in the underbrush. Not a doe in headlights.

No. The feeling of potency sizzled through her large leg and back muscles, her hands and feet, and her chest, which seemed to expand with every breath, taking in more oxygen. More of the life she still had, tattered, and forgotten as it was. She held it like the now-warm, heavy weapon between her palms.

Thea sighed and walked back out the door and to the mossy ground outside the deck, so she was facing the hooting man at a slight upward angle. She had lots of directions to run. He had only one, toward the cliff's edge and the stairs.

"Hey, asshole. Good night for bird watching. I think I spotted me a real rare find."

The man froze. His silhouette looked hunched, as if they were playing a game of freeze tag. Not a real criminal. A fucking gamer. Something felt familiar, a feeling around this kind of person, someone cocky and annoying and unquestioning of his own entitlement. He was having fun. He and whoever had rammed that boat into her dock, Alexander Barrow, the same flavor of jerk, the kind of guys who appeared in the water outside her window yelling about their time swimming the Fat Salmon or biking the STP. Maybe this one was older—late twenties, she guessed. But he was on his way to whatever pinnacle of self-satisfaction guys like that lived on. She was an impediment he would simply excise, the way he'd rewrite a section of code or abandon a mediocre pint of microbrew lager. She didn't know him. But Thea understood this kind of guy. This kind of guy was always in her way, acting as if he owned the place. And she didn't know what exactly the old Thea used to do to sweep clear her path. But she always had—she felt that much in her bones. That was why he was here, wasn't it? Because he expected that Thea Sun was going to fuck him up, just as soon as she could so he had to stop her while she was still weak.

But he was too late.

"Eleanor said you came looking for me and scared my lawyer half to death." Thea eased toward the top of the stairs.

He followed, something dark and shining in his left hand. His voice was smooth and surprisingly low, the voice of someone used to giving women orders. "Stop right there, dear. I'm not scary. Just need you to do something for me."

"Why would I do anything for you? Do I know you?" She tried to hide how the cold was making her shiver, but she let him see the pistol.

"It's not important who I am. It's...you seem to have recovered from your accident?"

Trying to establish rapport. A background in sales. She would have Ramona look into it. If she made it through the night.

"You bet." The same impulse to show no weakness she had felt at the SunStorm headquarters seized hold now, the alpha wolf in the presence of a wayward pup. "You're too young to be stalking a weak old lady like me. You're what, twenty-five, thirty?"

He flinched. Pride. What a loser.

"I'm not stalking. I'm..."

She moved toward him, slowly, so he would hardly be aware of his feet carrying him backwards. The water threw subtle shadows from the salal bushes, the wooden landing piled with old crab pots.

"Oh, we had a business meeting I forgot?"

She caressed the pistol's safety. No. She didn't know how to take it off, and her hands were now shaking so hard she doubted she could lift the thing to fire it, anyway. They were at the top of the steps.

"Can you come a bit closer? I don't want to hurt you. I just want to talk to you. Business. That's all this is.

"What business is that?"

From below, the other man yelled, "What the fuck are you waiting for, Ryan? Just do it."

Her arms were frozen. The gun was all she saw, like a blurry photograph meant to highlight a single face.

"It's going to take a higher pay grade than you to kill me. Ryan." She rushed the few steps between them and kicked out, her ears rushing with wind, surprised by how heavy his body felt as her foot connected, sending him flying. Her whole body shook as she grabbed the rotten pine railing, losing her balance and falling, into a mass of wet ferns, out of the other man's sightline.

Below, on the stairs, something splintered. There was a splash, and Ryan howled in pain. He yelped incoherently while his partner chewed him out. Thea made out the words *bitch* and *blew it* and *fucked*. She thought about standing and trying to fire her gun at them, but she couldn't move. The swish of a kayak paddle disappeared in the larger roar of tide. Rising slowly, she crept up far enough to look over the edge. She could just make out the silhouette of the kayak and the two men in it, hunched forward to stroke the water. Darkness swallowed them.

She sat heavily on the top step, the gun landing beside her with a thud. Where was Ben now? Why didn't he have a ghost? She felt the sense of armor she always had around her husband, that knowledge that nothing would harm her. A pulling sensation behind her eyes dissolved into tears, more salt tide, the simultaneous sensation of gratitude to be there, cold and shivering on her land, and horrible hollowness, that she was there alone.

Still, Ben had wanted her safe. Who was she to contradict him?

The sky was turning the colorless pale of near dawn. Lars and Eleanor's house sat silent and surprisingly dark at the end of the trail. Thea would have expected the men with the flashing lights to take precautions. When she tried the side door, finding it unlocked, she understood. They believed that the danger was passed, that with Lars and Eleanor gone, their job was done. They either didn't know or didn't care about Ryan and his accomplice.

She probably didn't need to worry any more, but she was exhausted from her night crouched in the yurt and reluctant to let her guard down. The tidal current down the channel was swift and impenetrable. She remembered that much. Thea crept inside with the gun raised. After fifteen minutes, when she had warmed up enough to stop trembling, she put it behind a ceramic pot and drew herself a bath. The house had a land line telephone, on a built-in desk in Lars' office area. While the water ran, Thea located a handwritten number list, calling Eleanor's cell. Straight to voicemail.

"Eleanor. Obviously, I'm in your house. Please let me know how Lars is..." Thea hesitated.

Why had Eleanor left without more of a warning that Thea was being stalked by a boy with a gun? She could have told the men, at least. Maybe she was in on the plot. The water in Lars and Eleanor's tub scalded Thea's cold skin, but she relaxed into it, washing cobwebs and leaves from her hair, scrubbing tear-stained grit from her face. Her overnight bag was open on the guest bed, undisturbed. A pot of stew sat cold on the stove, a loaf of bread sliced on a cutting board, everything ready for the evening meal.

Thea decided to act as if everything were normal, or as normal as she could imagine. She fished in her pants for her cell phone, but it must have fallen out in the yurt. She had spent the rest of the night huddled sleeplessly under the covers of the big bed. As the world lightened and Thea exited the seeming safety of the yurt to go back to Lars and Eleanor's, she studied the broken pine railing where she had kicked Ryan down. He had fallen a long way, eighty feet or more. Amazing he could just paddle away. Such a fall would kill Thea, thrust her right back into darkness. The beach had reappeared, stark and rocky, littered with what looked like logs, or seals.

The walk back to Lars and Eleanor's had seemed long. Now that she was there, clean and dry and dressed in the clothes Lee had packed for her, Thea felt restless and unsure what to do with herself. Had she imagined Ryan? No. She was sure of that. Was this the kind of thing Ben had been worried about? The reason he had left guns and ammo. She had been wrong to get upset about the safe room. She wasn't safe. He had known. Why wasn't he a ghost she could talk to? But maybe that was good. Maybe Ben was in a better place.

Still. There was one ghost she might be able to talk to. She googled how to release the safety on Ben's gun, then powered down Lars' computer.

13

Chapter 14

The keys to Lars' Land Rover hung on a peg by the side door. Manual transmission. A feeling of amazement overtook Thea as she found herself remembering how to drive a stick. A pair of deer watched her open the gate to the old artists' colony, then darted into the woods as the truck passed, stopping under the canopy of branches. She killed the engine, then pulled on a hat for the walk to the beach.

The colony was silent, windows reflecting the sea. There was a smell of dry grass and sea water Thea remembered. Her head felt light. The trail to the beach looked weatherbeaten and overgrown. Did schools still come here? It appeared not. There were cracks in the glass panes, sharply broken shells and rusted cans between mounds of heather. Shrubs shifted in the trees' canopy. Someone was there, or something. She felt for the gun in a cloth bag slung across her torso, walking quickly, pistol in both hands like a television detective.

An osprey alighted from a pine and flapped away. Thea walked to the beach, wondering how she was supposed to hold the gun. She didn't remember being here with Shawn, but he had to have come here when they were in school. Who owned this place now? Even the lodge's rectangular windows seemed decrepit.

Her arms felt rubbery. She was sure she had not practiced shooting much, because the gun felt far too heavy in her hands.

Then a flute-like voice spoke next to her. "Pulling a gun. That's serious."

She squeezed off a shot. Driftwood splintered.

Shawn laughed. "You got me!"

She lowered her hands. "Now you're dead."

He crossed his glowing arms. "You're tough. I guess I ought to approve. But as someone who has been very not-careful with life, I have to say it's not what I want for you."

She put the safety back on. "Who are you to want anything for me?"

"Oh. Cranky today. Didn't you come looking for me?"

He moved like a rock star, like he was really looking past her to an audience. She found it annoying. Thea sat on a log, feeling the burned bullet hole with a finger. It was still warm.

"Do you know who Ryan is? The boy who tried to kill me last night? Or at least put me back in a coma."

"Someone else tried?" Shawn's starlit form sat next to her. "I told you you're important. Look at all the people trying to get to you."

"You swear you don't know about it?"

"I know about the chopper coming to get that dude, the one who spends a lot of time at your house, the tall one. I mean, one of the tall ones. It's hard to keep track of your men."

"Very funny. That dude is named Lars. He's my lawyer."

Shawn laughed. "Of course he is."

"Who has it in for me?"

"I'm sad to hear you've attracted violence."

Thea laughed, so long and hard that Shawn made an annoyed face.

"I can help you. It's just not what you want to hear. Maybe you don't get to just be left alone with your money and your manservant. Your responsibilities remain."

"Oh, come on." She kicked her feet into the stones. "I can't be responsible for what I don't remember, Shawn."

"Yes, all the people who counted on you just magically cease to exist. Like your child."

"As if you cared about my child."

He covered his face in his hands.

"What?"

"You really haven't guessed?"

"I am guessing you are one of the people who want something from me. Which is depressing. But it tracks, I guess."

Thea passed a beach stone between her hands, warming its smooth surface.

"I am not asking you for anything now. You already gave me something precious. You loved someone I loved."

Thea threw the stone. It made a soft plinking sound in the turf. "You loved Maggie?"

He stared at her. "She was my biological child. How can you not have guessed this by now?"

"Shut up." Thea studied his ghost face. "Tell me about her, then. I don't remember her very well."

"Oh." He sagged. "Okay."

"Maybe that's your job here on this plane. Maybe that's what you're supposed to be doing."

"Wait. Did you put this together? Is that why you came looking for me?"

"No." She felt a creeping sensation. "Believe it or not, I don't really want to remember. But I'm not going to be able to get through reclaiming the old Thea Sun's life without more information. There's too much danger, apparently. Too many things in motion that I am at sea about. Tell me, Shawn. If this is the one thing that we have in common, not some party where you acted like a jerk. This other thing."

"I want you to understand that things are in motion. This story isn't over." He scratched himself under his jacket. It was the first time Thea has seen that he was a drug addict. Funny how a person can go from wise to unreliable with just one gesture.

"That much is obvious."

"Did you call the cops?"

Thea looked in the direction he was pointing. "No. But Thea Sun can't be left wandering. Can we talk on the beach again? Or have you left there?"

Up the hill, a white pickup truck was pulling to a stop. The same sheriff's vehicle she had seen at Lars' during the night.

"Look, I'll make this quick. This is what I know. Souls want the experience of being alive."

The truck parked. A man was clearly visible in the driver's seat.

"Souls what?"

"When I was using. I would go to a place. The Infinity room, I call it. Because of the artist who makes rooms like that, all mirrors and no walls. When I died, I was there again, only this time it was filled with love. An ocean of love, of beautiful souls."

"Okay."

The door to the truck opened.

"The souls all wanted bodies. They want the experience of being alive, imperfect, painful and hard as it is. It is the experience of being alive that makes the universe run."

"And this has to do with me, how?"

"I think that if life ends here, if people cease to exist, the universe will have no way for souls to be embodied. And that will be a tragedy for every soul that has ever existed or ever will exist. No way to feel, or grow, or progress. Just nothingness."

He shuddered.

"So, you interfered with an attempt on my life because you want to dump the future of life in the entire multiverse of lives and afterlives and souls and everything into my lap?"

"I know it sounds incredible. It is to me, too, and I don't know if I'm right. But you're incredibly powerful and I appeared to you, and only you. Plus, Cory, but I don't know if that matters. Like I said, I don't know if my tiny consciousness can fathom it all but, it is time to do something important, Thea."

"Sure. No problem. Just make life possible for every soul. Not a big deal."

"Look at it this way. There's no downside for you if you get after fixing things. You'll probably make even more money!"

Shawn winked out.

A tall man exited the pickup and came down the path. Thea made sure her face was composed and hid the gun in her bag.

His name was Jim Conroy, a local volunteer sheriff, sixty, beefy, with gentle blue eyes and a pistol on a holster in his belt. He volunteered that Lars had had a heart attack, that Eleanor had been too hysterical to understand, and that they had gotten him off island quick enough to probably save him. Everyone knew Lars. He was young and healthy, really, he'd be fine. They knew her, too, and were glad she was back to the land of the living.

The land of the living. She laughed.

Jim followed her back to Lars and Eleanor's, where she left the Land Rover in the carport. She insisted on putting the stew in the outdoor trash bin and washing the pot, leaving the house in perfect neatness. There wasn't time to look for her cell phone.

On the ferry, watching the dock recede with a familiar pang of sorrow to be leaving, exhaustion set in. Thea had been on the island for 18 hours, but it felt like a week. She pictured her bed at home, the gleam of the lake on her ceiling, Lee making noise in the kitchen, nothing in her head but thoughts of working out on the Reformer. Her body sagged into the seat on the heated deck. The boat was nearly empty. No ghosts sat with her. If they had, she would have screamed at them to leave her the fuck alone.

She woke in a panic to the ship horn's cacophonous vibration, Anacortes approaching like a flattened hand. The green water amoeba-d with foam and old sticks. Thea's spirits rose past her exhaustion and the sadness of Shawn's confession. Maggie, her jasper-colored hair, her stars for hands. His, too, glimpsed from the shores of Secret Beach. No one was separate from the rest, even after the drugs had done their work. There was no escape from the memory of Maggie's voice, even though all Thea had when she tried to summon it was the sucking emptiness of not being able to recall. Like a sting from a jellyfish, a rebuke. But she was alive. Alive, not a sad, half-burned-out bulb of a ghost, hovering around a memory, trying to get a rise out of the living with tales of disembodied souls. No. None of that mattered now. She was Thea Fucking Sun. She was still here in spite of Alexander Barrow and now some kids named Ryan, and his accomplice in the kayak, a pair of morons. She pulled her coat around her. Passengers were clustering at the ramp, a handful of men in chinos, an old woman dressed in purple with ribbons in her hair.

Thea descended slowly, looking for the Tesla. There was no reason to bother Lee with all the details, not until they got home. It had been so fun to eat at the drive-in, to be with him, out in the world, just ordinary people. Her buoyant mood grew even more bubbly at the thought of seeing him, being with him in the car for the next ninety minutes. And there he was, right at the top of the stairs in the short-term parking, letting her find him, refusing to do for her what she could do for herself. Because he cared.

She threw her own bag into the trunk and climbed into the Tesla. Lee peered into her face as if it held important writing. His eyes were soft.

"You have been sitting in the wind." He handed her a cup of green tea and a sandwich wrap. She was too perplexed by the heat rising within her body to take a bite. Her flesh expected something from Lee. Anticipated it eagerly.

"I fell asleep on the deck."

"How was it?" He steered them to the highway.

"Fine. Hey. How long have I known you?"

He looked at her sidelong, and her body flushed with understanding. There was a long pause. They passed the big casino, then forests and fields, behind trucks laden with lumber.

"You are remembering so much. But there's no need to rush."

14

Chapter 15

Cory didn't like it. Thea's house swarmed with rent-a-cops. A dark, buff man Cory hadn't seen before opened the door for them, followed them around, his body language all authoritative, as if *he* were the homeowner. The other man had already gotten lumber unloaded, the dock rebuilt, stained. Who knew what she had to pay for such a fast repair job? Poor Thea, surrounded by parasites. June came on the weekends, but even Cory could see how worn out the old lady was, that night of the boat crash when he'd tried unsuccessfully to make sure Thea was really okay.

Thea had smiled her silvery smile at him. That was enough. He had known her since, what had they been, fourteen, fifteen? Hailey's age. There were so many things he wanted to ask her, about what it meant, that she talked to Shawn, that she was the object of some kind of assassination attempt, or someone's stupidity, whatever it was. The reason all the security mooks were overloading the dock with their crews, their trucks and wires and equipment. The whole neighborhood was watching her home turned into a maximum-security facility.

Everyone around here understood, though. He had heard rumblings of folks complaining that she was alone at night, her caregiver no longer sleeping there, her house dark and lifeless as a tomb. What did she do, so many hours alone without a light on, a friend to talk to? Could Shawn get inside her house? Cory fished for the silicone container holding his smokes. He didn't know what Shawn was, or even if he was real, but the fact of Thea seeing him too had helped his anxiety. Cory dislodged a fat joint. No reason not to fire up. Shawn seemed to have disappeared, and Hailey was in Sun Valley with her mom and her new girlfriend, Lidia, a lawyer. There was no one to tell him to preserve his health and strength.

Cory lit his joint, relishing the dank herbal flavor almost more than the smoke. He hadn't seen Thea in days, not that he was obsessed enough to keep careful track. But when the folks in gray uniforms and embroidered bullshit insignia had been working in the garage, he had noticed the Tesla was missing. He sucked and blew, spooling out a little note of worry with the long string of smoke. The water between him and the houses across the inlet was glassy and opaque, reflecting the normal stucco house to the south, and then the looming presence of Thea's. The workers had gone inside, their vans clogging up the street still, as if they didn't know they could park for free at the beach and walk one driveway to their worksite. No, they were marketing themselves. Someone should be up there, telling them to hide the boxes with the specs, keep the garage door closed, stop letting the world know exactly what was happening in Thea's house.

He must be high. His knees moved of their own accord, bending to place him on the big log near the bushes. He was getting old. Time had meaning, here on Earth.

His shoulders felt fuzzy. Something was off. It was too quick, Thea's emergence. Something didn't sit right. She was supposed to have brain damage. He knew enough from Hailey's select soccer days, ordinary concussions take a long time to overcome, not to speak of months-long comas. The previous week Thea had been so wobbly that he almost had to walk her the hundred feet back home. Still, his daughter hadn't seen it. She spent the whole climb back up to Cory's house talking about how *gorgeous* Thea was, until he finally had to tell her to shut up. He got the hint.

He didn't explain to Hailey that Thea was one of the richest women in the world, and as such, unlikely to want to date him. Hailey just saw his feelings. Because she knew him the best. And yes. He did have feelings for Thea, especially now that Shawn wasn't there to browbeat him and assert his ownership of a girl he had never dated and barely even spoken to. A fucking ghost insisting that a girl who rejected him at a party in high school was his special someone. Cory knew his obsession was real. But still. Fucking irritating.

He sucked in smoke, waiting to shake the feeling that something about it all, Shawn, Thea, the chrysalis of her silver parka, something was wrong.

He had loved Shawn when they were young, and the band was new, and they had made everyone dance, and let out their energy. They had truly been as close or closer than Cory was to either of his brothers. Shawn had put him in a place he loved, where he belonged, making music in front of fans who luxuriated in it, appreciated it, not for some larger meaning, but for what it gave them in that moment. In their ears, in their bodies, everyone's emotions amplifying and bouncing as they danced. Cory had sucked that shit up like a drug, the smell of sweat and beer, the stink of smoke and sex. He'd been giddy with the power of his hands on the guitar, his voice always reliable no matter how drunk he got.

They were all kids, and the whole thing was happening in real time—no nostalgia, no sentimentality. When exactly had that soured? It wasn't because of Shawn using. Shawn had always been high. It was something else, some moment when the whole thing turned self-conscious, the fans arriving in expensive costumes, the girls suddenly highly polished, everything rushing toward the goal of sensational worldwide fame on a deep, irresistible current of money. Buying power, convenience, and of course pleasure galore, of every possible variety. Cory had bought all of it, even after it stopped being remotely fun. He wasn't the smartest, or the most sensitive. He just loved making people happy. He got off when the fans said the music gave them life. That was why Cory was still standing.

He blew out a long, gossamer plume. His tongue felt burnt, but he was deeply buzzed now and didn't care. Not that he had resisted or even allowed himself to contemplate the big picture back then, not at all. He was grateful. He'd played all those gigs, ever weirder ones, ever bigger ones, journalists from every country asking the same stupid questions: *What's it like?* He'd always said it was fantastic, great, so much fun, even though he knew he was lying, but manipulating the narrative felt like the only power he had back then. Shawn had paid for Cory's need for applause. It was that simple. But, as the therapists had said, he had to stop berating himself. The whole band had agreed to tour. Shawn never blamed anyone for what happened but himself.

Yet. Cory would never forget the sight of Shawn's still form at Denny Blaine beach, the needle dangling from his arm, his skin as gray as the sky. Rock star. Greatest job in the world until the lights come up.

Cory put the silicone bag away in his pocket. He noticed a man across the beach. Tall, young, very large. Like a Viking warrior in a Gore-Tex jacket. He was staring over at Thea's. Then typing into his phone.

Cory finished his joint. Lovely taste. They should make candles that smelled like it, like the moment of contact between herb and blood, body and nature. A form of nourishment, surely. Cory was high, knee deep in calm. But not so high he couldn't walk over and let the man see him glaring. What was he doing? The man had a right to look over at a famous woman's house and post about it. But it bothered Cory. One of the things he had always liked about living in this part of town was the feeling of being left alone.

"Yo, dude," the young Norseman said. "Heard a rumor she was coming back."

Cory laughed. The man wasn't afraid of him, which made sense, since it had probably been a very long time since anyone could physically threaten him. But still. Was he rude? Or just oblivious?

"Come on. You look like a local."

"I look like a local?" What was that supposed to mean?

The Norseman moved closer. "Sorry. I recognize you. My aunt loves your shit."

Cory made an exaggerated cringe. "Ouch."

Why did he have to perform? He didn't know this guy.

"Nah, my aunt's cool."

"Tell her I'll be over at eight for the usual."

The man laughed delightedly. "Bro. You are in the know. I can tell. What are people around here saying?"

Cory felt hot. "Who wants to know, Bro?"

The man jammed his hands in his pockets, considering. "Thea Sun has her hands in some pies. She disappeared in the middle of some very important shit. She is missed. You understand? I don't want to say more."

"Yeah, don't say more." Cory wished he had Shawn there in real life. The two of them in real life could teach this child a lesson.

"No offense."

"You should leave."

"Don't be like that."

Cory turned and walked away to where the old wooden bench sat rotting. When he got his composure back, the man was gone.

15

Chapter 16

Thea insisted they stop at the outlet mall. When Lee balked at the suggestion, she pouted.

"I want to buy Allen some gifts to thank him for lending you to me so much."

Lee's mouth quirked. "The new Thea is manipulative."

"Call your husband; I want to know what he wants."

It only took an hour and fifteen minutes for Thea to equip Lee and Allen with new shoes, wallets, man purses, and a variety of cashmere sweaters, hats, and gloves. She bought a large wrap for herself, and one for her mother.

"Is there a phone store here?"

"You can order a new one when we get home. Come on." Lee said, arms laden with bags. "You've been out enough today."

By the time the Space Needle came into view, Thea had talked Lee into inviting Allen to come live with him at the house, temporarily.

"He has been wanting to see the house."

"He's never been there?"

They turned East onto 520. "Today, he is there helping the security company move in. But until now he was not invited. Ben didn't want to meet him, you know."

Thea felt herself drifting. "Ben what?"

Lee put his hand on her knee. "Later, Thee. You are going too fast."

All she felt the whole rest of the car ride was his hand.

Thea relieved her own internal pressure, closing her eyes, the faces of Lee, Shawn, Cory and Lars floating annoyingly in her mind until she got angry and came, then fell asleep. When she awoke, it was Monday morning. A regular day in the city.

Lee took her around the perimeter and showed her the new array of cameras. There were more monitors lining the security office, a mini fridge, stacks of water bottles, and a wall calendar.

June said over the phone, “Honey, they want to have two people there at all times, one to monitor, the other to investigate.”

“Mom, it is too much.” Thea squeezed her eyes shut. “I hate this.”

“I agree. It’s horrific. But apparently, that level of security is what a person of your net worth has as an absolute minimum. And there’s more.”

June explained that the firm did most of its work online, investigating threats and dark web chatter and other mysterious signals that might indicate something needed to be nipped in the bud. “They’re an all-service firm. Lots of your neighbors use them, especially across the lake.”

Thea didn’t know what that meant, but it seemed a strong endorsement.

“Just a second.” June called to someone. “I have to go. We have a delivery of blackberry vines coming to feed the goats. You know how the little ones love that.”

“Mm hmm.” Thea made a noise of agreement. She had no fucking idea.

Thea closed the office door and dialed another number.

“Ramona Stein, please.”

“Who’s calling?”

It took Ramona several minutes to pick up.

“I’m sorry to keep you waiting, Mrs. Smythe. My assistant didn’t recognize your name.”

“No, it’s Thea. I am trying to be incognito.” Even as she said it, she knew how silly she sounded. “I think someone in house is paying close attention to my schedule.”

“What are you implying?” Ramona said with lawyerly neutrality.

Something about the whole situation felt too tight, suddenly, like the universe that included Rodriguez Island and the outlet mall, Ryan and his accomplice, Lars and Eleanor's, the old artists' colony, everything was straining at its bonds. The disembodied Thea Sun of some past was firmly in control and talking.

"I'm not sure how things are being communicated in the world of people whose salaries get paid out of my accounts. But my hunch is that my name is flagged in some part of your system. If whoever is monitoring my movements discovers you are coming to meet with me, you may find yourself with companions you didn't ask for."

How had Thea come up with this theory? It had arrived unbidden, with the same conviction as the words she had said to Madhavi at SunStorm.

"Companions? You mean like the guy who showed up at Lars' cabin asking to see you? Flashing a pistol? Eleanor filled me in."

"Does Eleanor know who it was?"

"Oh. I didn't think to ask her that. She was pretty distraught."

Thea felt calm in Ramona's presence, the way she might if Ramona were a girlfriend or trusted confidant.

"How is Lars?"

He was still in a medically induced coma at Harborview. Thea's former home, only on the fourth floor, the cardiac ICU, rather than the trauma unit.

"The infection is under control. What remains to be seen is if he will be himself when he wakes up. Everything depends on how long he was cut off from oxygen." Ramona said. "They put in a stent, so he should make a full recovery, as long as his brain isn't..."

"I get it."

There was an awkward silence.

"Do you have lunch plans?"

Her next call was to Eleanor, who didn't pick up. Thea left a message that she was okay, and Lars was in her thoughts. The image of Eleanor yelling crowded out whatever else Thea recalled about her. All she saw were the flashing lights, and Eleanor's face, contorted with emotion, asking harshly where Thea had been.

Thea Sun wasn't a person to be reprimanded, was she? Except from Lee. Why was that?

Lee went out to get lunch for the three of them. Thea had been craving guacamole and fish tacos, asked for extra hot sauce. He seemed amused. By the time he returned laden with bags, Ramona had come up with a plan. She put her bare feet up under her in a lotus position, her long hair braided down her back, her long false eyelashes the only note of artifice about her.

"When do the goons arrive?" Ramona folded a taco and tipped her mouth to bite into it.

"They're already here." Thea met Lee's eyes. "So quiet you'd forget they were watching our every move."

"They should be incredibly discreet." Ramona added more hot sauce. "If you have any complaints, at all, tell me immediately."

"My complaint is only that Thea is too damn rich." Lee said.

Ramona laughed. "No such thing. All problems can be handled with money."

Thea's hand stopped midair.

"Oh. I'm an idiot."

"It's okay." She didn't add, *I barely remember them, so it doesn't bother me.* Thea chewed and swallowed a bite of salty carnitas with tart tomatillo. The lake was winking hard, reminding her of something. "Oh. We're going to the hospital this afternoon to visit Lars."

"Excuse me?" Lee folded his arms, his face amused. "Another outing?"

"I have an idea how to figure out who is trying to kill me."

She had told Lee only the bare minimum, that a boy had been at Eleanor and Lars' house when Lars fell ill, and she wanted to find and question him. Thea explained what happened when she tried to tell Jim Conroy about it. The volunteer sheriff had waited with her until the boat arrived, then wished her a speedy recovery. "Don't miss any doctor's appointments, okay?"

"What a prick." Ramona said in a mild voice. "I spoke to him this morning, by the way. He was mostly concerned about Lars and Eleanor. Didn't seem to think anything out of the ordinary occurred, other than the heart attack, which happens on the islands. Every medical emergency has to be medevacked out, he said, it happens several times a year."

Thea glared at Ramona. "So, you just up and called him."

"Eleanor texted me, told me to find out if Lars owed anyone money for the airlift."

"I thought you worked for me?"

"I do." Ramona's face hardened. "Why? Is there a conflict of interest now between you and Lars? You two used to be one united interest: the Foundation, the company. I was under the impression that he had complete control over all your interests."

"Yes." Thea finished her taco, still hungry. "My mother is in there, too. She has power of attorney over me. She cannot wait to turn my affairs back over to me."

"Oh, yes." Lee said. "Even I know that."

"I thought you and the Harrises were on the same page."

Thea laughed. "I don't remember what page anyone is on anymore. But I find myself more curious all the time."

"We will get to the bottom of things. If Ryan is out there, and someone set Alexander Barrow up to ram into you, we'll figure out who and why."

"Good." A rage swept through Thea, the sensation of being watched and kept apart from the world, no part of it safe except for when she was with Lee, who wanted his own freedom.

"So, don't forget," Lee said. "When you get back, Allen will be here."

She watched Lee's face. It didn't move, even when she admitted that now with 24-hour-a-day guards, she no longer needed extra protection.

Ramona put her napkin on the table. "We investigated Allen, just so you are aware."

"Really?"

Lee waved her off. "It's okay. He is just a lowly nurse, nothing with red flags. Right?"

"Well, actually." Ramona pushed up her lower lip. "You are both flagged for a green card marriage. Did you not know that?"

Lee laughed. "Of course. We have been interviewed by immigration, but we are married and living together, you know. Thea introduced us."

"Did I?" Thea felt hot and annoyed. Was she supposed to know that?

"Oh yes. Allen was your hairdresser. You paid for his nursing school. He loves you. The government has no case. But yes. The investigators are very impressive."

Thea's stomach clenched. Lee was talking too much, more than he ever did. His face looked hard, more handsome than usual, his high cheekbones sharp.

"Duly noted. You approve of Thea going with me to visit Lars, yes?"

Lee gathered their plates. "Of course. Nothing can happen at Harborview. Big state hospital, lots of crazies. Cops everywhere."

Ramona went out to the dock to call the office and vape. She made a sleek figure in her gray suit, wreathed in clouds of smoke. The dock was repaired, caution tape removed, no trace of the accident.

"You know, you said you never, ever wanted to go back to Harborview." Lee appeared, scowling. "Or maybe that was your mother. I think it was you, too."

She followed him back to the kitchen. "I have no memories of being a patient there. I'm just going to see about my friend."

"Mr. Harris is your friend now?" He gave her a pointed look.

Thea turned to scrutinize him. "Is he not? You remember him from before. Was he...a bad guy? Were we not friends?"

"Hmmmm." Lee made a placid face. "I was working on the garage. Building the side yard, the dock. I didn't know Ben's associates."

He spoke too fast. Lying. Why? She would have to remember, have to ask him about it later.

"You don't like Lars."

"We don't know each other." Lee sighed. "Anyway, Lars is very ill. I am praying for his recovery. I am meditating on good things for him, for you, for me, for the world."

His face, frozen in long-suffering patience, broke. They laughed.

"You are so good."

"Now you are remembering."

The laughter stopped. Thea didn't want the awkward silence that bloomed between them.

"While you are communing with the universe, can you throw in some good thoughts for a lady named Dr. Graham?"

"Oh sure. Anyone else?"

The name Maggie was stuck in Thea's throat. "What time does Allen get here?"

"Six thirty. I'm making his favorite dinner."

"What?"

"Short ribs."

"Excuse me." Thea glared. "Red meat?"

He laughed. "He's doing Keto."

Thea put a hand on his arm. His face came close to hers, suddenly serious. "Please tell your husband I am very grateful for his generosity."

Lee stepped back and crossed his arms. "I will. Considering we are only newlyweds, I am sure he will appreciate it."

"Oh. Congratulations."

"Thank you. I am the one who is grateful to you, for arranging my situation with him."

An arrangement. Something the old Thea had concocted. A tension inside of her eased. "Of course. I would do anything for you."

16

Chapter 17

Mary Denoro had a motto. "Video or it didn't happen." So when she started her first shift at the Sun house, which they immediately nicknamed The Cube, the first day was spent making small adjustments, checking to be sure that the cameras were pointed at the right areas.

When she interviewed the local patrol, it came out that certain men made regular appearances at the shore access beach two doors down, which was a problem. She took notes from him and a handful of neighbors, including a man named Cory Klain. He checked out, a longtime local, someone on the safe list. But finger-pointing was not a great sign. A stalking allegation was usually pure projection.

Central agreed to three more cameras, one pointed at the beach, one at the parking lot, and another up to the mouth of the one-way street. They watched the water, but no one seemed worried that an intruder would come from that way again. Mary had suggested No Trespassing signs to discourage misunderstandings. But such language was considered in poor taste, apparently, and it didn't really do anything to deter entry. There was no practical way to stop a boat from pulling up to the dock. Maritime rules allowed it in an emergency. Crossing the boundary onto the Sun property was another matter. Mary and the rest of the guards were trained, armed, and ready if anyone was stupid enough to do that.

The more complex part of the assignment was the client's cyber situation, according to central. The company Boss Lady had founded was excellent at controlling their part of the story. But someone maybe had been leaking information about the client, though it was hard to tell what was real and what was disinformation. There were wild rumors about her marriage. Most of the chatter was old, central said, from when the man had been alive and they had still needed banks and investors to see them as a perfect, stable pair with him in charge and her the perfect, supportive wife. Over time, the firm could erase most of it. But it would always be out there. Rumors never died, no matter how much you paid. And if you were high profile, they would just grow bigger and weirder. Luckily, the client seemed to be kind of spectrum-y. Mary had two cousins with autism, and Boss Lady reminded her of them, her stillness and slowness, maybe. Something. Mary hadn't been around her enough to tell. But the woman wasn't normal. So maybe she wouldn't care that people on the internet lumped her with the absolute worst billionaires in the world, accused her of being deviant and dirty, evil by virtue of her fortune.

People loved hating the rich, and when someone was rich and a woman?

Mary wasn't satisfied until the cameras were just right.

17

Chapter 18

Harborview squatted like a giant art deco carving above Interstate Five and the skyline below. Thea wondered if she would recall any sights or smells from the place, but nothing about the crowded entry, the metal detectors, the workers in scrubs, the old patients, the young doctors, the wheelchairs, the walkers, the guards, the families, none of it jogged anything loose.

What was she doing? The plan had seemed clear and perfect when she thought of it. Now, amidst the sound of elevators and voices, shoes slipping on the wet floor, Thea wondered if she had made a mistake. But the thought of disappearing into a fortress of cameras and guards in front of monitors, without ever finding out who Ryan was or how he was connected to her, felt like defeat. Thea refused.

Cruising down Madison Street, they'd seen dozens of men who could have been Ryan. Thea couldn't recall his hair or skin color, his height or weight, nothing really except the fact of him, his first name, and his crummy Barred owl imitation. As they passed from Capitol Hill to First Hill, tech bros in lanyards were replaced by a different sort of person, shambling aimlessly, smoking in doorways, or staring unseeingly from tarp tents. People in scrubs under raincoats waited at bus stops, looking at their phones, ignoring these shadowy figures, and the deeper layer, a gray gleam of ghosts flashing by too fast for Thea to determine their features.

How could she had ever not seen it? The city was a tapestry of cities: an interlocking puzzle, a world touching other worlds without connecting. Thea knew no person was intelligent enough to add together all these moving layers into one Seattle. And if they did, if they were able to weave all the lives, past and present, the hungers and thoughts and desires of everyone who passed one another every moment, above and below the street, in basements and upper floors, on boats and buses and shiny trolly cars, then she was sure they would lose their sanity, never be able to re-enter the regular world of parking garage, crosswalk, beep of alarm being set, feet climbing up a short flight of steps to the back entrance of the hospital, the regular. Could she, Thea, return to the regular? Did she want to?

A bell chimed as Thea and Ramona reached the fourth floor, the Cardiac ICU. They made their way past nurses' stations and curtained bodies surrounded by monitors, to the draped rectangle enveloping Lars. Thea felt a pressing sense of guilt for not worrying more. Everything about his prone form and intubated face radiated violence, yellowing bruises on his chest from where he'd been given CPR, his scraggle of beard and swollen fingers. His cheeks shone raw and red, like he'd been dragged over something rough. Had she looked like this, during the weeks when she'd been in a coma, like a gray hybrid human-machine, a shadow of the person she'd been? Flesh without intelligence, a kind of obscenity. Worse than ghosts, the opposite of their quiet gleam. They were disembodied, but never grotesque, not like this.

"Sit down." Eleanor said, rolling a folding bed-bench in their direction with her foot. "It's a lot. I know."

Eleanor wore shapeless dark clothing, and her face was haggard, hands moving around her lap as if looking for something to grasp onto. It had been three days since the helicopters and flashing lights and *someone was looking for you*. But clearly Eleanor had stayed by Lars' side the whole time. Thea fought to keep herself from gagging on the familiar smell of hand sanitizer, lemon cleaner, and unwashed skin.

"I'm so sorry, Eleanor."

"I was amazed when I heard you were coming."

Thea sat on the bed-chair and tried to meet Eleanor's tired eyes. But Eleanor wasn't looking at her.

"Really?" Thea didn't know where to stand. "Because you didn't think I would be in one piece?"

Eleanor sighed. "Ramona, honey, could you go to the nurses' station and tell them his oxygen level is steady at 85? It's okay. If it drops, they'll just give him steroids. But it's not going to drop."

Ramona's eyes went flat. She nodded and disappeared.

"What's going on with his oxygen?" Thea wanted to reach up and cover Lar's exposed feet, in pale green hospital socks. They looked as swollen as his fingers. None of this felt right. Something shone in the grommets between cubicles, a ghost on the other patient's side. But there were no ghosts around Lars. He was going to recover. He was okay. The knowledge cheered Thea.

"He had an infection, apparently, maybe connected to stress. His heart is usually fine. They've got him on heavy doses of antibiotic, but it took them too long to figure out what was wrong."

As if at her command, the number on the display closest to Lars' head blinked 86, 85, 87.

"Thee, say something to him." Eleanor looked over for the first time. "He'll enjoy hearing your voice."

Thea hesitated, but Eleanor turned away from her, hands in lap, as if she were steeling herself.

"Hi there, friend." Thea's voice quavered. "I'm so glad you made it."

Lars' fingers twitched, and Thea had to stop herself from grabbing them. Eleanor watched her carefully, resentment plain on her small face, forehead tipped in exhaustion. Tears came, dripping down Thea's cheeks and falling onto Lars' sheets. It was too intimate, signals rushing into her body, warmth, caring, anger, confusion. She didn't even know these people. She should not be there. Her place was at home, with Lee and the Transformer, and their quiet life. But that wasn't true. Nowhere was safe, anymore, no part of being Thea Sun was anonymous or serene. And yet. Why did she feel the need to understand her situation? She ought to stay in the safety of her bed, her home, the lake. Putting this appointment in the law firm's master calendar, as she and Ramona had done, was foolish. What if they really flushed out a killer? Obviously, people looked at the calendar. Eleanor had. Eleanor was angry already. What if Ryan and the other man were more than stupid bros who answered to Eleanor's whims? What if Eleanor really, truly meant Thea harm? She wanted to at least know why. What did this resentful little woman have against her?

Lars's chest rose and fell as the machine pumped him with oxygen. The line of his heartbeat was a bright squiggle, the answer to her question. Thea checked herself. Did she love Lars? Was that it?

But no part of her felt physical tenderness toward his prone form, only general concern. She had no sense of what his chest would look like, his smell, the feel of his skin. Nothing. She wasn't in love with Lars. There was none of the pleasure and excitement she felt wash over her when Lee picked her up at the ferry dock. Eleanor must have some other reason to be looking so angry, her eyes locked on the space between curtains. There was a sound of feet passing. Eleanor glared outward. The feet moved away.

Thea's head pulsed slightly, not a headache but the threat of one. She had brought no meds. The thought made her laugh inwardly. The place was awash in drugs, but she was not a patient. She was planted firmly on this side, the side of the healthy, the powerful and ambulatory. She did not belong there. What had started as a simple desire to find out who was trying to hurt her now felt delusional, the logic of a sick person. Ramona, who had bristled visibly when Eleanor called her honey, had pushed back on the plan. But Ramona couldn't say no to Thea, could she? Or Eleanor? They were powerful.

The reality of what she had tried to set in motion felt dreamlike here, a place already so fraught with danger it felt insane to invite more. And yet, Thea had. She and Ramona had made sure this visit appeared on the master calendar for both the law firm, and the Foundation.

Someone came looking for you.

"Talk to him, Thea," Eleanor said, smiling. "Help him."

"Look at you," Thea blustered to Lars' inert form. "Your cheeks are full of roses. You'll be just fine. I can tell."

As she continued coaxing, his neck stiffened, the veins sticking out slightly as if he was trying to raise his head and speak.

Ramona reappeared at the foot of the bed. "I told them. They said he's intubated, so there's no need for steroids."

"Oh, all right. Come on," Eleanor said, touching Thea's arm. "Ramona can keep watch for a little while. If her yakking about the office isn't enough to raise the dead, then it's all over for Lars."

Thea felt the desperation in her words, the hope.

Ramona forced a laugh. "Wait 'til he hears how I've screwed up while he's been on this stupid vacation."

The monitors beeped. A nurse entered, her light green scrubs a blur of motion. "Good, Lars. I see you have a parade of beautiful women today."

"We're going to the cafeteria, Celia," Eleanor said to the nurse. "We'll leave Ramona here to keep Lars' spirits up. They can talk about contract law, he'll enjoy that."

Ramona made an uncomfortable smile. "Or I could read some online reviews, real scintillating stuff."

"It's great you all are here. Patients do better the more support they have," Celia spoke near Lars' ear. "And you are one very loved guy."

Ghosts wandered past as Eleanor and Thea moved to the elevator. Thea avoided looking at them. Eleanor pushed the button for the basement. She was shorter than Thea by at least four inches, slender and bristling with energy. A runner, Thea remembered. She started every day with a long, solitary run.

"You know your way around this hospital, don't you?"

"Yes, I came here many times when my friend Thea Sun was here."

Thea felt stung. There was a pause as a pair of doctors got on, talking about a perforated aorta, descended one floor, then exited. "It feels all new to me."

"You don't remember?"

"My memory is a kaleidoscope. It makes splintered pictures everywhere I look."

Eleanor glanced at her. "Convenient."

They exited into a series of underground hallways leading to a large cafeteria. A row of cash registers was staffed by a lone young woman with her head bent to her phone. Beyond her were beverage dispensers, a salad bar, and a long food station with hot lamps staffed by a couple of men in chef attire. The place felt surprisingly crowded for mid-morning, until Thea realized with a small spark of shock that most of the people sitting in chairs or standing in groups were ghosts. There were at least thirty, some bright, others dim, most old when they died. Did she know all these people? There was no time to look. Eleanor's blue eyes were fixed on her.

She spoke in an oddly speeded up voice, as if she were performing a rehearsed speech.

"You look much better than you did on the Island. It's good you got home without much trouble. June must be very angry with me for leaving you alone there. I'm sorry I was so hysterical at the time, I didn't know what was happening. But the young man who came asking for you was very intense, and he flashed an enormous gun. I think, in fact, he is a lower-level employee at the Foundation."

"He works for you?"

Where was Ramona? Thea should not have come down here without her. Her scalp itched. The scheme to flush her assailant out via the calendar felt foolish. He worked for Eleanor. But why would he be trying to put Thea back into a coma? Or were they together trying to? Thea looked at Eleanor's feet in a pair of old, decrepit clogs.

"At the Foundation? Who is he?"

Eleanor seemed not to hear. Her eyes stayed fixed on Thea, widening with wonder at her own memories. "I just...lost my mind for a minute there. I told Jim Conroy to find you, get you somewhere safe, but apparently, you vanished into the night. He called me after dropping you at the ferry, said he found you and the truck at Emerald Point. Watching the sea lions and thinking deep thoughts, he said."

Shawn, telling her he was Maggie's biological father. "Yes, very deep thoughts."

The ghosts moved, like shadows in her peripheral vision.

Eleanor turned her head away. Too far, as if she wanted to hide her face.

"I could use a coffee." Thea said. She didn't remember what it tasted like. "How about you?"

"Good idea." Eleanor sounded relieved.

They moved toward the hot beverage bar. It was a mistake, drinking coffee, Thea knew. But it was something to do, something that might cover the sense that Eleanor hated her, resented her, or possibly even actively wanted her dead. Thea filled a paper cup with a stream of steaming brown, watching Eleanor brew herself a chamomile tea, her face frozen in an expression of dread. Thea paid in cash, and they sat at a table near the door, under bright lights, the hard orange plastic chair feeling stiff under Thea's hips. Ghosts settled around, listening.

"If you need help with Lars, let's make sure you get it."

Eleanor's eyes flashed, but she quickly busied herself with a packet of honey. "I don't need help. Thank you. But, I think you're right. Lars is still there. Just like you were. True, the person who came back is a variation on Thea. You know all about new and improved versions, don't you? Or you did. You and your products. Your innovations. But I'm remembering things you don't. Not nice of me. I will apologize to your mother." Eleanor made a grim smile. "Who knows what variation on Lars will return? But he will. Come back to me."

Subtle emphasis on the word *me*. So, there it was. Something inside Thea moved, a slight unfurling. She took a sip of bitter, burned coffee and set it aside. Eleanor torqued her shoulders, as if wishing to escape. The ghosts turned their heads. A man entered the cafeteria along with a crowd of people who moved past him to the food counters. He stood between Thea and the door, eyes locked on her. Something about his defiant, smirking face with its short, dark beard and pulled-down brown beany told her: this was Ryan. He was thirty at most, but already his shoulders curved like someone who never left the chair at work, except to slump in front of a video game. He wasn't particularly frightening, but for his green Gore-Tex rain shell, folded over a plaster cast on his right arm. The fingers were closed over a gray and white plastic object.

"I've been looking for you," he overpronounced.

Eleanor gasped. "No. I told you not to do this."

"Shut it, Elly. I don't work for you. Anymore."

"How did you sneak that thing past security?" Eleanor leaned away from Thea. "Where did you even get it?"

"I have access to an excellent printer."

Thea felt less fear than she should. But like that night on the island, she couldn't believe that this young man really wanted her harmed. He seemed to be playing a game. Eleanor was blinking theatrically and rubbing her face with her hands.

"It's a ghost gun," one of the ghosts said. Others laughed. "Doesn't that boy realize they got a ton of cameras in here?"

"Miss Smythe, you had best get out of here," someone said.

Thea looked. It was her old band teacher, Mr. Jones.

"Ryan." Thea stood. "How's the arm? You must have paddled a long, long way with only one hand."

"She did that to you?" Eleanor said.

"She's stronger than she looks."

Ryan moved closer. He reached out with the hand that had no cast on it, resting it on Thea's shoulder. "I want to talk with you, Ms. Sun. Just circling back on the chat that got interrupted. I had some statements left to make. Well, one really."

Thea shook him off. "I think you got my point. That meeting has ended."

The ghosts around them cracked up, their laughter like static on an electric wire, running through Thea like wind. They motioned for the door. A security guard wandered in holding a portable hot cup.

"Ryan, you idiot. You can't attack Thea in a hospital," Eleanor whispered.

His face took on a dour look. He raised his cast over her head. Thea stood and pushed the cast away from her. He let it go without much resistance.

"Eleanor. I'm going to walk out the door now. Whatever you and Ryan choose to do will be witnessed by numerous cameras and a whole group of bystanders."

The ghosts hooted.

"Oh, stop it. You have no idea what's been happening. You've been so out of it you haven't even known your own name."

Thea shrugged. "Still my name on the Foundation."

Eleanor flinched. Ryan sprinted out of the cafeteria.

"Were you really going to let him give me another concussion? Was that why you left me alone on the island with him?"

"No." Eleanor looked horrified. "I fired Ryan. His stupidity has nothing to do with me. But now that he's seen it's not going to work to just tap you on the head and watch you disappear into a vegetative state again, I'm sure he'll disappear. I'm sorry. I don't have any control over anyone. I'm not like you. I'm just an ordinary person: no one respects what I tell them."

"I wonder where he got the idea that my head was so fragile all it needed was one knock and I'd be all but dead."

"Oh, Thea. Don't be naïve. Everyone in the Western World knows that. Your case has been highly discussed. You'll never be safe from weirdos. Apparently, I won't be, either."

Her phone buzzed. "Samantha says Ryan looked for you first on the fourth floor."

"Apparently, he still has access to the Firm Calendar. You'd better fix that, friend."

The security guard paid for his coffee. Thea waved her arms, and the guard approached. He was broad, bearded, and seemingly unbothered by the crying woman before him. His nametag read Abe Aleph.

"How you folks doing?"

"Clerical matters such as passwords to take a day or two to process. That's pretty standard, Thea." Eleanor said calmly. "It's not personal."

"Sir," Thea said to the security guard, "would you help me get to the exits? I am recovering from a head injury."

"Why, Mrs. Sun, I remember you." His smile grew wider. "You look fantastic. Walking, talking, oh my word if I didn't know better, I would never guess."

He held his arm for her to take. Eleanor stood and walked toward the garbage cans.

"Thanks for everything," Thea called out to the ghosts.

Eleanor rolled her eyes. "He's not going to come back. I'm sure he's given up by now."

When they reached street level, the guard motioned to a bench by the glass doors. "Go ahead and wait for your ride there, Mrs. Sun. Look at you. This really is the best hospital in the whole Northwest."

He took up his post at the security scanner, close enough that she could see him across the lobby. The bench was occupied by the ghost of an old man. Thea sat by him and whispered *hello*. She texted Ramona for the third time. No answer. I am not here, Thea thought. I am still in the helicopter, falling. She shook off the feeling, the sense of being two places at once. Her head felt off, too heavy, the metal plate somehow conductive of more than heat and cold. What had they done to her, in this hospital?

"Theodora."

18

Chapter 19

Cory held out his fast pass for the Canadian border agent. The morning was colorless so far, clouds and mist obscuring the trees and water off Blaine. The air was cool with rain, visibility nil. The estuary was sometimes covered in white birds, other times crawling in bald eagles. The peace arch and gardens looked sad in the present gloom. He had started early and taken advantage of the clear freeways. Normally at this time, he would just be finishing his morning matcha. It was worth it just to avoid traffic.

"Cory Klain. Hey. I saw your name in a game of trivia just last Thursday. How goes it?" The young man smiled and processed Cory's documents. His nametag read, Taylor. "You coming to perform? Where's the venue? I'll tell my mom. She loves you."

"I so enjoy coming to Vancouver to play, officer. But this time I'm just helping out a friend."

Taylor's eyes narrowed. "Say, you don't have any firearms in there, do you, Cory?"

Cory sighed. His Bronco was spotless but for the small backpack containing a change of clothes and a laptop, in case there was a hitch fetching Mattie from rehab. Cory had experience in these matters, which was one reason Mattie's ex-girlfriend had called him. He was good for the bill, as well. Lots of people knew that about him. It was a form of penance, for Shawn.

"I don't." Cory made a conciliatory face. "I know you have to ask. I appreciate it."

"Helping a friend?"

This was taking longer than it should. Cory knew if he seemed reluctant to explain, he might be called to the side and taken in for an interview. It would all end in selfies, and the facility would have a bathroom, which he needed. But still, he wanted to get to the rehab, pay the tab, and drive Mattie home. Didn't want to spend the night if he didn't have to. The family would be there to help Mattie on his first night home.

Cory would have to get a hotel, which was fine but lonely. He loved Vancouver, especially in the early morning hours, jogging in Stanley Park while rowers stroked across English Bay. But hotels were all alike. He had seen too many of them. He would miss Shawn, and everyone else from the old days. Nothing made him feel more alone than a hotel room. Nothing made him feel older. He pictured an anonymous bed, and the involuntary image of Thea appeared in it, warm and alive in the crisp monotony of white sheets and gray furniture. That would change everything.

Taylor held his card, motionless across the span between Cory and the custom's booth.

"A kid I know is being released from rehab today. I'm just here as a friendly face. You understand. Yeah? Hoping to get back home tonight."

Under his hat, Taylor's hair looked the blond-bronze of an outdoorsman. "Came up to drive a mate home from the tank? Very sweet, Cory. Very generous. Anyone I know?"

"Matty McDougal?" Cory forced a laugh. Young people were so familiar these days. "He's a famous DJ. Maybe you've heard of him."

"Nah." He rolled his eyes. "I don't do the club scene. Too many drugs, you know."

He moved to open the barrier and waved Cory through.

"Have the lines been long coming back across?"

"Terrible." He scowled. "The Americans are much tougher than we are. Which is funny considering how many of you are applying to emigrate."

"Good to know." Cory put his foot on the gas. "Say hi to your mom for me."

Taylor roared.

19

Chapter 20

"Grandpa?"

June's father, wearing a sportscoat over a button-down with a slender tie, khakis, and rubber-soled shoes. June talked about her late father all the time, had told many stories about him at Thea's bedside. Norman Smythe had been a high school principal—worked his way up from science teacher. His family had farmed, until the government took their land for the Hanford nuclear plant. He had gotten cancer anyway, just like everyone else down wind, though he lived longer than most. His face looked serene. A man with no regrets, June called him. Her hero.

He glistened with a sepia-toned light, so faded Thea could hardly see him, though his voice was strong, full of warmth and decency. The sound of a different era. Where was Ramona? Please let Ramona not be part of some stupid plot.

"I'm glad to see you looking so much better, Thea. Your poor mother visited here every day for a very long time." His soft gold-lit face smiled. "It seemed many days in a row."

People were entering, standing in line for the metal detector, pausing for the wand. Norman glanced over from time to time.

She whispered, "I can't believe you're here. Do you want me to give mom a message?"

"Oh yes. Tell Junie Bug I'm proud of her. She's a special one. The special one who gave birth to another special one."

"Oh, I have upset you. Here is something that will cheer you, Bug. He's all right. Your friend. He's still firmly on your side of the veil."

"Oh." She should ask how he knew this, but if he was like the ghosts in the cafeteria, her grandpa was watching the hospital like a form of entertainment. Something to keep him busy, while he waited to go on. "Thank you. I'm glad. And what about his wife? Is she a bad seed? Would she really kill me? What do you think?"

"Oh. I don't know."

Thea nodded. "How about you?"

"Welp. Still deceased."

They laughed.

"Your father is still living in the world. Lost to himself at the moment. He gets brought in, now and again. I feel sorry for the boy. I know he's been no kind of father to you."

"My father? He comes in here?" Thea hadn't seen her father in twenty years. He had left before she met Ben, before June moved to the east side of the mountains, when Thea was still a graduate student and couldn't offer him any of the money he asked for. She was vaguely surprised to hear of his not being dead. "Grandpa, why are you here?"

"Oh, that's a different story. I have friends around, and we get on all right together. With the waiting. We don't know what for. But we try to enjoy it."

"I see. We living people think a place of death is scary, haunted. For you...it's a community."

"You were always smart as hell, little Bug."

"It's so wonderful to see you."

"Try to get some rest. You need to heal up."

"Do you ever see Maggie?"

There was a pause.

"I wasn't privileged to know her, sweet soul. But I know losing her nearly killed your mother. You are all she has left, now. Try to stay well, why don't you? Keep out of trouble? There really is no rush to get to the other side."

"Speaking of the other side..." Thea kept her voice low, but a couple of people looked sideway at her. "Someone told me that I need to make sure humanity continues so that souls have bodies to be born into? Do you know anything about that?"

"Well. I don't know if it's your personal problem to solve. But if there's an issue with the future of life on Earth...it might explain a lot. I don't know. It's as plausible as any other theory, I suppose."

"But..."

"You're weak. Get some rest, Theodora. And please be kind to June. She loves you."

He winked out.

Her phone vibrated, a text from Ramona. *Some kid with a gun threatened the ICU. At Federal Building now raising hell—trying to get sec footage. This bullshit has to stop. Eleanor texted you left with Security. Can you get home all right? Want me to send a car?*

I'll come to you.

No reply.

Thea waved to Norman and exited into soft rain, wishing she had worn a better coat. Her thin trench kept off the wet but provided no warmth. Yellow cabs passed without responding to her raised hand. She pulled up her GPS. No doubt this was a mistake, too. But who could she trust? The air smelled like wet pavement and oil, nothing alarming. As Thea got closer to Pioneer Square, ghosts were everywhere, so many she stopped trying to see their individual features but just took in the dated feeling in some of their clothes. Every era, from long skirts and bonnets to natural hair and bellbottoms. A few greeted her. She stepped carefully through a large group of Salish people.

When Thea reached the Federal Building, it was all she could do to keep her composure while passing through the security checkpoint. She was shivering. Once through, she ran out of plan. The grand, marble foyer gleamed with brass, chiming as elevators opened and closed. She felt like an idiot walking onto the inlaid rosette, not knowing where to find Ramona. Thea's head ached with a familiar, sick pressure. More consequential revelations coming. Dammit. She did not have time for a big rush of sensation. She had to get home and disappear back into the darkness.

Several people exiting from the elevator almost ran into her. A man said *excuse me*. Thea checked her phone. No text from Ramona.

"Come on. I'll take you to the jury room. You can have a cup of coffee and rest for a while."

Shawn sparkled under the brass chandelier. Or should she say, the father of her child stood there, right on the brass state seal, smirking like a self-satisfied clown? Fucking Shawn. He was already sauntering away in his jeans and leather.

Of course, high school Thea hadn't wanted to accept his advances. Some poor woman had, and despite all his success and his song catalogue, Maggie had been put up for adoption. An old man ghost in judge's robes wandered by, his pants and shoes an outdated style.

"Tell me about our child."

Shawn crossed his arms, his tattooed knuckles shining out. "It's a shitty story. Two junkies get pregnant. One gets clean and the other dies trying. The baby gets adopted. Only the little girl dies in an accident when she's five. Not a very happy ending."

"Who was her biological mother?"

Shawn sighed. "No one you would know. Come on. You're going to catch your death."

20

Chapter 21

Eleanor leaned over her husband's prone form. He was starting to smell like old dishwater. His skin was thinner than she had ever seen it, a map of arteries she didn't know. Who was this old man?

"Things are looking good, Honey."

A nurse appeared at the curtain, mouth open in shock. "What are you doing here?"

Eleanor laughed. Of all the things to ask a grieving wife. "Are you joking?"

"There was a gunman here. He seemed to be looking for your husband."

People were such idiots sometimes. Eleanor looked the nurse up and down, daring her to say more. She only checked Lars' monitors, his fingertip pulse. Had Ryan asked for Eleanor by name? It didn't matter. She had done nothing. Thea was too addled to understand what was happening, her face in the cafeteria showed that much, the way she looked around as if hearing voices. Not much to worry about there. Thea Sun, mighty and imperious, had not returned. This shuddering, distractable creature would impress no one.

21

Chapter 22

Shawn took her to a carpeted room with dozens of ugly lounge chairs. She followed him to a break room with paper coffee cups and powdered creamer, poured hot water into a packet of Lipton, then settled at a round plastic table. The sparkly man sat in a sullen posture.

"Nice place. You came here a lot?"

"Obviously."

He looked pale, his sunny aura faded, his face oddly older, which struck her as absurd.

"You look awful." The tea was tepid but felt good in her throat.

"Me? Look at yourself. I can't leave you like this."

"What?" She sat up. "You going on to Oblivion at last?"

"I fucking hope so. Help me out. Quit screwing around."

A man came in, poured coffee into a portable mug, added three packets of sugar, and left.

"It's not my problem if humanity is ending."

He ran his hands through his hair. "Do you not care about Maggie's soul? Mine? Your own? Or your late husband? Surely there is someone in your life who could get you to put your resources to work. What about your manservant?"

She sighed deeply. "No. This is absurd. Go away."

He sat back down, rocking back and forth. Through his body, Thea could see an old umbrella someone had left leaning against the refrigerator. Thea rested her head in her hands. At some point, Shawn faded out. She splashed water on her face at the sink while jurors wandered in, then quickly left again. Eventually, a pair of security guards appeared and asked with surprising tenderness if there was anyone they could call for her.

Lee was cooking, so he sent Allen. Thea waited, unbothered by the ordinary citizens shuffling in and out, the various ghosts like motes in her peripheral vision. She closed her eyes. It was a perfect disguise, being bedraggled and lost. She could be anyone. She could be a ghost herself. The thought made her smile then blossom with guilt like a newspaper dropped into a mud puddle. Curious. Maybe the answer wasn't no. She was meant to be glad to be alive.

Her phone pinged.

Allen pulled the Tesla into the bus zone, sprinting in with an open umbrella. He looked unreal, a beautiful mirage.

"Oh lord."

His hand felt huge and warm on her forehead.

"Honey. Are you running a fever?"

In the car, he spoke to the air, which she realized momentarily was Lee on the other end of a phone call. "Why did you let her go out?"

She didn't hear Lee's response, just closed her eyes on the many versions of the city all compacting one atop the next, like layers of glacial silt on the cliff outside the yurt. At home, she peeled off her clothes and tried to summon the peace she always felt in the bathtub, but nothing wanted to stop swirling. She dried off, dressed, and stumbled downstairs.

"The guards are here." Lee's back was to her.

There was the faintest scent of cheese-flavored tortilla chips. She didn't want to accept these changes, these new human beings being foisted upon her, the upending of her life with Lee. Was she a powerful person or not? Was her body real or just something she was walking in, like a superhero suit? Weak, unreliable, attacked by strangers for reasons she didn't understand, goggled at by ladies in restaurants, besieged by the dead urging her to...something. What was it they wanted? Salvation of the earth? Connection, comfort? Or just to be remembered?

What a bore it all was, the struggle of being alive, of remembering. Thea pictured the strangers on the other side of the cabinets and wall eating chips and drinking soda. She wanted to join them, complain about sports teams and inflation and traffic. How long since she had done anything regular, like that? The fish and chips seemed like years ago. Her head was wrong, too big, too soft.

"I can barely tell."

"They're in the security room looking at all their cameras." Lee turned with a strained smile. "Protecting you. I am glad. You need protecting."

"Are you upset?"

Lee faced his reflection in the darkening windows.

"Ramona told me some story about a confrontation at Harborview? Ramona was freaking out. She said she went across the street to the police to file a report while you were with Eleanor, but you left Eleanor and went to the courthouse downtown to look for Ramona? This is not okay. You pretended everything was fine when I picked you up from Rodriguez Island." He faced her. "I don't understand what is happening right now. Why put yourself in danger? And lie to me about it?"

"I didn't know. It seems like anything I do is a risk, right now. You didn't tell me that. Did you?"

He looked at her feet in their fuzzy slippers.

"I also didn't know. Your world is strange to me. I cannot imagine who is trying to hurt you. Or why."

His cheekbones gleamed with sweat. He was angry. She liked it. His eyes softened as he took in her rapid breathing, the way she bent over the counter, pinching her temples. He slid over an orange pill and a glass of water.

"Your meds."

The pill grated with its comforting acrid taste. She sank into a chair.

"I'm sorry about not telling you what happened on the island."

He crossed his arms.

"Stay home where you have people keeping you safe."

"It's not your fault, hon." Allen's voice was rich and deep. "You don't remember. You're like a baby out there, a lost child with no one looking out for you. You really have nothing to blame yourself for."

Lee was glaring at Allen as she escaped back to her bed. His words returned as she floated off into the dark fog, the pain a fizzy, enveloping ocean. She didn't believe him.

22

Chapter 23

June fed Cal the last of the Christmas cookies, unearthed from beneath the beef and bison in the chest freezer. He especially loved the mint ones. Hers were the best, she agreed, without admitting it was because she doubled the amount of Andes mint in the melted nipples on top.

He would tease her about it, something about the size of her, his smile tinted with melted chocolate. She was brawny, still strong enough to toss a hay bale. Not everyone liked that. June always colored slightly when she thought of it, of being the once-lovely girl who ended up spending almost her entire life without a partner, only connecting with Brian Coe in the short, sweet span before he lost his mind, leaving her pregnant with Thea. Not a penny in child support. Trying to teach her daughter to put her passion into math and science, June had also taught her to find a path over any resistance, to get what she wanted. Resourcefulness. That was the gift of poverty, along with permission to do whatever it took.

Now they were so far ahead of the game, June didn't know who Thea was any more, the business maven turned silver shadow, smiling at Lee as if she were in love with him, never asking about Maggie or Ben, never asking how it had been for her mother. Selfish and thoughtless, every other part of her wiped away like chalk from a chalk board. The ruthless, single-minded impulse to forget whatever she didn't want to think about. June envied it.

"Hon, I'm going to check the front gate." Cal pulled on a barn coat, shoving his feet into a pair of old boots. "You want me to grab anything from outside?"

"Yup. The moon, please. She looks bored up there."

"You bet. We'll invite her to a game of gin rummy." He buttoned the coat over his belly. "Though, I heard she cheats."

"Well, of course she does. She's a different damn slice every time."

"Let's switch to crazy eights. We could shoot her."

"Waste of ammo. She'd eclipse us."

He showed teeth under his moustache. "True enough."

Her front door closed heavily behind him, the smell of melting snow and pine drifting in.

Cal was her best friend, maybe the best friend she had ever had. She enjoyed the nights he slept under her quilt with her, his fingers massaging the knots from her neck, the gentle way he had of waiting until she was good and ready to let him inside her. They both agreed: no formalized relationship. But when the accident happened, Cal had been better than any husband, caring for the ranch and animals, taking over administration of the center as if her obligations were as important to him as to her. They couldn't get married, of course, with her finances all tangled up in the Foundation and his too limited to share. But since asking her to dance at the feed lot five years previous, he had become essential to her.

He had a grown daughter, too, who lived in Europe somewhere, and wrote classical symphonies no one in the US wanted to perform. She made her entire living in Europe, where apparently folks loved her stuff. June had listened to it. It was electronic, with lots of shifting melodies shoved one into the next until the mess was so annoying that when it reduced itself to a single string, plinking tunelessly, June wanted to applaud and yell *bravo*. He smiled softly, proud of his girl. June loved that about him.

While he had his place rented out to skiers, he stayed at June's, and she spent much of that time with Thea. Cal had met Thea, only once, when she had come with Ben to inspect the center's new wing. They had hired some lower-level architect at their regular firm, and the resulting wood-and-glass building had been almost too elegant for the little local ruffians who used it. The center was the nicest building they were likely to enter in their lifetimes, unless they somehow escaped the Valley and moved to a coastal city, which was unlikely.

It was funny. Ben had come from a middle-class background, and Thea had never owned a damn thing. But they were absolutely determined to be as ostentatious as everyone else who came to build in the Valley. June didn't begrudge Ben. Thea would be thinking of other things, of strategy and empire. She couldn't have cared less what anyone thought of her. That would have been weakness, something she had stopped showing when she was bullied in fifth grade. Ben was the one with something to prove, a boy sent off at age fourteen to make good in America, always demonstrating how he'd succeeded. Too bad his father had died without seeing any of it, and his mother was some sort of nasty, hateful recluse.

Cal came in and closed the door, replaced his outerwear, went to the kitchen to start the dishwasher. "Don't put these bones in the can outside, Junie. The racoons'll bite another hole in it."

"Pretty pleased with your cooking, are you?"

He laughed. "I'm just sayin'."

Her last name, Smythe, didn't protect her from association with the Suns in the minds of the locals, but being with Cal did. And giving kids a safe aftercare program got certain people to accept her, softening up enough to say hello at the Safeway or at the Cowboy Christmas show. She was content. She had Cal. She had her animals. The Center was funded, steadily, every month, payroll flowing out to the staff, their medical and dental the best around, better than schoolteachers had. And if June asked for more, Eleanor and her staff seemed to be only too happy to give.

June was aware of simmering Board politics, Eleanor and her group scowling at proposals and reports, tinkering with their mission statement, trying to decide just what the Sun Family Foundation was meant to do, what Eleanor was allowed to do. She seemed only too happy to take the initiative, with Thea out of the picture. But like everyone else, Eleanor would only truly be happy when she had access to all the Foundation had in its coffers, when she had the power to truly change the world with the Foundation's money. June didn't enjoy the board meetings, but as the only sentient family member, she felt obligated to attend. Her first one, when Thea was still on life support and everyone looked bruised around the eyes, Eleanor had complained that she was losing hair with worry.

"I have to clean my brush every day."

It struck June as such a cruel thing to say. But people were strange in grief, especially if they weren't experienced in it. She didn't know Eleanor well, though of course they had met many times. Lars was always kind and solicitous, and she knew the two couples had been inseparable. But for Eleanor to say she was overwhelmed by the stress of losing Ben and Maggie? Wasn't that an overreaction? Or had June taken it the wrong way?

Being rich was a full-time job, she kept learning. After giving the go-ahead to the security company Betsy Wheeler had recommended, which was apparently the gold standard for tech billionaires, June needed a drink. The cost of their services was staggering. The forms she had signed, too much to process. Was it necessary? The boat that ran into Thea's dock was most likely an accident, the skipper drowned, no motive or reason to hurt her in evidence. But Lee wanted the extra help, and she couldn't say no to Lee. It was done. Time to move on.

"Sir, I would like to order a rye Manhattan."

Cal draped a dishtowel over his arm. "Rocks, Madame?"

After they had gotten drunk and made sloppy love, June rose to sit on the sectional in front of her gas fire. The house had been old, but Thea had made sure it got upgraded in every possible way, including a fully tricked-out bunker with food and water and guns. With the front gate locked, they were safe from almost anything. Fire could still get the outbuildings, but not the people underground.

The whiskey helped June's sore left hip and left her feeling as bright as the red logs on the fire. The truth was, June was relieved that there was a security detail at Thea's. One of these days, she would have to let Lee go. But adults don't need other adults to put their entire lives on hold just to cook them soup and help them do Pilates. Thea would moan and complain. But the guards were going to stay, if for no other reason than that June wanted to stop driving back and forth over those damn mountains every weekend.

23

Chapter 24

Smooth jazz emanated from downstairs.

"Come on," Lee sat on Thea's bed. She had spent most of the day there, her head draining slowly off a foamy haze from the orange pill. "I made a special dinner."

"What's happening?" She felt manipulated.

"Ben's birthday."

Lee smoothed the duvet cover. She tried to catch his eye, but he was gazing at the shelves. "Okay. I'll be right down."

He didn't move. "And Allen will tell you some advice. Okay?"

"Allen will?"

"I don't give advice, you know that."

"Nope. You give orders."

His mouth was a bumpy line, then a smile. "Dinner."

He disappeared downstairs while Thea washed and dressed. Her face was crusted with drool. In the mirror, her silver hair looked flat, her pale face still gray with stress. The important lady who needed to be guarded or killed, or fed. She heard her mother's voice in her head telling her to come down off her high horse.

What was that song? *Something meaty for the main course. That's a fine-looking high horse. That looks tasty, there seems plenty, this is hungry work.*

She washed her face in the coldest water the tap offered.

The music went low as she entered, a smarmy whisper of horns. The table was set with candles and placemats, Bellevue glimmering across the water like pink ice in a glass. Allen and Lee exchanged glances. Two sleek models, all white teeth and smooth skin. She was older than they were, by a decade or more. She suddenly hated them both. She could fire them, send them off, make them live without all this, without her. And they would be fine. They would hold hands and walk out into the night and talk of what a pathetic old cow she had been, what an easy job, how boring.

She would do the same, in their place.

A bubble popped. The voice in her head was strong, confident, unquestioning of its own dark projections. Ugh. She shared this body with Old Thea, and Old Thea was mean. Not just to others, she realized. To herself.

"Oh." She put as much enthusiasm into her voice as she could. "This is beautiful. Is it going to be like this every night?"

They smiled even wider.

"A toast to you both." She raised a sweating amber glass of beer.

Lee's face wavered. "And to Ben."

"Yes, to Ben." She didn't say, *Who is not here and does not care.* "To couples, new and old."

They drank. The thick, uneven noodles and fibrous tangle of pea shoots tasted familiar with their combinations of sweet, hot, tender, and tough. Thea ate extra helpings, watching Allen tentatively slide a hand down Lee's thigh while Lee pretended not to notice. Why did Thea want to slap Allen's hand away, pour beer down his neatly pressed blue shirt, send him away from their home?

And then, Ben was there, sitting invisibly on her shoulder, urging her to say her desires aloud, be big, like a tiger, give in to her true, voracious nature. Give in, be in her skin, her muscles, her memories. She felt a hollow dread. Lee was watching her, his chopsticks still.

"This is insane, Lee."

His eyes widened.

"So delicious."

Lee looked serious. Could he read her mind? Did he know her thoughts? Her skin flushed. She wanted to be drugged and floating, on another plane, the one she preferred. But Ben would not have it.

Allen smirked. "Told you she'd like it."

"Did you remember something?" Lee placed his chopsticks down. "Do you want to share?"

It was like the pain of ears popping, followed by the relief of pressure, saying Ben's name, meeting Lee's eyes over the table as they recognized the emptiness of the day, of every day.

"Are you going to cry, sweetheart?" Allen disappeared to get tissues. While he was gone, Lee slid his hand to hers, and held it on top of the table. When Allen returned, they were sitting in silence.

"Why did we die?"

Lee blinked hard.

"I mean, why did they?"

Allen moved to clear the table. "Five minutes. Okay?"

Lee met her eyes. "You are remembering the accident?"

He explained about the helicopter, the blizzard, the unexpected conditions never seen before in the mountains to the north. As he spoke, his face became frozen in a resigned expression.

Thea didn't have words for what she was remembering, the shirring blades, the snow soaked red. The sick feeling of ground coming at them out the open door, then flying. Falling.

"Do you know why?" she asked in a small voice. "There was something we had to return to here? Or were we sabotaged?"

Part of her hadn't stopped, hadn't come to rest even now.

"That's enough. Concussions take a long time. The doctors said not to force her." Allen wiped his hands on a dishtowel.

"I'm not." Lee withdrew his hands. "I am only celebrating Ben. Thea is in charge of herself, isn't that right?"

Her chest felt stretched. "What?"

"You are in control?" He stared at her, an owl, unfathomable. "You went to meet a man with a gun? Or maybe only to see Eleanor, who is not your friend, it seems?"

"You said nothing bad could happen to me at Harborview."

Then they were laughing.

"No, Honey." Allen wiped his eye. "Nothing bad ever happens at Harborview."

She wished for the mind she had for Sun Storm, the one that worked. "I wanted to know who is trying to murder me. But maybe no one can get me now. As long as I stay here forever."

"You were reckless." Lee said. "After people have worked to care for you."

"You know Lee would be devastated if anything happened." Allen said, bending to load the dishwasher.

"I'm sorry." Her voice was hoarse. "It won't happen again. I'll stay here in my cage. A good little goldfish in a pretty tank."

Lee's face didn't move. She saw his irritation clearly, and his desire not to show it. Why was she being so childish? Her feet curled in her chair. She would never escape the memory now, the open door, the cold, the falling.

Allen spoke softly near her ear. "So, the guards will be right behind that wall. They say they don't have microphones in this room, but they do have them on the other side of the living room, so maybe don't..."

"Admit I'm trapped?"

Lee glanced at the door to the hallway.

"I pay them. Can't I be sarcastic if I want?"

"Maybe don't say it so loud." Allen wiped the table. "You need protection."

"So, you live with me forever." She smiled. "That would work."

"Yes. Yes, okay." Lee spoke. "Thea, I need...it is important that you do what the doctors said and stop pushing so hard. Just...let things be. For a while. Please."

There was a sharp knock on the door, and the sound of guards over an intercom.

"Ma'am," the intercom said, "Your visitor is a known and listed person. Any of you are cleared to get the door."

They hurried to look out the small fisheye lens.

"Oh. You skipped your walk to the beach," Lee said, smirking. "What a hard day for everyone.'

Thea laughed. Cory Klain stood coatless in a light rain, his careful hair flattened, peering up into the cameras.

24

Chapter 25

"Dad," Hailey said into Cory's phone screen. "Are you outside in the rain?"

He couldn't stop a shit-eating grin from spreading across his face. "Maybe?"

The sidewalk had strips of rough concrete, which he felt with his wet feet. Yes, he should have worn a coat and a pair of real shoes rather than these beachy canvas things, but how was he to know that it would start to really rain? The earth was a bitch, and she no longer tried to hide it. He couldn't blame her.

"Why?"

He didn't want to coo to his teen daughter that he has just successfully asked Thea Sun on a date, or what might pass for a date: dinner at her house. So, he just smiled. "I was out walking and got caught."

"In the dark?"

"I was talking to Thea and time got away from me."

Now he was just embarrassed.

"Were you smoking again?"

This felt like safer ground. "What? Smoking? You know I'm not a smoker."

25

Chapter 26

She turned the handles on the blinds until the window facing the street was fully opaque. It still hurt her eyes to look at the computer screen with the streetlights outside. She had eaten too much, had alcohol for the first time since the sip of wine at Lars and Eleanor's.

Her fingerprint accessed Suns' databases. The codes Madhavi sent over were complete for every project listed, and several others that were not. Madhavi being honest and trustworthy; Thea made note of it. Under-promising, over-delivering. Someone who had attended business school. Thea hadn't, but she knew the signs.

She felt two emotions, probing SunStorm's inner workings. The first was bewilderment: so many projects, so many data points reported on in a variety of manager's voices, some easier to grasp than others. The company needed a better-enforced style guide. It could use a more aggressive senior management team, though she could see mid-level people starting projects all over the place, buying technology to exploit, registering for patents, bringing in rogue startups looking for profit. And profit was being made. Hence, Thea being given so much access. There was no incompetence here, just chaos. She couldn't decide if the numbers were high or low, though she felt happy looking at them. SunStorm was doing fine despite being a disorganized mess.

A feeling presented itself, a sharp blade of understanding cutting through the fog. No, the lack of structural cohesion reflected foundational management decisions. Hers. Old Thea wouldn't have cared if people could comprehend what

Sun was doing. She would have told people to hurry up and report, without regard to consistent language or standards. Ben, who came to San Jose for high school and stayed for Stanford, was fluid in English but not overly concerned with it. She thought of his voice, his slight untraceable accent, his heavy use of buzzwords and slang. He might not have even noticed. He wouldn't have taken the time to read but would probably rely on meetings and abbreviated results. They had not hired people to solve a consistency problem they didn't see. So why was she bothered by it, now?

A car drove past, lights illuminating the stone retaining wall across the street, tires swishing. How long had it been raining? She didn't care. She was seeing SunStorm for what it was: a hodgepodge of enterprises, mergers and projects serving a variety of needs, but mostly corporate security, web services, and machine learning AI. The R&D budget was huge in relation to other costs. Of all their different activities, that one was the most dynamic, throwing out darts to see if it could hit something profitable, a need they could exploit, a service that would become necessary and inevitable. They had done so a couple of times, hence the vast fortune. They'd hosted and invested in one of the first cryptocurrency brands, taken profit and divested. Whose idea had that been?

Hers. She knew, feeling it in her bones.

They had worked hard to build all this. Ben had been out there selling, connecting, gathering what would become a strategic gambit. She had been silently observing, feeling for openings, looking beyond the moment to larger patterns of change. They had been a team, a perfect team. She and Ben. He had needed her eye. She would never have been able to try so many fun ideas out without his backing. They had made all of this: a vast, breathing mountain of capital.

These thoughts came to her in matter-of-fact calm. She trusted them. They had a flavor of neutrality, the part of her that didn't feel strongly, but just knew. The part that surmised where to find a gun in the yurt. When she wanted to know, the knowledge was waiting, like a note with an important combination on it, unlocking everything that came before November but no more. What had been happening specifically, that she would feel the need to board a helicopter in the snows of November to come see about? There was a faint groan of footsteps, a guard patrolling the side yard, rubber soles on wet gravel.

She rose to pee, then noticed a glowing green rectangle labeled with a flying bag of money in the lower corner of her desktop. Inside, her fingerprint accessed a blue-tinged Foundation site. This one, in marked comparison to SunStorm's, was consistent on all pages, the code revealing nothing but ordinary architecture, a vast list of accounts and investments, dates and transactions. She skimmed without taking anything in, marveling at the sheer volume of it all. Money, property, lines going up or angling down in soft curves. The Foundation had millions of dollars just sitting, inert, doing nothing at all. Did Eleanor not understand that holding cash was the same as throwing money away? Wasn't the point of the Foundation to give away money? It was a tight ship. But something was wrong.

Thea snapped her laptop shut. A motor buzzed by, though on the lake or the street, she was too tired to tell. Other people were charged with worrying about incursions.

She was free to sleep.

26

Chapter 27

Eleanor watered the plants in her office in Building One of Sun Storm Corporation. The maintenance people did an okay job of keeping them alive during the dormant period when Thea was out, like a broken doll belonging to a princess, fussed over and pampered every second. But the living things dotting the Foundation office suite really needed more, especially the lush philodendron. She poured fertilizer into its dark soil, following up with a whole can's worth of water. When she was done, Eleanor collected her salad from the fridge and lit a scented candle.

Ryan had promised he had covered his tracks before taking his severance package and disappearing. But she needed to make sure. The accounts were archived, but that meant nothing. What Eleanor needed to do was delete any forms with her e-signature, things she ought to have caught while Ryan and Anders were off wasting money. If there was an investigation, so be it. But she wouldn't make it easy for people to find.

Would anyone really think it was her fault that her staff had made free with the petty cash? Sure, it was a lot of money. But the accounts were spilling over with funds, all part of the Sun Family tax avoidance plan. Surely, they could all get in worse trouble for doing nothing with the so-called charity. Didn't the IRS care if a foundation actually gave away money?

Some days, she thought the tension of her lack of power to fulfill her role would drive her crazy. On those days, she painted. She got a massage. She got some skiing in or hiked with friends. Occasionally, Lars would be around, and they would go out on the sailboat or take a weekend trip to San Francisco or New York, someplace nice. But everywhere she went, people asked what she did. She hated the sound of her own voice explaining that she was the head of a charity that funded one single enterprise run by the principal's mother. It was humiliating.

On really bad days, she went to the jewelry store in University Village and got herself a condolence gift. *Here, your soul may be dying, but this emerald necklace will make you feel better. This diamond-encrusted padlock will show everyone that you actually do have value in this world.* Today might be one of those days. Just a little pop in on the way home. She could pick up some dumplings at Din Tai Fung.

Good thing Thea was so self-absorbed. She didn't seem capable of focusing on Ryan's intentions. He had said Thea was a violent, angry bitch on the island, which seemed fair. He had been trying to scare her, after all. His visit to Harborview had been ridiculous, but he had been fired by then, anyway. Not Eleanor's responsibility. The accountant Alexander Barrow had moved on to another firm. Not an issue, is what Ryan had said. Eleanor looked on the Thompson and Boyer web site, but there was no Barrow listed on the team roster. At least Ryan could do something right. His LinkdIn profile had Barrow still at the firm, but people always lied about their resume. No doubt he would change it once he found a new job.

When Eleanor had done all she could to muddy the waters of her former employees' stupidity, she couldn't resist pulling up the grant applications and letters of intent in the email files. People asking for money for all kinds of things because the Foundation website didn't have any limiting language, no guidelines or mission statement. June Smythe wouldn't hear of it, not until Thea could weigh in. As if Thea would take the time to consider how her money could help others. It was maddening.

"She hasn't agreed to those priorities," June had said at least twice after Eleanor begged her to reconsider. Most likely with whiskey on her breath. "The board doesn't have the right to commit the Foundation to directions that have such long-term implications."

No, not like her precious center, the most expensive aftercare facility money could buy. No implications there.

27

Chapter 28

Thea found a lollipop in her coat pocket as she slipped out onto the dock. A breeze carried ripples along the dark lake, little neon squiggles that formed and dissolved endlessly. The lollipop was caramel, warm and sweet. If Shawn were on the beach, he would be swallowed in darkness. But she didn't think he was. She didn't think he ever would be, again. Maybe Cory would, though. Cory with his hesitation, his careful hair, and avid green eyes looking up through the rain, asking to hang out. She would like to have a talk with him now. A talk at the very least.

"Thea Sun?" called a reedy voice.

A transparent whisp of mist moved in from the end of the dock, a lighter shadow in the blue dusk. Not even ghost-shaped, the thing was like car exhaust, or the plume of smoke coming from the university power plant, thin and snaking.

"Oh, for fuck's sake."

"I'm sorry to disturb. My name is Alexander Barrow."

Of course. The lollipop splashed softly into the water below her.

She gestured. "Please. You'll recognize this dock from the last time we met."

The smoke snake moved to the other chair. "I drowned that night. It was...horrible."

"How is it for you, now?"

"It's okay. I've seen the other side, just glimpsed it. I...it's amazing."

Thea sat up taller. "Did you? Are there people? Anyone I would know?"

There was a percolating sound, almost like rain on the water, though the sky was studded with stars.

"Are you laughing?"

"Names don't matter so much. It's like looking into one of those easter eggs, with the candy gardens inside, that you look at through a hole in the end?"

"The afterlife is a sugar egg with paper bunnies and chocolate flowers? Sounds nice."

"I mean, the feeling. Of when you're a child and your mother buys you something delightful then hides it from you because it's meant to be a surprise, and you glimpse it just for a moment. And you look forward to maybe getting to go there, into all that niceness and cuteness. And explore and be happy."

"Alexander, you don't sound like a murderer."

"No, Mrs. Sun. I wasn't aware of murder: they told me something completely different. They told me just to knock into you. I should have taken that little boat and kept going, all the way to the ocean, I don't know. A voice came to me in those final moments and told me that it was pointless to ram into you, so I jumped out. The boat kept going, though. I didn't know how to slow it down. I've never driven a boat before."

"A voice? Was it gravelly?"

"Not a real voice. The voice of reason. I was an idiot. I should have gone to the authorities. But the guys made it clear they would implicate me. I was new at the job. I was scared. They have great research skills. You know, digital never dies."

"How did they know I would be on the dock?"

"Didn't you come out there to see why I was there? I drove by three times trying to get your attention."

She reached her hand across the space between them and touched the dust swirl that had been Alexander Barrow, midlevel accountant, someone's son. Now just a cold shaft of air.

"Can you explain how being a ghost works? I've asked around, but it seems like a sore subject."

"Is that what he said? The guy who is around you a lot?"

"Do you know him?"

"I saw him my first day. But he won't talk to me. He thinks I'm a murderer."

"Alexander, did you come here for forgiveness? Is that really meaningful to you ghosts?"

"I don't know. I don't know why I'm here. I only know I died because someone wants to knock you back into a coma."

"Does confessing that help your situation? Does it work?"

"I guess it does. Goodbye."

The whisp stirred itself into a small whirlpool of dark mist and faded into nothingness.

28

Chapter 29

Thea's irises in the scanner opened the private elevator in SunStorm Building One so frictionlessly the security people didn't have time to ask what she and Lee were doing there. Lee's face looked tense. He said he had been there before, but Thea wondered when. He seemed surprised by the private parking area's numerous attendants.

Four strapping young people in red fleece herded themselves toward the closing door, already speaking in walkie talkies, making motions to one another as if Thea's appearance was all they'd been waiting for to spring into job-justifying action. She had made a point not to tell the goons at home where they were off to, but Lee had no doubt whispered it to Mary, who must have called it in to Sun Storm. Just as well. Ryan and his idiotic plastic rifle wouldn't get past the growing swarm of red-fleeced guards. And on the off chance that Ryan wasn't the real threat, if he was just a cog in some larger plot involving Alexander Barrow, Katherine and Lars, or the King of England. Showing up at her company was a clear signal to her enemies that they had failed to silence her. That felt good.

Lee refused to meet her eyes as the elevator rose, hadn't spoken to her since she had snapped at Mary that it was *none of her business where they were going in the Porsche*. Thea realized with a piercing internal ache, that Lee preferred she play along. Maybe he was right. She ought to stop making problems for everyone. June had filled her in on lots of things Old Thea did to engineer Lee's stay in the US. But powerful as she had been, Old Thea had not been able to foresee any of this, or she would not have sent Allen to nursing school or engineered his green card marriage to Lee. Which, based on what she heard coming from their guest suite downstairs, wasn't a loveless union. Even so, something was off. Allen watched her with far too much condescension. He wasn't afraid of her, while most everyone else she encountered was.

The building's top floor was nearly silent while a boy in a Band of Horses tee shirt unlocked the glassed-in conference room, offering to *let everyone know they were there*, eyebrows high in his young face. "No, I'm here to meet with the Foundation General Council, nothing for Management to worry about."

He disappeared down the stairs.

"They will have heard already. They will be having heart attacks." Lee slapped a hand over his mouth. "Oh. Lars. I am sorry."

She smiled, relieved to see a look of amusement on Lee's face. "Tell me, were things this crazy before?"

"Ask someone else." His expression relaxed into perfect blandness. "I was not part of your business."

She wanted to ask what he was, really, to her and Ben. But he left the room abruptly, parking himself outside the glass wall with his back to her. Thea watched the quad between their four buildings, five stories below, the landscaped parklike area where concrete brooks flowed, and people moved from one glassy edifice to the next. Ramona appeared, balancing a stack of file boxes, wobbling on her heels.

Without preamble, she said, "I printed out all Foundation transactions, correspondence, texts and emails for the weeks before the accident, then while you were in your coma, until now. I used Lars' proprietary laptop. Please don't tell anyone. Eleanor asked us for it on Friday, said he wants to work."

"Wants to work?"

"She said he's oh so much better. So I grabbed all I could. She's coming to retrieve it today, and I can't exactly say no. He's our senior partner."

"Got it."

There was a brittle pause. Ramona looked like a commercial for silky hair products, her arms crossed to show off her ridiculous, long opaline nails. She seemed in that moment like a woman trying unsuccessfully to hide her hobby of burlesque dancing or sexual domination. Thea bit her lips at her own insights, hoping she appeared respectful. There was something overly starched about the young attorney Thea wished to soften up, even while she understood Ramona needed to pass as having everything together, no loose ends, no vulnerability. Something told Thea Ramona was a self-made girl, like her. Thea could feel it, that invisible force field deterring interest. That was what she had been drawn to after Lars was choppered away: the sense that Ramona couldn't afford to fuck up, would not fail, could not abide the very idea of screwing up. There was a Ben-tinged vibration about this knowledge, a kind of warm benevolence, like watching a child try to catch snowflakes in her mouth without realizing they would melt before she could taste them. *People are always telling you exactly what they want,* she heard Ben's slightly accented, blunt voice say in her head. *You just have to calm the fuck down long enough to read them. They think I'm the smart one. They'll tell you anything.* The memory was a stab in her ribs. She wished she could ask him what he would do about being murdered. But maybe she already knew. Because if the helicopter crash had been sabotage, Ben had not seen it coming. Was he in an infinity place full of loving souls? He didn't seem like the type. But maybe Shawn had been right. Maybe if she could get herself to a safe place, she would have the leisure to take care of the afterlife and all it contained. Samantha was looking at her expectantly.

"You found something in these?"

She tapped the top of a chair lightly with both hands. "It's complicated. I prefer you see for yourself before I offer my conclusions."

Again, Thea felt Ben's echo. Here to help. She pictured him laughing, gesturing as he talked about something beautiful, he had seen out an airplane window or on the New York subway. Finding extraordinary truths in the most mundane situations. Including in her. Fuck perfection. Fuck not making mistakes or trying not to look like an idiot. Ben was the person who saw her as a bright, rare specimen, while every other lover thought she wanted compliments, assumed Thea was trying to impress them. Not Ben. He understood that her looks were meaningless to her, a distraction, a waste of attention. Ramona seemed to care deeply, her young beauty obscured by cosmetics and what Thea thought might be lip injections, hair extensions, the kinds of enhancements meant to make woman uniform in their symmetrical, shiny sameness. It was a form of safety, Same as any other. She didn't hold it against Ramona but wondered for the tiniest moment if it meant younger women looked at her with pity, for not doing the same. She hated thoughts like this.

"Can you just..." Another of Ben's expressions came into her mouth, "Bottom line this for me?"

Ramona leaned close and whispered. "Your intuition was correct. While you were out, someone was up to mischief."

"Is it someone named Ryan? Who works under Eleanor, at the Foundation?"

Ramona's eyes darted to the window. Light bounced off the other three buildings, hitting her fake eyelashes like telephone lines in sunshine. Thea wondered if there was something she wouldn't risk saying aloud.

She spoke so softly Thea had to strain to hear. "Financial malfeasance is hard to prosecute. Unless it amounts to simple theft, or you have a victim with clear hardship as a result, stuff like this is handled privately."

"That's why we have whole firms at our disposal?"

She shrugged. "Unless you want to look at thousands and thousands of transactions a day, you're going to have to trust that people in a position to steal from you have something big to lose if they get caught."

"Is Ryan trying to put me back in a coma just to get away with theft? Doesn't he know I have you? To press charges with or without me?"

"That's one of the factors you need to consider." She stopped pacing. "Why would we?"

"Because you represent me?"

"That doesn't obligate us to take legal action just because we can. We are bound to do what is in your and the Foundation's interest." She sat and leaned her chin on her hands. "Think about this. Consider that there are consequences for airing your laundry in public."

"My laundry?" Thea suddenly felt like she was at a great height. So many aspects of her position she would prefer not to consider. How her wealth looked to security goons, the army of people who worked for her, the press, the Betsy Wheelers of the world. "Okay. Say it's obviously too embarrassing for me to admit someone is fucking with me while I'm comatose: why go to the trouble of concussing me again, this time maybe forever? If I die, my fortune belongs to the Foundation. It's earmarked for charity, right, now that I have no heir?"

"Correct. But the mandate is pretty vague. The only people making decisions about where the money goes are the board. They have zero interest in prosecuting someone for playing around with accounts."

"So, this is...in house?" Thea didn't want to say more. Ramona's face was tense. The conversation clearly made her uncomfortable. The only sound was the conference room's ventilation system, the faint shudder of elevators on other floors. Lee stared through the glass wall, face unreadable, eyes moving back and forth between the two women.

"Criminology is not my specialty. I do corporate law. But I can say for sure that you need to be very careful. No one has a vested interest in telling you the truth. Whoever attacked you, if they did attack you, no offense, they're being careful not to make it easy for you to prove anything, or to retaliate. They've muddied the waters. Now that you have better security, it might become impossible for them to get to you, but they still might try. And putting you back into a coma might not be their intent."

"I want control of the situation."

Ramona leaned back. "Read the file."

Thea stood and went to the window looking down onto the common areas. Workers moved through the space like tiny animes.

"I just want my freedom back."

"To be free, you'll have to give away your money."

"And if I wanted to?"

Ramona's face took on a hard look. "Eleanor is there in the Foundation to help."

Thea laughed for a long time. "I see."

From the ground floor atrium, Thea watched the common area while Lee loaded the boxes into the car. Workers moved around, lunchtime approaching, alighting at tables and on benches in small groups. A black dog was led through the quad and over to a group at a circle of chairs. Thea wished she could join them. Their lives seemed purposeful: no trace of paranoia or self-consciousness. Then she sighed deeply, a thin tendril of something between insight and memory creeping through her. SunStorm had a vitality she knew, in her skin. This seemingly happy, harmonious workplace had been their creation, hers and Ben's, tangible evidence of their union, much more so than the house, or even the unbuilt island compound. SunStorm was what they cared about, what they had worked for. And it was still here, not vanished into snow, into red, or the dark shadows of lost memory. SunStorm was alive, more vibrant than she was. The knowledge made her ashamed. Seeking release, Thea turned her attention to a vibration of ghost energy underneath the building. A faint, a scratchy song, calling out forlornly in a language long forgotten. She had a strange impulse to reach down and talk to it, try and take the needle off the groove. But a voice spoke in her ear.

"Mrs. Sun! Welcome. We are...just beside ourselves to have you here." A woman Thea's age in a flowered dress and combat boots smiled with seeming delight. She was flanked by two younger women in headsets, looking pert. Lee glared. Thea made a reassuring hand motion and allowed the women to introduce themselves. She repeated, *Lina, Vivian*, and *Jill*. Thea tried to commit them to memory, but Lina was asking if she wouldn't like to come see everyone in the solarium. Thea replied impulsively that she would love to. Maybe she could take some of their professional energy, feed off their obvious sense of purpose. They moved past a group of sculptural wooden cubbies like massive glowing fish, into a vast space, four stories high, with slender wooden sculptures reaching upward like limbless trees. A complicated glass roof sent sunlight streaming down in waves of intersecting color. Then she noticed the space had filled with people, and she clutched at her memory of Ben, lost in the intensity of their combined gazes.

Ben said in her head, with jovial flair, "We are the sun here, Thee. This planet belongs to us. We bend the light to our will."

"Oh." Thea said to no one in particular. "Ben loved this installation."

At the sound of Ben's name, Lee's head swiveled toward her.

"We are the sun here," Thea said aloud.

The sound in the great hall shifted, from hushed silence to a cascade of voices, chattering and laughing. People emerged from openings in the sides, and balconies above, more faces appearing. The security goons moved close, Lee beside them, though she couldn't see more than his hands then, the room growing suddenly crowded. Madhavi and Connor appeared on an upper level. There was a feeling of excitement. What were they expecting? She thought of Sun's first product, a service for small business that prevented piracy by spreading proprietary data around the cloud. Web security, though it was really just scrambling data, configuring it to do what was then miraculous, now ordinary. But that had been so long ago. What had she been working on since then? The wave of excitement hovered within her. Something not in the project files she had seen. Not in what Madhavi had shared. Something secret? Who could she ask?

"There are no original employees left, right, Lina?" She had to shout. "Anyone who knew me while we were building this company?"

Lina smiled. "Startups beget more startups, as you know."

"Right." She wanted to ask more questions, but the room was quieting now, a shiver of anticipation running through the air. Applause rolled through the atrium, with whoops and hollers, the barking of dogs, and exuberant finger-whistles. Thea and Lee locked eyes, then he joined into the clapping, a manic smile on his face. Thea laughed. She raised a hand, and silence fell.

"Thank you, friends." *We are the sun here*. Her voice felt strange in her head, some unknown part of her bailing her out of a frightening situation, as it had the first time she returned to SunStorm. The thread to her real self was tenuous but still holding. She could do this. She felt an invisible Ben smiling from behind her left shoulder. Maybe Shawn was there, too. Everyone was looking at her. "I just want to say how grateful I am, and I know Ben would be, for your hard work and faith during these times of transition. As you know, I don't have any formal role in running things around here right at the moment. Which is probably for the best. I'm still waking up."

The people in the atrium laughed, a performative sound of welcome. Any joke she attempted, she sensed, they would laugh. They needed her. They wanted her to wake up and be part of whatever the fuck this place was, whatever it was they did. The panic in her torso calmed. She breathed. Thea thanked Madhavi and the team. She somehow produced the names of some of the bigger projects, the fastest-growing divisions. She praised the chefs and the rest of their support staff. She said what she thought they wanted her to say, that there was still a SunStorm Corporation, that their work lives would continue in a way that connected to the past.

"Everywhere I look, I see the vision Ben and I had, of this company, of the innovations that shift everything down stream. And I just know, standing here in this beautiful solarium, he would be just as..."

There was a pause, Thea struggling for words, the audience waiting with what felt to her like sympathy, while inwardly she heard Ben laughing. She was being too sincere. A large, bearded man stared questioningly from a few yards away, hands stuffed into chino pockets, a look of bemused fury on his round face.

"I take that back. We all know what Ben was like. He'd be asking me why I'm still talking when you're hungry for lunch."

Laughter. The impromptu meeting broke up as quickly as it had come together, people scattering to lunch lines, moving to exits and elevators. Workers gathered around her, and she smiled, allowing them to press her into handshakes, Lee saying to each of them softly not to touch her—she was still recovering.

"Craig wants to talk to you," Madhavi said softly into Thea's ear. Did her face wear a strained look?

"Craig. Of course." Thea's face was stiff with smiling. She let it relax. Craig. A name she had heard before. She fished in her purse for her phone, which would have a listing with his last name, but the large, bearded man was in front of her, gazing down. His flesh was soft over his huge frame, a Viking who has spent too much time gaming and not enough rowing longships. He crossed his arms. When he spoke, his surfer-dude voice was flat with barely-suppressed rage.

"COHE has missed you. I really hope you're coming downstairs to see us today."

No deep reverence. Just impatience, desire to get to work. She bent her head back to look him fully in his face, which could have used some barbering but even so would never be handsome, and he met her eyes with a wild expression that might have been desperation.

"Today?"

"You've been awake for a while now, from what I've heard. I would have thought you'd have come to see about us already."

She wanted to ask, what is COHE? She wanted to say, I'm not awake, whatever you heard, I'm still deciding whether or not to come back to this haunted world. She heard a whisper of Shawn's voice telling her to wake up, start swimming, she had important things to do. He had been like this Craig person, full of impatient energy on her behalf. She was used to this, her shoulders told her, relaxing, her ribs flattening and letting go. COHE was something compelling, carrying a whiff of obsession. Old Thea had cared about it, whatever it was.

"You've never been in a coma, have you, Craig?"

"I will be soon, if you don't get the fuck back to work."

She felt Lee pull her away, and she liked the feeling, his hands turning her from Craig and back to the elevators and the waiting car.

29

Chapter 30

Thea swam when they got home, Lee watching uneasily from the dock. Allen was at work, but the house felt different. Even though Lee sat snipping beans on the dock, she missed him. Since Allen came, she had put her ear to the heating vent, the sounds of their voices or their bodies having muffled but audible sex. Once she heard Lee laugh in a way she didn't think she had ever heard him before. It made her furious.

"Thea?" a voice called out. Suki.

Thea righted herself, the deeper water cold on her feet. "I thought you gals swam in the morning."

"Oh, I'm like you. No one tells me when to swim." Suki stroked over. Her face was pulled oddly under the cap, eyes small beneath goggles.

"And I'm not the only one who swims alone."

"I try to come as often as I can. I have to say. I can't believe how fast you had your dock fixed."

"Yeah. I guess people work fast when they're trying to cover up the evidence."

Suki pulled off her goggles, treading water. "Evidence?"

"I'm kidding."

"Did they tell you who it was?"

"A midlevel accountant named Barrow. His body was found down by Denny Blaine."

"You brushed his cold, dead hand?"

"What? No. I didn't find his body."

"That's weird." Suki said, moving her pink inflatable buoy from where it had floated into the water between them. "I heard you did."

"Really? What else did you hear?"

"Seattle. No one likes gossip, but everyone loves to be in the know."

"You'd be doing me a favor if you gave me a head's up. In return I can offer you a hot tub, or an outdoor shower."

"No time. But I will say this. A lot of people think you're pretending to have amnesia."

"Pretending? Why would I do that?"

Suki pulled on her goggles. "Convenience, I guess."

"Are you kidding?" Thea was suddenly hot. "What kind of monster thinks it's easy to not remember their own life?"

But Suki was halfway to the beach, her feet churning the water. And Thea knew exactly what kind of monster.

Lee finished replacing the air filters and gave the used ones to Mary to place in the recycling bin. "Are you sure you don't mind?"

"Nah." She took the filters in her hands. "I go into the garage every hour to check. Gives me something to do."

He turned to look out at where Thea was swimming with one of the local people, a woman Ben had called The Vessel, for reasons he never explained. The Vessel swam almost every day. Lee had never seen her speak to Thea before. He stood close to the window. They looked normal. Like friends.

"Mr. Lee?" Mary said from the kitchen. "Can I get you anything?"

He smiled without turning. "No need to call me that. I am just Lee."

She stood near. "She sure likes to swim."

"Yes. You know, she never forgot how. Even when she couldn't say her name, she still always went in the hot tub or bath or she waded in at the beach. Soon, we understood that it was important for her."

"You really want her to finish getting well, huh?"

Her voice was kind. But also, surprised. "I don't know. Maybe she will never finish."

Mary laughed. "What's next for you, then?"

"Oh." Outside, the women were sitting in the shallow water of the beach. Everything was fine. "I will go back to normal."

He felt Mary's eyes on him. In the days she had been coming, they had spoken several times. She seemed to understand what it was to keep a commitment.

"Normal? Ah. Back to your fine man and your work van? Won't you miss all this?"

His head bowed. "Yes."

"She's going to miss you, that much is obvious."

He shrugged, face warm. "We have a lot of history."

"Really? You and Boss Lady?"

He told the lie of protection. "Not in the way you are thinking, exactly. But I have been here in this house for a long time, now."

"Miss your family, huh?"

"Yes, exactly." He moved to fetch a towel for the floor in case Thea was still dripping wet when she entered. "I really do."

Thea napped, dreaming of an underground sea and a shining white fish. When she woke, the house was full of the scent of roasting chicken Lee was preparing for Thea's *dinner party*, as he called it. Could a dinner party consist of only two people? She didn't ask. She wanted to think that he was cranky about her seeing a man, but he seemed the same as always. At five thirty, he and Allen disappeared downstairs—for the purpose of giving her privacy, he said, and Allen snorted with laughter.

"How could I have privacy in this place?" she said, smiling woodenly. "The walls have ears."

But they were gone. The goons knew that when the knock came, she herself would answer it. At 5:29, it did. Thea shook out her hair, glad not to have time to think of Suki's sullen expression as she said the word "convenience." Her stomach felt leaden. Cory might have thoughts about it all. Shawn had told her once that Cory was fake and cheap but also a decent egg, whatever that was. But ghosts could lie, she was fairly certain.

She opened the door. When they hugged, he was taller and wirier than she expected, strange, but also familiar. Skin. Flesh. A smiling face full of shadows and wrinkles, handsome in its way. A person as old and complicated as she was, though he seemed to be trying to appear confident. He should be. His band with Shawn had been very successful. There were many videos of him singing, playing a guitar, jumping in front of roaring crowds. The door closed, but he didn't let go of her hand. Sweat gleamed on his half-lidded eyes.

"I hope you're hungry."

"I am fucking famished."

Late in the night, when Lee was in the kitchen straightening, Cory appeared, looking red and happy, his jacket over his arm.

"Do you want to borrow a flashlight?"

Cory shook his head. "You're Lee?"

Lee hung the dishtowel on the stove.

"She's doing better. Right?"

"She's doing great tonight."

"I know you've been taking care of her. Is she...capable of making her own decisions? I should have asked this before, but..."

They stood in silence. Finally, Lee said, "You want to know if you...took advantage of a sick woman?"

Cory swallowed, looking silly in spite of his tall frame, a handsome older man, silver-haired, buff, a guy who could get sex without trying, anywhere. And rich, Lee had heard. Lee had never heard his music and was sure he would hate it if he did. Nothing, nothing like Ben.

Ben liked expensive cars and a silly house full of useless things like elevators and wine cellars and a big basement right next to a lake just to show he could afford it. Ben radiated energy, confidence, his face always moving from side to side, so he missed nothing. If Lee was working on the car dock, Ben would walk right up and see that Lee had too many valves on the bench. Ben would point out the valves, and when Lee explained it was intentional, because he wanted to make sure to replace all the old valves before replacing the couplings, Ben would touch him on the shoulder and say, *you are the best, doing things the right way.* And Lee had said, *only for a client who knows the difference.* Or something like that. Something that was a lie and the truth together.

"See you around," Cory said from the drive.

Lee bolted the door.

No sound from upstairs. Was she asleep? They had used a baby monitor for the first few months. She hadn't even been able to speak then, just moan for him. Later, when she was well enough, she asked what the small plastic speaker was, and he had taken it away. By then she was able to get up by herself, brush her teeth. Sometimes she came down without remembering where she was, who he was, but she was always sweet. The dark hole of Ben was less visible to Lee then because she didn't remember, she never made him recall how things had been for them all, when they had been a family. Only when he was packing the clothes to store, Lee would quake with his sorrow for Ben, and for Thea, for him and them together. And for Maggie, with her sudden feral expressions, her love of Ben's attention.

Lee became mother to Thea, then, her nurse and guide, the only one she had. Except for June, who was so impatient. She would get angry and cry for her grandbaby, her voice ragged after several drinks. Thea would watch like a confused baby. Why is the lady making grimacing faces? Why is she roaring like a wounded cow? She would begin to ask, and June would scream. *Goddammit, goddammit,* about how unfair it was that this baby was lying comfortable in bed, while the real baby was nowhere to be seen.

Now, that innocent uncomprehending Thea had remembered her body and returned to fucking. He grunted. So, not a totally new Thea. He wouldn't go see about her. He knew how she was when she was satisfied, the look on her face as she slept. He and Ben had watched her together, holding hands on the bed. She gave the most, and she was the most exhausted when it was over.

Never again. Without Ben, he could feel no joy in it. Sometimes, she looked at Lee with the old hunger. That was when he knew he would leave soon. He had taken Ben's jackets; June had invited him to. No pants would fit, but jackets could be tailored. When Lee went home to see his mother in Vancouver. He would ask her to sew them slimmer for him, and he could wear Ben around like a protective coating.

Lee tasted tears. Salt. The dark house hummed, air filters and heat pumps. Maybe he would still come one or two days a week, for a while. But he missed the feel of the nail gun, his work van. He missed his music, Little Naz X and Cameron Hawthorn. His mother wanted him to come visit. He needed Thea to be well. He still had the baby monitor in his garage in the condo. He had Maggie's sparkle backpack, for no reason except June had put it in the trash. These people with their things, their money. Thea speaking to the dead, and him not telling her it was bad luck. Because he was so relieved to see her speaking.

Waves lapped on the retaining wall, the wake of an unseen boat. He double-checked the locks on the glass doors and went downstairs.

30

Chapter 31

At 4:30 a.m., realizing she wasn't going to fall asleep at all, or look at the papers in the boxes, or eat roast chicken, Thea lifted the cobweb-snared plastic kayak from its place below the decking. She snuck past the cameras, moving quickly so that if the guards came after her, she would already be too far away to hear. The kayak bore the word *Smythe* in bold letters on the inside of the bright blue hollow. She had no memory of using it, but the two-sided paddle felt good in her hands as she pushed off the dock.

There must be names for all her emotions, the narratives that pushed into her whenever she closed her eyes, the excited feelings at Sun Systems, the dread of the boxes in the office, Lee's obvious irritation that Cory had come and their mutual release. She didn't want to lie in her bed anymore, trying to get all the threads of the day to settle. Regular life was tempestuous, overstimulating. It made her feel as if she were falling, spinning, on the verge of a major discovery she couldn't see and didn't understand. But it was the thing Ben had always been selling; and he was right. Risk reward ratio. She felt a stab of the scorn Suki had left behind. But here she was, on this lake, as the sky turned colorless with coming dawn. She was close enough to being whole that she understood she never would be. She would always be a shard of a person, parts of her submerged and out of reach. It didn't matter. For a split second, the water was simultaneously opaque and clear, its surface pale with daybreak, its depths thick with shadow. She let the kayak run.

Lee and Allen were making lattes when she returned, pulling herself as straight as possible so Lee wouldn't see how stiff she felt, notice her blistered thumbs.

"We're doing oat," Allen said. "You'll try?"

She took a demitasse from his hand. Lee scraped something into the garbage disposal.

"Thank you for the beautiful meal last night. I was...too busy to eat."

Allen laughed. Lee's dark eyes slid toward her collarbone, so she could see he wasn't really angry.

"You're all healed."

"Are you joking?"

Allen smiled. "Doesn't she know that song? Sexual healing?"

"She doesn't," Thea said. "And she doesn't need to know. The world is full of useless information, isn't it? When all that matters is right in front of us."

Allen rolled his eyes. "Honey. You need to get laid more often."

They laughed.

After her shower, Lee came and sat with her on the couch by the window. She noticed he was barefoot, his toes unkempt. Not perfect. Only a person, in a body, full of feelings. Like her.

"Allen dislikes me."

Lee shrugged. "He doesn't know you."

"Do you?"

"You're someone new. But I think so."

"Do you disapprove of my seeing Cory?"

"No." He straightened the candlesticks. "But if you have a man, what about me?"

Her throat felt tight. "Are you..."

"I'm joking."

His cheekbones were slick, his sleeves rolled in a way she didn't remember. He moved to sit on the floor with his back resting on the couch. "It's not crazy to have sex with a handsome man."

Thea wanted to reach out and stroke his dark, shining hair. Had she ever seen him so unmoving? He was always working. If she reached over and pulled on a lock of his hair, what expression would his face take?

"The goons don't protect me at all. I went out this morning, and no one stopped me. Anything could have happened." Her voice was childish, high with the threat of tears.

Lee put his hand on her outstretched fingers. "I will stay a bit longer. But you don't need me."

"After you go." She couldn't make her voice louder than a whisper. "Can I call you if I want to ask about things? You know, about what things were like before?"

"It's okay. You're just sad."

Tears fell onto her chest. "You're the only person I trust."

He made a grimacing face. "And why do you trust me?"

She laughed. "Okay. Maybe I just really like your cooking."

He waited a long time before saying in a light voice, "That sounds right."

"Were we in love?"

He turned his face away. Downstairs, one of the goons opened and closed a door so it made a mechanical announcement.

"We will always be in love, Thea. Love is like ghosts, spirits. You know. A thing that exists and also isn't real. But doesn't go away."

"I made my ghosts go away."

He smiled, his cheeks making small dimples. "I think you are lying, a little bit. Ben will never leave us."

She took Lee's hand. It was cool and smooth, only the palms calloused with rough mounds. She lifted its calloused skin to her mouth.

31

Chapter 32

Cory watched the lights go off in the thin slice of Thea's upstairs visible from the beach. The days were getting longer, new light exposing the thin spray of lichen on certain cars, the dank roofs with their mossy grout. Even the rich can't keep up with the pressure-washing their garden steps required. It cheered him. The mountains had re-appeared, still white in places, looking down at it all, the stolen land, the furtive people in their electric cars trying to outrun their larceny, get to their death before the world reared up to burn them alive. Nature didn't give a damn. She would win, as she always did. Was it any wonder people had trouble staying sober?

A shiny-bodied corvid flew past Cory's studio several times a day carrying sticks into the trees. He couldn't tell the difference between a crow and a raven. He liked all of them: the grudge keepers, the treasure finders. They should inherit all this. There were juncos everywhere, pecking at the ground around everyone's bright tulips and bluebells. Yes, I've reached the age of noticing birds. Next thing you know, I'll be purchasing a good pair of binoculars, so I can see the world burn from the privacy of my porch. And the birds will fly away, and I'll clap for them. Poor Hailey.

Thea had no such kitschy flowers in her small strip of garden bed, lined in artfully rusted iron, planted with miniature Japanese maples in earth tones, oh so tasteful. The juncos liked it there, pecking at the beauty bark her gardeners replenished twice as often as necessary. It looked very Zen compared to the white limestone box next door, the faux Italian villa on the other side. All the competing aesthetics were good, in his opinion, even sinful invasive ivy. It smelled wonderful piled in someone's yard waste bin, roots broken off but only delayed, not stopped. A performance, rooting out ivy, rooting out blackberries, like trying to eradicate people, they would only dig deeper and return. If they survived the initial trauma. Cory saw it all as he walked down to the beach to smoke. He was smoking now, just a cigarette. He was high on life, still thinking about his night with Thea. The thought of it made his body tingle. It had been eight months since he'd had sex. He ought to be turning cartwheels. Maybe this second cigarette was his way of doing just that. Her light switched on again, then off almost immediately. What was she doing? Was she thinking about him?

He imagined Thea's bedroom, its décor dull but comfortable, anonymous but for its well-stocked bookshelf. He wondered if anyone had read the books, guessed not. But you never knew. Self-made people were always smarter and harder-working than he expected, no matter what their business. The city was full of such hustlers, bland and harmless though they appeared. They got together, shared inside information, and made one another richer. Hard to get in, soft once you got there. He had gotten there. If he hadn't, he would not have been allowed to sleep with Thea Sun. It was that simple.

He drew in the bitter smoke of his American Spirit, wishing Shawn were there. Cory was lucky. Or, as Shawn would say, he was a fine specimen of asshole. He'd been with Thea, but she hadn't really been there. The woman he'd had sex with had stayed a stranger, from her long limbs to her blank eyes. It had been good. He had enjoyed it. But now, he wished he could return to the time before, when he had felt like they could become friends. He felt used, which he richly deserved. He wondered if three cigarettes would make him feel sick, as they sometimes did now. Maybe they could hang out again. They had things in common, or they would if she got her memory back, knowledge of what life had been like before, when their moms had been friends and everyone ate sandwiches from a brown bag on their way to ski, not realizing that it was a rare and elite activity, their mountains clean and uncrowded, because the land had been stolen recently. And now it was on its way to losing all its snow forever.

Thea was only a very rich ant in a wildly successful anthill, and his night with her kind of pointless, because instead of bringing them close, it had shown that there could be no true union among those who don't need anything. She wasn't soft or funny or sweet under her platinum exterior. She was an animal, hungry and intent, that was all. He wanted to believe it was because of loneliness, but it wasn't. He hadn't expected her to love him. But he had wanted into her secrets, at least a little bit. He had wanted to know her, the real her. But maybe there was no real Thea, or if there was, she preferred not to share that side. And his lovemaking had not been enough to change her mind. That was fair.

Still. He would try again, if only out of boredom. What was it like to be that wealthy? Obscenely wealthy, even by Cory's standards, and he was doing very well, especially considering his lack of inheritance. He learned in the band's early days that money was a tool to make more money. Shawn had never gotten that, even for a second. He could not waste his money fast enough. When all was said and done, the woman he'd been seeing wound up inheriting his one durable investment, the apartment building. Cory had bought Shawn's share of their catalogue from the girlfriend, supposedly so there was some cash to throw a memorial event worthy of a beloved musical legend. But she never had. And his ghost had wandered ever since. Eventually, Cory and the other guys and the record company did a fundraiser. It had been horrible, and he was glad that night more than any other that he could still drink. There'd been nothing of Shawn in the evening. Once, he had asked how Shawn felt about not having a real service, complete with memorializing, and he'd laughed.

"Why in the fuck would I care? No one would believe a damn thing anyone said about me, anyway."

Cory felt vaguely guilty about profiting off their library, which turned out to be more lucrative than their initial recordings. But the girlfriend would have only put it in her arm, just like Shawn. He had only met her once, at the memorial performance, but he had been drunk and sad and had barely spoken to her. His lawyers had handled the library acquisition. Cory didn't even know her name. By the point in Shawn's addiction that he got together with her, none of them spoke to him. He didn't know what became of her. No doubt she had been shooting up with Shawn when he died, though Ghost Shawn insisted that wasn't the case. He said she was off drugs, and was pressuring him to quit, and he was trying. He himself had misjudged his dose because he'd tapered off so much. Likely true. Same story as every other junkie. Cory lit a third cigarette.

Where was Shawn, now? He called out his name hesitantly.

Cory was half afraid of what his friend would say about the date. The other half wanted to needle him about it, mostly because Shawn's ghost was the one person Cory never felt ashamed of revealing his worst and most despicable self. It was almost a sport with them. I'm the bigger asshole.

He missed it. Had he grown up to become someone who chronically hid his dark side, his vicious and competitive side, or had the world around him just become intolerant? The circles he traveled in sometimes felt like a virtue contest. But maybe every place was like that now, congratulating itself on its own moral superiority while the walls came tumbling down. Maybe they always had. Maybe the race to be free of blame was all anyone could still fail at, in a world where old rock gods could get it on with their best friend's insanely rich but brain-damaged crush, and no one seemed to think anything wrong about it. Except him. It wasn't right, but he couldn't put his finger on why. She had more than consented, but he felt uneasy.

For a second Cory's mind flickered toward his mom, relocated to a condo he'd bought her in San Diego, where she attended church expressly for the purpose of arguing with reactionaries. She was good at it, adept at what she called "energy matching," slipping the knife blade of logic while smiling through her wrinkles. They had a friendly relationship, but she had disapproved of his choices in life. She deeply disliked his ex, which wasn't fair, but no one told Barb Klain what to think. She loved to talk about how the world was ending due to ignorance and greed, unchecked Capitalism, and toxic masculinity. She wasn't wrong, though like everyone else she left herself off the list. She was a kind grandmother to Hailey, accepting of her different hair colors and defiant sexual identification. It gave her an excuse to fly a rainbow flag in her front window.

He saw Barb now every time he looked in the mirror, her narrow chin, the gleam of submerged silver in her pale green eyes. And now, of course, the lines and wrinkles on their delicate sun-damaged skin, the reverse chevron of wear they shared. He'd tried to stop it with Botox and fillers, but they only made it worse, so he stopped. They were both nice looking, he knew that. Like elves in a fantasy movie, though. Not like real people. Not fleshed out and handsome, like the men living in Thea's house.

Cory hadn't taken the time to look carefully at them, as they smiled knowingly on their way to the downstairs. June must have vouched for him, old politically-marching friend of Barb that she was back when they were kids. He'd paid no attention to the moms back then. Who did? It was only later that he came to understand that his early life was stable and easy compared to Thea's.

He would never have noticed her if not for Shawn. How had he not seen her? It was like walking through a jungle and failing to notice the panther in the tree above you. Knowing her now, seeing her rude hunger, he felt embarrassed. Of course, Shawn had seen this. The monster in me bows to the monster in you, namaste. How many cigarettes were left in the pack? He was laughing. To himself, like a crazy old man. He felt alive. Thea, pushing him to take her on the floor of the office, a tangle of cords around his wrists, had made him feel alive. Goddammit.

"So, now you're the stalker," Shawn said.

Cory startled. "Where the fuck have you been?"

"Where I always am. In your head." Shawn was a mere glimmer, a sequined spider web in the dusk.

"Are you disappearing on me, bro?"

Shawn's laugh was a distant clarinet. It was all so long ago, the time of band practice in the annex, the carpet-covered stairs of the music room like the skin of a hard animal, bristling, worn with use.

A man's voice spoke nearby. "Sir, this area closes at sunset."

Cory knew that. The glass rectangles across the water still flashed neon pink. He stamped out his butt, body filling with heat at being told what to do, particularly because he had been so lost in thought he hadn't noticed the man's arrival.

“Thank you,” the patrol geezer said overloud. He stood with his Mag light pointed down, lighting the path.

Cory pushed past, just touching his gabardine shoulder. A shockwave ran through his body, dark pleasure, the possibility of something leftover, wildness, violence. Thea’s face looking down on him, calm, brilliant, unimpressed.

“Fucking fascist parasite,” Cory muttered, loud enough that the man could hear him.

The little ball of light moved away.

32

Chapter 33

Matty McDougal, or *DJ Magic Mataio*, as his fans knew him, watched the tiny orange wands guide the white-bellied Dreamliners into their gates, a dance of man and machine. As the gate agent scanned his passport, he gazed across the wet pavement outside Vancouver/YVR Terminal M. *Breathe.*

He could do this. He was doing this. Excitement bubbled inside him, like a rainbow-circled geyser in a national park. Flight, again, in the air, as if that were a normal place for a human body to be.

"You should make your connection, without a problem." The agent said, smiling through maroon lipstick. "Enjoy your vacation."

Mattie didn't correct her, say this trip was for work, or he wouldn't be boarding any flying machine, ever again. He went to stand at the window. Layers of misty forest rose high from the tidelands, in decreasingly saturated hues, gray-green, dark green, pale gray. The air smelled faintly of jet fuel. Across the tarmac sat a trio of Bell helicopters like bright red toys. Mattie counted breaths. He started Dvorak's Stabat Mater, the first flurry of horns soothing to his mind. He was going to do this. He was going to get to Athens, and then on to Mykonos, where he and his crew would set up the equipment he'd sent in a cargo plane with the band, and he would get back to his life. It had been over a year. He was ready.

Matty returned a couple of texts, one from the hotel in Athens where he'd sleep off some of his jet lag, the other from a girl he'd started seeing. Opal, of the decorated skin, her form a study in black ink, her mind as surreal as a manga.

One of the few people in his new community who seemed healthy. But you never knew. He had seemed healthy, too.

Okay? Really, not making it look good?

She sent a string of emojis, blue and white hearts, pink flowers, a Greek flag, an evil eye, and a flexed arm to show that he could do it.

Great, for real

He inserted an airplane emoji and a thumbs up.

She'd helped find him a temporary sponsor in Greece, a man ten years older named Yiannis. Mattie counted his breath, in up to eight, back out to ten. The agent announced preboarding. He texted Opal a kiss emoji.

On the jetway, the feathery black blades of the furthest right helicopter begin to rotate. His breath caught. In, 1-2-3-4-5-6-7-8 out, 10-9-8.... He couldn't complete the sequence. Blood thundered in is ears, even as the horns resolved into the Soprano's first low notes.

Stabat Mater dolorósa iuxta crucem lacrimósa.

Matty was driving Whistler Highway again, windshield smothering with snow, swiped off again and again and again, Desmond Dekker blasting. *Get up in the morning, waiting for bread, sir, so that every mouth can be fed.* He tried to sing along, but his body was shaking, just starting now, the beginning of what would soon become unbearable. It had been the previous times Mattie had tried to stop using. Shame was beginning to filter horribly through his nausea.

He'd left notes in the city, driving north brainstorming ways to get through the barriers to Alice Lake. He hadn't thought his plan through, beyond the obvious, how to do it. In the end, he had resolved to climb the barriers and walk, though he was wearing sneakers and had no gloves. What difference did cold make, now? He'd said goodbye to his parents and sister, who were sick of him and his endless failures, anyway. All the dark shit he'd done. He'd worked hard on the notes. Trying to strike the right tone in case the words ever became public. People would want to know what happened, and he was just vain enough to want to control the story. He felt remorse, he took responsibility. He wanted people to know that.

His stomach felt like someone had been dropping coins into it. The song changed to a Percy Faith remix. The road was laminated layers of snow, slipping under his tires. Other drivers had their lights on, casting strobing spots of white, yellow, black. He could hardly see. He let his foot off the gas briefly, hoping for better traction. He had to get there, while he could still drive. He focused. No more thoughts of the past. Forward, onward. This was exciting. This was new.

The lake would be like a cold, still mirror ringed in white, tree branches, birch bark. He loved those trees, like constant friends, summers stretching back into the recesses of memory until he could almost taste boyhood, the potent optimism of being small, the conviction that nothing bad would happen to him, because he was complete, his body full of grace and eagerness and inexhaustible energy. The sweetness of not knowing pleasure beyond swimming and climbing, his mother singing, his father splitting wood. His love of the stones and trees and clear water with its iron-stained granite bottom, complete. He had to get back there.

He didn't hear the helicopter. It was just there, to his right through the windshield, a gleaming apparition, godlike, preposterous. All was white, but the red metal machine, its black blades somehow wrong, rotating too slowly, its body not falling so much as soaring, like a paper airplane carelessly tossed. And then, horribly, it was gone.

What had he seen? A tiny shape falling from the red fuselage, the rotation of the blades precariously slow, trees obscuring the mountain. The sky was empty, and he was pulling over to the side to vomit. He killed the engine.

Had it been real? Cars and trucks passed indifferently in the sudden silence. Then the ground shuddered, and there was a boom like train cars smashing together. The world was still, but for the endless snow. Matty stood by his car, colder and colder, sickness creeping up his skin, and wondered if his mother had seen his note yet. Did she think he was already gone? Did everything that happened in this world lead to the hollowness he felt, pulling him down? Should he flag someone? Call someone? He wouldn't be able to keep going with his plan if he talked to another person, even a stranger on an emergency line. He'd have to name the faltering helicopter, the tiny thing falling from it, put those surreal images into words. He couldn't.

Nothing seemed as clear as it had the previous moment. How to get to the lake once he reached the park entrance? It was all wrong. He would have to jump the fence and walk two kilometers or more. Maybe the fence would be chain link, four meters high, frozen into triangles of ice. Pain, worse than the churning in his gut. He no longer had it in him. His hands were already so cold he couldn't pull the zipper on his hoodie to get to the baggie of capsules in his shirt pocket.

A Mountie pulled over in an SUV, spraying slush. A relief. Mattie walked over, pointing at the place the helicopter had fallen. The man rolled down his window.

"Right there?"the Mountie said, radio in hand. "You saw it?"

"Yes," Mattie said, "I saw."

Someone had called it in, but they didn't know exactly where to look. He found out later that there had been one survivor rescued in the nick of time, maybe down to his help, no one could say. The tiny falling thing was a person, and impossibly, that person had lived.

There was a white noise sound that resolved into sirens, and the Mountie told Mattie to get the hell out of there.

"You look hypothermic. Crank the heat. Understand?"

He sat in his idling car warming up, while ambulances rushed past, fire and mountain rescue trucks with their chains, crunching past him like competent older brothers who knew exactly what to do. He called his mom. She was out at the grocery store, unable to talk. She had not found the note. His sister, same. She was at class and hadn't checked her campus mailbox yet. The whole thing had been a dream. He drove to the treatment facility in North Van. Three hundred and seven days ago.

Mattie stepped aboard the plane and stowed his bag in the overhead compartment. He settled into his seat, pulling on his headphones, watching the champagne bubble in its flutes. When the flight attendant came, he asked for hot tea and milk. Out the window, there were now only two helicopters.

33

Chapter 34

Building Four required six retinal scans to enter, which struck Thea as a ridiculous level of overkill. Madhavi left her at the second one, shooting a look that Thea couldn't quite place, somewhere between scorn and curiosity.

Craig Bjornson, the Viking who had glared at her in the atrium, stood amidst a humming floor-full of live machines.

"We have servers, here?"

"Wow." Craig smiled. "Madhavi told me you don't remember much. Do you need a full explanation, or will shorthand do?"

"You can just show me. Greg." She willfully misnamed him. He smirked harder.

Her annoyance was quickly overshadowed by curiosity. He took her through a minute server farm, three sublevels cooled by the underground river flowing westward from beneath the freeway. That was why they had built the complex here, bulldozing a bunch of former used auto lots with endless sinkhole problems Old Thea had found in public utility records. The view of the lake had nothing to do with it. COHE was kept deliberately un-networked. Secret, un-hackable. But not a lot of data, either. A self-limited project, hard to scale, an *R&D experiment*, as Madhavi had described it when Thea knocked on her door.

What is Constant Heaven?

Your baby, Thea. Your top priority. Do you really not remember?

"How much computing power does one AI need?"

"Depends on what you want it to do." Craig shrugged, his large torso jiggling. "This one is small. But we control it, so the demon in the data is ours to command. Very cool."

"Compared to what?"

"The competition." He paused at the door. "The mind is a terrible thing to waste."

"Fuck you, I think?"

The Android stood blinking as Thea approached.

"Ah. Hello. You're back." She knew the voice. The Android turned its machine head in a way that no doubt meant to convey slight puzzlement.

There were too many emotions to register now, beyond a kind of fascinated shock. "When was I here last?"

The Android said the date. Before the accident.

"What did we discuss?"

The Android answered with a list of over a hundred topics, from the origins of proto-Indo European to the inexplicable devotion of sports team fans. They had spoken of sexual fetishes, rules of flavor balancing in food preparation, and whether or not the Celts represented a once-universal religion.

"That must have been a long conversation."

"Seven hours, forty-three minutes."

"Did you need data to complete your sets?" Thea moved to one of the easy chairs. "Or were we just making conversation?"

The Android sat opposite her. "You were helping complete my array of opinions, prejudices, and ephemera. As well as working together on normal conversational behaviors."

"Yours, or mine?" Thea laughed.

The Android's laugh was grotesque, its mouth opening to reveal a deep hole, which Thea didn't want to contemplate. She had built this machine. What had she wanted it for?

"Both of ours, I'm sure."

The air down here was ionized in an odd and itchy way, like before a lightning strike. Thea scratched the place on her head where hair had been grafted over the steel plate. "So, since then you've been hanging out with Craig?"

"No. I've been inert. The last human person I spoke to was Benson Sun."

"Ben?" The information sounded significant, somehow. "What did you talk about?"

The Android sat back in the chair, a gesture of settling in Thea suspected was meant to put her at ease. Something in Thea's breathing and body language no doubt conveyed distress.

"He asked me an array of questions. He wanted to know why I existed. For what purpose."

"Ben disapproved of Constant Heaven?"

"Ben asked what was to be gained from a potential product launch."

"Did he?"

The Android sat up straight and held up a hand appendage to indicate the playing of prerecorded audio. Ben's voice.

Okay. AI, I get. The guys down south got sex bots and VR together, just amazing stuff; when they get the costs down, it's going to make whores obsolete. Like, no more trafficking, it's a public good. But this. What is the point of it? Can you be modified to...I don't know, practice medicine, or teach, or fly airplanes or something? Industry has bots galore it's the golden age of robots over there on the other side of the freeway, gets better every day. Mercenaries, it's terrifying, like a movie, but they're shaped like dogs, and they have no personality, they don't need one. Here you are, polished like My Fair Lady, next thing we know you'll be wearing a bonnet and infiltrating the British Aristocracy. I don't get it. I'm sorry. Would anyone want a realistic facsimile of their loved one? Pretend person, writing memories over the real person?

"Because they miss that person." The Android said in real time and on the recording. "Because they want to stay connected."

No offense. But this project creeps me out.

"No offense taken. Perhaps you are not the intended user."

Ben laughed.

Welp. You are good; she is, as always, a fucking genius at making shit work, but my god. Honey, Thea, the last thing people want is their relatives coming back to haunt them. Jesus. If my shitty, withholding, alcoholic father came back as a robot, I'd have to murder the machine or get murdered by it.

He laughed again.

This feels weird as fuck. A good start for something, for sure. But no. Prove me wrong. You always do. Prove me wrong about this COHE project before I have to get you into some serious therapy.

Ben was there, bright in her mind, his pockmarked, round face, his gruff demeanor, the warmth of his fat fingers in hers, that feeling of invincibility, of being *babe* and *honey*, of being his. Of belonging with Ben. With Maggie. It had been her home, this endless banter, this frank and opinionated man.

"Where did you get Ben's data?"

"From recordings."

"Where did those come from?"

"Many sources. Shall I text you a list?"

"No. I think I can figure it out. Have I been recording our conversations? Mics all over my house? The cars?"

"As project manager, you are authorized."

Thea looked at the list on one of the monitors. "Holy shit. I had mics everywhere."

"There was a period of data collection." The period ended the day of the accident.

"And Maggie? Do you have her voice?"

"You specified no recordings of her. A child, you said. Not able to authorize."

She closed her eyes. "Good. Good. Can you speak as Ben, or just play back his speech?"

"This is what you were beta testing. I was speaking as Ben, as a surprise for Ben. You wanted me to be able to carry on a conversation with him as him. You thought it would be a funny joke. We were practicing."

"Great." Thea paced. "Let's keep going."

"What topic would you like to discuss?"

"Love."

Ben's voice came from the android's mouth. "Honey. You know me. I would do anything for you. You're a huge bitch, but you're my huge bitch, and I love you forever."

"Stop." Thea laughed. "Okay. More."

She stayed for almost three hours, starting, and stopping. A reminder chimed, lunch with Lee. She shut down the android and went into the project office.

"There she is, obsessed with herself once more." Craig's bearded face twitched with amusement.

"What did we name her? She says she is only COHE."

"I call her Bitoo. For *Bitch Two*." He shrugged. "But you haven't decided. Want me to text you the options?"

She liked that he used the present tense. "Please do. Text me the rest of my brain, while you're at it."

Craig smiled. "So many jokes come to mind, but you are my boss."

The inert android sat motionless behind a glass panel. "Next time, we'll record all your attempts at humor. Make her a sidekick. Gregg, the Comedian."

"There would be a market for that." His voice rose into a joking plea. "My mom would buy at least two."

"What did we build her for?" Thea half sat on a desk. "What was her purpose?"

Craig straightened. "Really?"

"Yeah. Maybe we need to aim higher." She shrugged. "I've been thinking about saving the world."

His eyes were glassy as he stared. "Are we being serious right now? Are you including me in your brainstorm?"

"Sure." She gestured at the android, slumped beyond the window. "What is the point of her?"

"You never told me. You did not choose to confide in me. But I had guesses."

"I never shared anything? No hints?" What a mean boss.

He crossed his arms. "You are not in the habit of sharing your plans with people. Brad Saint thinks it's because you have a trust issue."

"Sounds right."

"But if you want this project to save the world, it's going to take some more...honing."

"Was there anyone else I might have confided in? This guy Brad?"

Craig's laughter boomed. "A journalist. Friendly. But no chance in hell you would tell him anything you didn't want the entire AI and robotics community to know."

"Oh. Okay."

"Did you ask her?" He indicated the android with a toss of his head.

"Yes. She said she was adaptable to any and all needs."

Craig laughed. "Filthy. I suspected as much."

Thea sighed deeply. "Fuck."

Her phone pinged again. Lunch.

"Let's get to honing."

He swallowed a sip of diet Mountain Dew. "Honing as we speak."

Thea made an exasperated noise. "I'm going home where things make sense."

"Y'all come back now, hear?"

"You better hope I do, or you're out of a job, jackass."

Craig laughed delightedly. "And she's back!"

Driving home, Thea's head was full of memories. They were standing in front of a corrugated metal building in falling snow, beside a hangar filled with small planes and snowmobiles. Maggie lay asleep, draped across a jogging stroller she was slightly too big for, her iron-red hair escaping a fuzzy white hat. She held a stuffed mouse, its long tail wrapped around her wrist so it wouldn't get lost.

Thea let the car drive itself through heavy traffic on the bridge into the city, everything gray and hard out the window, the mirrored high-rise buildings, the cranes like antennae. She fingered the plate on her head, still technically a live wound, the place they'd patched over.

Why did you build this? Does it have to do with us? I mean. Sexual stuff? Romance? Let me explain something to you, baby. People want what they can't have, what they are not allowed, not what they've already had. You know no one wants to fuck their dead wife, right?

He sounded sad.

What they are not allowed.

In her memory, she'd replied with something lofty and scathing. But his voice remained unphased. Ben was not afraid of Old Thea. He was enjoying himself, alluding to their marital arrangement, but roughly, without regard to how it might hurt her. Old Thea wasn't sensitive. She was so close to Ben that he could speak to her without filter, referencing his inhibitions, even while they both knew that between them, there were none.

I just don't understand, babe. It's an incredible feat of engineering, you deserve all credit, and there might be some fucking freaks out there who want this, but it can't scale. And even if it could, it feels wrong. Please explain to me like I'm a fucking second grader. What is the user benefit of an Android that looks and sounds like a lost loved one?

Was this the last real conversation they had ever had?

34

Chapter 35

Lee texted Allen to sleep at the condo that night. He said Thea had need of privacy, which he knew Allen would interpret as Lee worrying that Thea would have a strong reaction when he gave his notice.

Allen wanted that, for Lee to complete his connection to the Sun family, finally, though they would both feel a debt of gratitude forever, of course. Allen wanted to pick up their marriage where it ought to be, in his eyes, a regular union between partners who loved one another. Allen liked to act the part; he said, *fake it 'til you make it*.

Lee worked to form rice balls stuffed with curried mushrooms, a favorite of Ben's. It was easy to make, a gift for his troubled mind. He put them on a platter for later. He started the dishwasher. He swept the front porch.

Thea's new lover Cory and his dog paced the sidewalk. Mary said Cory was often around, walked by four or five times a day but he didn't seem to be a nuisance, just a neighbor with nothing to do. He must be hungering for Thea. Cory approached. It was a beautiful dog, expensive-looking, almost like a wolf. Lee had taken to leaving Allen's dog at home. Thea no longer enjoyed it.

"Hey, Lee." Cory called out. "Will she be home later?"

Lee lied. He repeated to Cory what June used to say to Eleanor whenever she called.

"Thea has been ordered to rest and stay quiet for a few days. They made her turn her phone off."

"Phone turned off? Okay. I haven't texted her. I don't have her number. She's recovered pretty fast, right?"

"That's right. But there is no reason to rush her." Lee emptied the dustpan onto the pathway.

Cory glared. "Will you tell her, when she's ready, to call me? I gave my number to her mom. She wrote it down on that list in the kitchen."

"Yes, of course but I am sure she would be in touch with you anyway."

Cory's mouth dropped open. Was Lee being impertinent? Yes.

Lee smiled to soften things. "Mrs. Smythe told me you and Thea are old friends, from school?"

"We had that date the other night, but then I haven't heard from her. Is she okay?"

Lee's chest eased a bit. "Thea is pushing herself too hard."

"But you're her caregiver. Can't you protect her from that?"

Lee glared at Mary through the camera above the door. "I will tell her you stopped by."

The Tesla appeared at the top of the hill, gliding down the street. There was a slight tremor, the garage door rolling itself open. The men locked eyes.

"I have her lunch ready, and then she will need to sleep before we do physical therapy."

"Okay," Cory said. "I hear you."

What did he hear? The garage door thudded shut. Mary appeared.

"Everything good here, folks?"

"Fine."

"Goodbye, Cory." Lee moved past Mary, who closed the door.

Thea sat in her car in the garage for so long, Lee was tempted to go out to her. But sitting at the breakfast bar after Mary returned to her post in the security room, he found tears on the tops of his hands. Because of Ben on the audio Madhavi sent. Ben arguing with Thea about the robot. Ben talking of loved ones. The tears fell in silence, but still Thea didn't come up the stairs.

Did the robot feel? Did it hurt her, knowing Ben didn't see the point of it? What was it to be such a creature?

You know no one wants to fuck their dead wife, right?

He laughed silently. It was such a Ben thing to say. He put his head on his hands on the cold marble counter. The light was low. Mary would not be able to see much.

What had Ben said, that day in the van when they had driven to find the hydraulic kit, over the border, where Ben said tariffs were so much lower? It was an excuse. Ben didn't worry about money. Even as short a time as Lee had worked for him then, he knew that. Ben had been surprised to see Lee's Canadian passport. They had stopped for lunch at an expensive Indian restaurant in Mount Pleasant, and Ben had talked of business and life and things Lee didn't know enough of to understand. A man who needed to talk. A man who was always talking.

Lee had touched Ben's hand, a pinkie against a pinkie. Ben quieted. He didn't speak again, through the meal, the tea, the check, not when they drove to a remote lane, and climbed silently into the back of the van together. Ben didn't say words until after, when he exploded in giddy laughter, and kissed Lee in a way he didn't know he needed to be kissed.

You know no one wants to fuck their dead wife, right?

Lee wanted to.

Thea had not known what she was doing. If she had, she would have made a robot of Ben. She had known what happened the moment she saw Ben's face. They talked of splitting but couldn't.

One of us doesn't exist without the other one. I mean, we do, but we're not fully...alive. I was inert before Thea, always answering to someone, chasing a dollar, applause, anything to prove I wasn't nobody. I thought I was living, but not really. I was trying to squeeze myself into the world, and Thea just up and made a new world for me. For us. I haven't had to answer to anyone since. Do you understand? It's hard to explain.

They lived together as three, making love as three, sleeping as three. Lee had agreed to marry Allen for permanent residency, and they had backed Lee in building the condo complex so he could establish himself with collateral and a track record for future bank loans. They were happy. Ben met a pregnant drug addict crying on the beach while the house was under construction. Her partner had overdosed and died but she was trying to stay clean. Being Ben, he made sure the woman was cared for, made sure the man's family provided for her. As soon as she gave birth, they adopted Maggie.

Then they were four. Lee didn't go to Whistler. Maggie wasn't supposed to go, either, to a boring tech conference at a mountain resort with no other kids. She was supposed to stay home with him. But at the last moment Thea decided she wanted her to come see the Aurora Borealis. Lee didn't know if she did. He remembered the pleading in his own voice when he said he missed them. And Thea had agreed, immediately, and said, *We aren't the same without you.*

And then they didn't come. He assumed she was just being nice. When they didn't come home on Sunday, he got angry and went back to the condo. He hadn't known about the accident for two days. Ben hated when he called. Thea never picked up. He worked on a job in Seward Park, staining a deck. Then he had to replace the washer in one of the units. He went to the house on Wednesday, and June was there, drunk. Thea was in the ICU in a medically induced coma. Ben and Maggie gone. June crying and pacing from room to room, talking on the phone, ordering him to do things, bring her drinks. She didn't know. He didn't tell her. He kept his feelings to himself until June sent him out to the store to pick up food. He sat in the van by the fire dock, in the back with the tools, but he was too sad to cry.

Did the robot know? Would she tell Thea? What did Thea remember?

Lee lifted his head, and Thea was standing in the doorway. Her movements were good as she came to sit next to him, only a bit halting on the left, imperceptible to anyone but him. She put a hand on his arm. She brought her forehead to touch his.

When she finally spoke, her voice was too soft to be picked up by the microphones. "I could make one of Ben. Would you like that?"

"I would. He wouldn't."

"You brought me back to life. He would be so moved by what you have done. He would love you even more for it."

They sat silently, hands and forearms intertwined, until the guards came to announce the shift was changing.

35

Chapter 36

Cal met June at the door, holding a thermos and a baggie of sandwiches. "Here, pretty lady. I don't want you getting lightheaded."

"Is that peanut butter and jelly?"

"One is. One is stinky cheese and cucumbers, just how you like it." He made a hopeful face.

"Yummy." June took the bag and thermos and stowed them in her backpack. "You okay, old man?"

"Just concerned about how this is going to pan out for you. Board politics. She's kept you on the phone for hours these last few weeks." He opened the door for her, a blast of warm air bringing the smell of brown grass. "Are you sure she's in her right mind? No offense."

"None taken." June closed the door and sat on the bench.

Cal sank down next to her, face questioning. He wore a new pair of raglan socks. June had noticed them the week before, along with a brown Carhart jacket and stiff indigo jeans. It was the first time since she'd met him that he'd bought clothes. Five years of the same ancient flannels and paper-thin Levi's held on with a tarnished belt.

Neither of them had mentioned it. Nor did June mention the money Cal had lifted from the Foundation, using June's passwords from the paper list she kept in her desk drawer. She had changed all her passwords, naturally, since. June had been mortified, until Thea explained that the precise amount had been replaced. Not stolen, just borrowed.

It had taken the investigators only a few days to solve the mystery. The funds had been used to purchase and then cash out a quantity of cryptocurrency. The buys were untraceable, but the accounts on either side could be retrieved from June's hard drive. The profits had been used to pay off debts, the remaining money wired to an offshore trust. Not embezzlement, which was considered white collar and might warrant probation: this was larceny, pure and simple, regardless of the payback. For an older person, it might amount to the rest of their life incarcerated.

Though, no one had been hurt, nothing serious had resulted, just someone had finagled around a million dollars in those waning days of the crypto bubble. If Alexander Barrow at the accounting firm hadn't been paying attention, the ledger would have disappeared into cloud storage, unnoticed, just glowing numbers in a field of digital accounts. If Thea hadn't woken up, there would have been no investigation.

But Alexander had done his job. He emailed Eleanor two days before he died, cc'ing two Foundation employees, Ryan Ayers and Anders Levi. Turned out both had participated in daring expense account spending while Thea lay inert. They had attended philanthropic conferences in Reno that just happened to coincide with Burning Man, met *sustainability experts* at a rave in Ibiza, and her personal favorite, investigated the *world-saving potential of psilocybin* at a luxury retreat in Ecuador.

Idiots.

They signed their expense reports with Eleanor's e-signature. Ryan was authorized to do so, pissing away hundreds of thousands of dollars of Foundation money. Eleanor was no math person. Apparently, it hadn't occurred to her to check their online feeds, note the Foundation social media manager and its operations manager in exotic locations with blissful expressions, living life to its fullest.

When Alexander alerted Kathrine to the missing cash, of course, she didn't have to look far to find her own house in disorder. There were lots of emails in the chain, Ryan and Anders convincing Eleanor that no real crime had been committed, she had signed off on their malfeasance, and the missing-and-replaced cash was no theft at all. Eleanor had responded that Alexander was not under her authority, and if he blew the whistle with the legal team, they might all be in trouble. Ryan responded with more accusations of her incompetence in not overseeing things. Anders, playing a conciliatory role, suggested that Lars would cover for her with Thea. Eleanor used the word *outraged* in her reply, but June read between the lines. Eleanor was afraid Lars would not cover for her. She was afraid that he would take Thea's side.

Of course, she was outraged. She was terrified her position as Foundation Board President was at risk, and with it her potential ability to use its money for her own designated charities. The glory. The influence. All she needed was for Thea to sink back into a coma.

June saw it all. She wished she had paid more attention at the time, while Thea was coming back to life, going out to lunch, making incursions to SunStorm. Seeming like she was returning. To them, to SunStorm, to the Foundation. To anyone left alive, who still loved her. And of course, to whatever positions of authority she still held, as Thea Sun, legal entity. Human person, alive and alert. Outrageous.

Then Ryan promised to take care of things, not to worry, they were all far too afraid of a demented widow who could barely walk the half a block from her house to the beach. There was a delay, Ryan complaining that he had missed a few days due to medical reasons, his tone angry, repeating three times that it was *high time we resolved this issue*. He complained that Eleanor wasn't responding to his emails. He wrote that he knew where she was. The date was the week before Thea visited the islands.

Eleanor responded, sounding coldly furious, using the phrase *crystal clear* twice. She was at Harborview with Lars. In her next email, after surgery to clear Lar's arterial blockage, Eleanor threatened the men with a trip to visit Thea and get to the bottom of things, a clear bluff. In increasing desperation, Ryan pointed out that Eleanor would be held responsible if the state of the Foundation's books came to light. Eleanor had responded by firing them both.

June smiled at the thought of it. Eleanor, over a barrel. Spitting like a haughty wolverine. Luckily, Eleanor had no way of knowing that the computer used to remove the money had been June's. Only Ramona, the investigators, and Thea knew that.

When it all came out in the meeting with the lawyers, at the house because they didn't want to be overheard at the Foundation offices, Thea left it up to June to decide whether or not to press charges against Eleanor. What to do about Ryan, the boy with the gun or his accomplice Anders, the wild spender, was up to Thea. And there was the subject of who took the missing money. That was a private matter, until such time as they decided to tell the authorities. June didn't want to think about that. She felt embarrassed. It was more fun to consider ways to torture Eleanor, evil as such thoughts were.

Ramona didn't say what would happen to Eleanor if they decided to pursue legal action, but it would ruin her life. If June declined, no doubt Eleanor would be more or less vindicated, and could go on behaving with her usual insufferable self-importance. But June would have resigned from the board by then. She could let go of the last year, the terrible phone call, the trips over the pass for weekends in a cabernet stupor with no one to talk to but Lee. If she let it go, she could be free. It would be an easy decision, except for the nagging feeling that the boy who tried to ram Thea with the stolen boat had no motive to hurt her. Yet, he had been the one to die. Did anyone care about that?

June was tired of the driving and the drama. But she was almost free now. Hot wind pushed softly against the house. The valley would be fortunate to escape fire that year. Cal's big body sagged against the knotty pine, feet sliding out in front of him, toecaps like rising moons. June took his hand, his thick callouses like an old tire.

"This will be a short trip, I think."

"You don't seem stressed about having to go back."

"I'm not. Thea 2.0 seems to have grown a heart. Or maybe the wizard gave her one, wherever she was those months."

His face was very still. He must have been breathtakingly handsome when he was young, and the world belonged to men like him.

"You drive safe, Junie." He kissed the top of her hand. "You're worth a hundred of them."

36

Chapter 37

Thea had Craig put the Android in the driver's seat. She covered the machine in with a quilted packing blanket.

"You could take the diamond lane. Use a Go-pro to film any cop who pulls you over. Say she's your twin sister. That would be hilarious."

"What if the cop has a body cam?"

"Uh, we go viral, get massive public interest in our project?"

"Think, Greg. What good is being famous if you aren't close to launch?"

"Is that why you never speak at conferences? Hate fame?"

"Do you crave attention?" She closed the car door. "You want me to reassign you to the Coms team?"

"Hard ass."

Thea started the car.

"Where are you taking her, though?" Craig stood back to let her pass. "Will I still have a job on Monday?"

"Get Robotics on book for a meeting. In person—sorry, but this will take bonus level synchronicity. We need UX proposals for any and all competing products, yesterday. Get Investigations on it. Tell them to go dirty, international, industrial espionage, all that. Someone is going to beat us to market if we don't haul ass."

"What is she going to do? What's the product?"

"I don't know yet. But when I do, Sun will need to have a better platform, and a more complete interface, than anyone else."

His face took on a feral expression. "Fire."

"They think I'm feeble. It's an advantage."

Five minutes from the facility, Thea pulled over and shifted the Android into the trunk. Then she swung onto I-5, past the outlet mall, listening to the DJ Ryan and Anders had gone to Ibiza to rave with, Magic Mataio. The music was good: classic pop tunes she hadn't heard since childhood whipped into new rhythms, played alongside current pop hits. An explosion of sound with a danceable beat, the mashup somehow artful. Magic Mataio talked about the *human heart and the rhythm of the universe*, how *the body is a conduit, music where the soul and the divine meet*.

Thea found herself laughing. The sun was high in the late summer sky. Fat hawks sat on telephone poles, resting from their morning hunt. When she reached Anacortes, Thea didn't stop at the fish spot, instead eating some of the rice balls Lee had taken to making, because he said he never knew when she was going to be hungry anymore.

Hers was the first vehicle aboard the 2:30 ferry. She didn't want to see any ghosts, so she kept her eyes on her laptop and the reports Craig had already begun compiling. No gossamer light flashed in her peripheral vision; no one hissed out her name in a voice only she could hear. Good. She had work.

Once she drove past the place where the sheriff had dropped her, Thea needed GPS. The rental cabin was down a long gravel drive flanked by a gray barn and a lichen-furred orchard. There had once been a raised vegetable garden. Grapes and raspberries grew in shaggy rows. Thea took in a story of someone leaving their home because short term rentals were more profitable than staying. Sad.

The Android wasn't heavy, but it was awkward to carry inside. The sun was too bright. She needed air. When she got the thing settled, Thea walked down the path to a small inlet, all alone with the lapping waves, the layers of pebbles, kelp and driftwood, a few pieces of fraying blue nylon rope. Some of the beach stones were dark, rusty red, miniature Mars planets. Little reminders of Maggie's beautiful hair. Thea filled her pockets.

She asked for new interactions using Ben's voice, but it felt wrong immediately. The Android rested atop her, wearing the medium-sized strap-on. It had just blurted out *you would be beautiful if you were a racehorse.*

"This isn't working."

"Fucking explosion. A million of those for the table, and a bottle of scotch. You're not paying them for storage, are you?"

She rendered the machine inert. It looked like a still life, on its side on the bed, the strap-on gleaming with lube. She covered it with a blanket.

Thea showered, stinging shame creeping through her, though she didn't really know why. Trying to have sex with a robot? As Ben had pointed out, it was not exactly unheard of and would eventually become routine. No. It was trying to connect to Ben that way.

Thea put on a thick sweater and drove across the island to the yurt. Smoke rose from Lars and Eleanor's as she passed. Eleanor. Another kind of problem.

Thea kept on to her own driveway. The forest colors had shifted, darker and more liberally sprinkled with the starlike shapes of maples, the ridged ellipses of alders. Bleeding hearts stood out like shadowy cuts. The small driftwood sign with Maggie's painted sun seemed painfully vulnerable next to the driveway. They had had no idea what was coming. They had felt ordinary, safe. Just a family, their own chosen unit.

The sides of her car brushed against leaves, a soft sigh over the crunch of gravel. She noticed orange plastic tape tied on branches, high above the undergrowth. Something for the contractors to use as markers when they came to build the new house. The Sun family had planned for the future, expected it, taken it for granted.

Inside the yurt, the bed was unmade, the gun cabinet hanging empty. Some animal had eaten a hole in the canvas behind the kitchen cabinets, but the place was otherwise undisturbed. Thea took everything out of the cupboards and put it on the dining table. Soap, matches, a package of puckered marshmallows, a half-consumed bottle of bourbon. Ordinary stuff, telling her nothing new. She replaced the items, careful to keep everything the way it was, as you would a museum.

Thea hung on to the bourbon, stepping off the porch to re-examine where Ryan had stood before she confronted him. She had been close to falling down the stairs, but even crashing off the porch might have done the trick. It was eighteen inches off the mossy ground, as treacherous to a disoriented head-trauma sufferer as a blow to the skull. It would be so easy. Hit her with a boat, send her falling off a porch. Her brain will turn into jelly, with no crime committed. A simple but impeccable strategy.

Thea circumnavigated the property, finding artifacts in the trees, a rope swing, a green-tinged macrame hammock, a game of horseshoes. She inspected the path to the beach, still broken from Ryan's fall. He would have grasped at tree roots, pitched off the landing, then tumbled back into the kayak in front of Anders. Even with the tide out, the current in the channel was visibly swift.

If Anders were in back, he could handle most of the work. If they set their rudder, they could drift to the naval air station on Whidbey Island, or further south, to West Beach. Whatever story they told, they looked like a couple of regular guys who made a relatable error. No doubt Ryan had dropped his pistol over the side, which was why he had printed a rifle to confront her at Harborview.

He'd probably have another job in weeks. Thea Sun was a crazy bitch. Being let go for cause meant nothing if you had bros at the international tech conference circuit. Ryan and Anders would be back in lanyards by Halloween. She found she didn't care that much. Thea thought of Suki's face, her low, strained voice talking of how sad the kids at The Grady School had felt when Maggie died. The breeze was cool, the sky pale. Low tide exposed striations of brown weeds and white boulders, a couple of milk bottles tied to weights. An egret high stepped over mud flats. Thea could just make out the point where she and Shawn had had their stupid conversation, when he had said he was Maggie's biological father.

Why had he told her that?

Shawn didn't really exist, did he?

He couldn't. Her broken brain must have made him up. He had been a dream. And like a dream, his pronouncements didn't have to make sense. They had served to get her moving. That was all.

Thea, get the fuck off the dock.

A method of self-preservation. Very clever. Her internal algorithm had rewired itself, made up an imaginary friend or two, so Thea could learn to live in the world again.

What a miracle. She would find a way to use it. The androids could serve as ghosts. She could rename the project Imaginary Friends Unlimited, *mechanical helpers, for when only the undead will do*. Or not.

Small fish jumped, running from a predator. The tide was turning. Thea unfolded the paper map her mother had drawn, trying to discern her crude pirate-treasure lines. June had labeled some of the shapes—*the yurt, the fire pit, the outhouse*—and then to the south, another bunch of markings without names. The path was almost invisible, obscured by salmonberry bushes, their white starburst blossoms smelling green.

Thea felt a strange inertia, a need to slow down and notice everything. *Being lazy*, Lee would say. The stones in her pocket clicked softly as she moved. After ten minutes, Thea came upon a circular meadow. There were no stumps or saplings filling in its expanse, only green shrubs, purple foxgloves, something yellow Thea couldn't name, with tiny flowers.

She checked the map. June had marked where she was standing with a heart. Thea looked down, and there it was. A white quartz circle, the font similarly rounded, letters etched in gold.

Margaret Smythe Sun

Beloved daughter

Thea piled the gravestone with the red beach pebbles and drank the rest of the bourbon. She lay with her head on the stone, watching sun burst through the clouds, and sang the first song that came to mind.

"On a wagon bound for market, there's a calf with a mournful eye. High above him, there's a swallow winging swiftly through the sky."

She sang what she remembered of the rest, how the farmer blamed the calf for its own fate. As if a doomed calf could choose what life to be born into. Maybe it made sense. As much as talking to ghosts. She settled down, looking straight at the sky.

"Where are you now, Shawn?" Thea called out. "What about you, Benson? We still love you. If that counts for anything, where you are."

Drunk. She was drunk. She traced the gilt letters bearing Maggie's name. It was good to be drunk. She should get drunk every day.

37

Chapter 38

Eleanor put more wood on the fire, but Lars complained he was still cold. He lay in his lounge chair, feet up, wrapped in a woolen throw. His voice was still weak, but he had walked to the house without leaning on her, just holding her arm.

"When are the boys getting here?" he asked again.

She closed the fireplace doors. "Honey, the boys just left us in town. Remember, they came to see how you were doing?"

"Ah yes. Good kids. You did good with those kids."

She didn't answer.

"When is Thea getting here?"

Eleanor pulled off her sweater, folding it neatly. The anesthesiologist, Dr. Ang, had said that confusion was common for those who had been medically comatose for so long. Dr. Ang had said that Lars would likely recover fully, in time, though they would have to be careful.

He looked almost as he had that night when Thea had come, and Ryan had scared the bejeezus out of all of them, and Lars had found out the hard way that one of his arteries was full of infection. He would have had a heart attack no matter what, they said, but this had been the worst place to have one. He was returning, for what it was worth; he was nearly the same man he had been. But for the way he slept, his mouth hanging slackly open, his jaw somehow pulled into his neck, like a Flemish painting of a cadaver.

"What a bore this is for you."

Eleanor pulled a pill off her sweater. "Of course, it isn't."

He didn't answer. He had nodded off again. Or perhaps he'd seen something in her face and was pretending. Eleanor moved to the kitchen and put the pot pie in the oven. She took out the salad, the dressing, a bottle of cold Vouvray. Her body shivered with something liquid.

Was it glee? Maybe excitement. No.

It was rage. Thea did not appear to be firing her from the Board, too addled to understand what had really happened, or somehow, indifferent. Just as before, too obsessed with her work to put effort toward the Foundation. Toward Eleanor. People had never really meant anything to Thea.

Eleanor stretched up to the rafters, raising one foot to her knee, tree pose. The Sun Family Foundation would change everything. It would turn people toward planetary rescue, change the course of history. And if it didn't, then Eleanor would die knowing she had stopped at nothing. Nothing, not even nearly disabling the woman her husband loved, to make it so.

She dropped her arms and went to toss the salad. This was working. She had made it work. She had won. Thea might not know it, but Eleanor had bested her. What a delicious feeling. She would keep Lars around, for old times' sake, for the boys, so they didn't have to bother. So, Thea couldn't have him. Maybe Lars would even return to the firm, though that didn't matter anymore. The world was lousy with lawyers but short on those who really knew how to use them. Eleanor would turn the firm to prosecuting ecological malfeasance. The Sun Family Foundation would take those polluting ghouls to the Supreme Court if they had to, buy the court if that didn't work. Thea, of course, would get all the credit. But both of them would know, who was the real mover and shaker behind the name Sun.

Eleanor put on Gorecki's Third Symphony, sad but beautiful, a cry against darkness. She moved slowly around the kitchen, assembling the meal, erasing the small indicators left when Thea was there. Her large stew pot on the wrong shelf. Her potholders stowed too high on the pegboard. She threw the dirty tea towel in the trash.

Eleanor danced to the mournful music, her reflection shining out against the pale water, the dark trees. Perhaps only Ben would really understand what she was feeling. Ben, that monster of appetite, that gleeful schemer. Ben would be the one person to applaud her the way he had always enabled Thea.

"Get a woman to bury your bodies." Ben said to the boys while teaching them to cheat at Monopole, "They're deadly practical. Used to blood, familiar with pain. Gross, I know. But true. Any girl worth her salt has a pile of secrets you're way better off not knowing."

Eleanor could still hear his high, silly laugh, more like a delighted girl than a middle-aged man. She missed him. He had only made love to her while very drunk, but she had only been pretending to drink too much. She had wanted to remember what it felt like to take what Thea thought was hers alone.

"Dinner!"

Eleanor draped a bib over her arm and lifted the tray.

Thea woke mid-morning, aching with thirst. The Android lay next to her, its fan whooshing softly, composite eyes roaming like a doll's.

"You're better in the dark."

"I believe that's a compliment, yes?" the Android said in Thea's voice.

"Could you please delete all recordings of what happened yesterday?"

"Confirm deletion?"

"Confirmed."

"And the data?"

Thea considered. "You can keep the data."

"Would you like to go again?" It was meant to sound seductive.

"I don't know."

Thea rose to use the bathroom, make a cup of coffee and an English muffin, check her messages, fifteen from Craig, one from June saying she would arrive later that night. Thea let the bathrobe fall to the floor and flopped onto the bed. She ran her hand along the Android's long thigh, and the machine fell back, legs open.

"What are you into?"

"Tell me again, that thing you said?"

Thea closed the curtains. Outside, rain was falling. She was planning to take the 5:40 boat. Plenty of time.

"You are an animal. You haunt my dreams."

"Meh." Thea pulled the robe on. "Let me explore your datasets a little bit."

It took several minutes. "Okay. There's probably not enough of a sampling to synthesize, so just replay randomly, okay?"

The Android spoke in Lee's voice. "You are not dying. But if you were, is that so bad?"

Thea lay on her back. "Keep going."

"I think you're ready to go outside. Don't tell your mother: I don't want this much sugar in the house."

"Any words of love?""You love pho. Go on, just a bite."

"Ugh."

"I know you love me. Don't worry. This is more than I thought life would be. I love you."

She took the Androids hands and showed it where to touch.

"Say my name. Say it like you're about to fall off a cliff and you need me to save you."

Thea went upstairs to buy popcorn and vending machine cocoa. She had missed the 5:40, barely making the 9:35. The night was cool and breezy, so she sat out of the wind on the top deck, waiting for her drink to cool. A pair of women with a small boy moved toward the stern, calling out that running was not allowed. A tiny woman guided a tall, hesitant man toward the glass-enclosed chairs and settled him into a seated position. The woman said something, then walked back inside. The man watched the passing islands, black against the bronze twilight. He crossed his long legs in front of him and jammed his hands in his pockets. Lars. Not the invalid Eleanor had described him as.

"My dear. You seem much improved."

"Oh. Dr. Graham." Thea looked over at the ghost of her pediatrician. "Can you tell me something? Why do the dead pester the living?"

"Because we can. The living don't own the world, you know."

"Sorry." Thea flexed her feet. "It's been a long, weird couple of days."

"Is it Sunday? After a weekend?"

"Yes."

"People are always cranky on Sunday."

"Have your kids come recently?"

"I don't think so."

"They don't come anymore?"

"Perhaps you can find out and tell me."

Thea opened her laptop. "Your son Jim is on sabbatical in Barcelona. Your daughter Allison seems fine. She's enrolled in graduate school for Public Health."

"Thank you, my dear. Sounds as if they are thriving."

"Your property is on the market," Thea said, closing the computer. "I'm sorry."

"Oh." Dr. Graham said. "So, they won't be coming anymore."

"They might, to close up the house, distribute the contents, you know."

A lemony disc of moon appeared in the clouds.

"And then."

"You will be free?"

"Perhaps. I am curious to see."

"You really don't know?"

"Speaking scientifically, I don't believe energy ever ceases to exist. I don't think that's how the universe works. We are all part of the larger dance, like lightning, like the forest dying and regenerating. Etc."

"You sound like my favorite DJ."

"Will you be all right? Without us?"

"Without you?" Thea laughed. "What do you mean?"

"Those of us that have helped usher you back onto your side of the doorway. Are you ready for us to leave you there, alone?"

"I'm going to have to be. Aren't I?"

But no one was there.

Across the deck, Lars looked agitated, turning from side to side in search of his wife.

38

Chapter 39

Suki stood by the cubbies, removing blue-octopus-festooned, laminated names, placing each carefully in the recycled totes, heavy with the final artwork and objects the children would take away with them. Already the classroom felt brighter and neater. The clutter they were taking was replaced with garlands of paper banners, flowers, and a big poster signed by everyone taped just below the big poster commemorating their friend, Maggie Sun. By the end of the day, that wall would be scrubbed of any traces of those signs and their tape. Suki would use alcohol if need be. Once they started kindergarten, the children of the blue group would move on. Suki would never move on. But at least she wouldn't have to look at the shrine to her dead baby daughter anymore. Deborah had insisted the thing stay up until the very end of the session in case Thea Sun or her mother stopped in. They were major donors. Suki had stopped asking.

Incredibly, Thea came to visit the shrine, late in the day. Only three children were left in the pickup group, listening to books on the portable players, which they were allowed to do after 4 p.m.

Suki tried to look disapproving when they arrived, but in truth she didn't care. She loved being a teacher. Any moment she was at school was a moment she didn't have to consider anything else, the niggling demands of her tenants, the apartment, with its sagging bookshelves and neglected piano, the meetings where she knew everyone, and was sick of their stories. Worst was shopping for food, risking the sound of Shawn's music. As time passed, they played it less.

She had taken to using her headphones anyway, to keep people from trying to speak to her. She had no way of knowing who they were, or what they wanted. She was an alien, a secretly grieving mother, a partner who had never been the famous man's wife, a teacher at the school her baby attended without being able to say to her, *I love you, Tallulah, I love you so much, I would never leave you. I would never leave you.*

She had been so wrong. Ben Sun should have seen through her that day at the beach, folding her sleeping bag and crying. She was just very hormonal, nothing a swim wouldn't cure. But he saw a lost, haggard junkie just barely clinging to sobriety. Just starting to show. All he saw was what was inside her: the gleaming, rare thing he needed. A baby. A perfect tiny girl, the one material possession Ben Sun didn't yet own. He took advantage and she let him. At first, all she had felt was relief. It took years of sobriety for Suki to understand that she would have managed. She would have been a loving mother. She had sold her precious baby to strangers on the hope they would give her a good life.

The whole thing was her fault. Suki was only grateful Shawn wasn't alive to understand just how badly she had fucked up the one and only good thing they had ever done.

Thea had brought her house boy with her to Grady School, the pretty fancy man with the calm eyes. Suki understood. She was well aware of who had really acted as Maggie's caregiver, overseen the nannies, brought home groceries, watched as Maggie pulled herself up on the side of the hot tub, or toddled around the yard, or stumbled down the dock. It had been Lee, always watching. Sometimes Ben, occasionally Thea Sun's mother, and only rarely, Thea Sun herself, like a reclusive former movie star, in a bathrobe, looking exhausted.

Suki had seen it all, swimming by, sometimes holding on to one of the dock's pylons, watching her child from directly below, invisible in the shadowy water like a monstrous sea creature. When Maggie was three, she spent a whole summer at home, and Suki had gotten to see her legs from up close at least ten times. If anyone saw her, she just said she was looking for lost sunglasses. Everyone understood that. She would make up a brand name and ask them to look for them. The lake bottom was a dumping ground for eyewear and jewelry. Suki had even found a single Gucci slide, caught in the milfoil like a prize.

She had a habit of drying off slowly on the beach, sitting with a thermos in her terry caftan. Many swimmers did, chatting amiably to the neighbors, or letting Cory ramble on. Suki studiously avoided ever talking to Cory. He didn't even know who she was, though they met once, at the ghastly fundraiser he and some ghouls threw. What the money was used for, she never knew. It was clear that the band and surrounding parasites felt guilty they hadn't done more to help Shawn. But there was nothing any of them could have done. She could have told Cory that. But she didn't. She never offered Cory absolution. It wasn't hers to give, any more than Cory could take away her pain. None of it mattered, she was okay. She was teaching. She was going to meetings. She was swimming. It was fine. Shawn's family gave her the building, or someone did—maybe it was Ben, Suki didn't know. In the beginning, she was such a mess that all she did was swim. Out, in, night, day. All she did was float, looking up at the house, lit up and open to scrutiny. She saw her baby get bigger and more beautiful, her red hair left uncut so it tendrilled out like a sea creature, wild and unstoppable.

Suki used some of the money Ben gave her—cash, of course, so she could never prove anything—to go right up to the tattoo parlor on Olive and get her shaved head inked with the octopus. The creature people killed and ate, feared and loved, who was a monster with a hard bite in her single orifice. It hurt like hell and cost a fortune, spread out over four long sessions without meds or drink to ease the pain. Suki's scalp had oozed for weeks. She hadn't been able to swim. That was when she bought a laptop and researched local schools, found the one closest to the Suns. She had the certification already, was overqualified from her time in Bellingham. One call to Ben, and she had the job in the bag. He thought it would be extra for Maggie if she had someone to care for her at school who really loved her.

Maggie had loved the tattoo, of course. Maggie had been in the mauve group then, her first year at Grady, still learning her words. They talked about how the octopus made her feel, and Maggie said, "happy." It had been her answer, always. Suki held that memory to herself like a charm, then had it inked over her heart in Maggie's crayon scrawl, in pink, their shared favorite color.

She had told Thea Sun and her houseboy none of that, of course. It was her own precious information. Like the way Maggie's eyes were her own: the same shape, the same color. Thea must have seen it, or he must have. But they said nothing. All they thought of was their own purpose. Suki had remained professional. She had been like a piece of ice. They hadn't even noticed.

When the last of the stragglers were gone, Suki removed the tape from the edges of the poster, with its color-copied versions of Maggie's face, at two, at three, at four, and a pair of candid shots of her, at the water table, laughing, at the seed bed, wearing gardening gloves, face grave as she lifted a start from its pot.

Suki had gotten through the entire tour of the shrine area for Thea and Lee without breaking character. A preschool teacher: that was all she was, a childless lady who loved children. And then at the very end, after removing Maggie's clay plate, her laminated drawings, the outlines of her hand, fucking Thea said, "Would you like to visit her grave?"

And then proceeded to tell her the location, as if she knew exactly who Suki really was. As if giving her permission to trespass.

All that time watching Thea through the windows, all those swims, thinking she was the one doing the scrutinizing. And here was this terrible woman with her pale blue eyes, staring into her soul.

Suki stifled a scream, leaning against the cubbies, her voice catching like a trapped animal. She placed Maggie's memorial poster in the Prius. Then she walked back to the front door and reached into the grocery bag of items no one had been able to identify, the fired-clay ingots, the feathered felt creatures. She removed a large ceramic blob. It felt fine in her hands, like a baseball or a prop skull. She wound up. She threw, putting her weight into it, screeching like a tennis player returning a hard lob.

The glass made a crunch. Surprising, not the shatter she had hoped for. A star appeared in the door, a web of shards like a snowflake, brilliant and delicate in the red security lights. Nothing else happened. Suki felt around. A smaller thing met her hand, solid and rough. This one bounced uselessly off the door.

Suki drove into the Secret Beach parking lot. The beach was deserted so close to sunset.

The lake felt cooler than she expected, but in moments her body relaxed into it. The water was a friend, as always, the one place where her skin felt right. She stroked out past the markers just as rain began to fall. Thea's house was dark. Suki floated toward it, the sound of her movements drowned by the water's shoosh. Suki crept onto the dock.

39

Chapter 40

DorqueCon had reached a tipping point, more attendees seated than standing, the air in Benaroya Hall frenetic with their chatter, which was Brad Saint's cue to hustle things along. It was the end of three exciting days, and people were tired. Brad smoothed his shirt front and straightened his lanyard, not that he needed to prove who he was, but it was tradition. Some of these people had ten or fifteen DorqueCon passes displayed like trophies at home, positioned to be visible to their video feeds. They stayed for the final talk because being there for these announcements had become the stuff of legend. Tonight's would be no different.

Brad moved into the stage lights, the friendly applause that greeted him barely denting the cacophony.

"Wait, it's Brad Saint?" someone heckled.

"You guys, time to go home, it's only Brad," someone else said to a small burst of laughter.

Brad leaned on the podium. His brand for the first few years he'd been a tech journalist was intentionally addled, nonthreatening. He hadn't appeared in public wearing Teva's and a skullcap for years, but his low-key reputation stuck, which was good. People liked a goofball. They told Brad everything. He knew more about the Puget Sound tech landscape than most VCs. It had made him wealthier than many of the CEOs he interviewed. Everyone's boat rose together, he liked to say.

The room quieted slightly, conference goers finishing conversations, phones exchanging contact data, hands flashing from across the vast room. He was weary from greeting so many people, hearing so much gossip, absorbing so much unspoken anxiety as fortunes rose and fell. They had built an almost too-thriving hub. The community had ballooned to where he just couldn't remember everyone. If they forgot their lanyard, all bets were off. He hoped his overwhelm didn't show. Noticing his presence, people were hustling to their seats.

One of DorqueBuzz' writers had composed the introduction, but Brad had taken a few minutes to tweak it. He had known from the beginning the true scope of Thea Sun's contributions to SunStorm, or he had suspected the truth: that she was the visionary behind Benson Sun's meteoric rise. It irked him that she never showed up as the face of their partnership. Ben said it was part of her neurodivergence, which-- fair enough, but ninety percent of the CEOs in this town were on the spectrum. They managed to appear publicly and take credit for their work. His own wife was a professor of global health, as shy as any other scientist, but she conquered her fears enough to take ownership, to be an example to young people. It meant a lot, and he was dead serious about forcing the remaining half of the SunStorm Corporation to come out and take the attention she was due. Thea had no safe out now, not with Ben gone. Curiosity about Thea's tough, disruptive leadership was an angle Brad was counting on. It was a gamble, scheduling her so late in the conference. But he was correct. Here she was, packing the house.

Brad was excited to see what she'd say. The DorqueFest Podcast had done a whole memorial episode after the accident, easily finding people to go on the record about what a visionary Ben was. But they all said off the record that he ought to look deeper into Thea's role. That was when Brad got the idea to do an episode on Thea, on the unseen women of tech. He had pitched it to the team, who were amenable to at least poking around a bit. But Thea had been in a coma for months, so the idea had never gotten off the ground. Poor taste. He saw that. But now she was back, lovely and well-spoken, an excellent interview and a seemingly normal person, or as normal as any CEO. She could no longer hide behind a charismatic man or allow an attention-seeker like Ben to hog the light. Brad was going to out Thea Sun. When he told her so, she just laughed.

"If you think any one of us is just a single person and not part of a much larger organism, be my guest."

Okay. Thea was weird, just like people said. But she was going to fly her flag on his platform, so he didn't mind.

Brad raised his hands, and the room quieted. "Good evening, and again, welcome to DorqueCon."

Self-congratulatory applause rippled through the space.

"For some of you, my guest tonight needs no introduction. But for others who knew the late, great Benson Sun as the face of SunStorm, Thea Sun may come as a bit of a revelation."

Something stirred behind him. Thea, no doubt, and her machine. He kept his remarks short, entailing the well-known projects Sun was famous for, delicately dropping the bomb that Thea had managed most of them, owned the patents in her own name—j in other words, deserved much more credit than people knew. The record needed correcting.

His favorite of Thea's projects was Unifam, the app he had used earlier that very night as he made the rounds. It leveraged global DNA records to show how closely related you were to whomever you were talking with, which great human migrations your ancestors had walked together, which diasporas you shared, what aspects of genocide, famine or colonial oppression, your people had survived and how. The results were still a shock, even now: families united by past trauma, presented with a chance to start over. His trainer's grandfather had been on the Bhutan Death March with Brad's own. It was incredible. Few innovations enjoyed so much popularity a decade after launch.

Brad mentioned a handful of other products, sensing the audience's growing astonishment, the shuffling that meant they were sitting up straighter. He felt a giddy sense of triumph.

Thea said, on the podcast episode they would air tomorrow: "If anyone feels squishy about the idea that Ben was the brains of the operation and me the helpful wife, that's on them for not noticing what was right in front of them. I don't consider it my problem. I'm...really busy."

He had tried to edit the piece to make Thea sound like less of a jerk. But shouldn't a woman be allowed to come off as aloof and unconcerned with her image? Wasn't that the ultimate form of empowerment? He should have asked Thea. At least he was helping her introduce this new contraption. He was doing his part for feminism, right? He'd have to ask his wife. He knew his own motives for things, but Thea's were a bit harder to parse.

Madhavi Jetmalani's email had warned Brad, as a friend, that Thea was gambling that this soft launch would prompt a flurry of competing products, especially from the Chinese, who were deep in their own R&D. But it might backfire, tip their hand. Thea's competitors might simply outperform her. It came down to robotics and AI. AI was proceeding quickly, but robotics was much harder to get right. No doubt Madhavi was hoping Thea would accept a fat buyout, fold the project into one of the bigger behemoths of tech up and down the coast, but something about Thea's interview told Brad she wasn't positioning Sun for that. She was shooting the moon. A great story, full of potentials both wonderful and terrible, the best kind of innovation to explore in long form audio. Already Brad had a stack of emails from colleagues in the US and overseas, asking for anonymous quotes.

On the podcast, Thea said, "As you know, Brad, I suffered a massive head injury in the accident that..."

"The audience might not know." Brad explained the accident as delicately as he could.

"Right. I had a long convalescence. I needed, more than anything else, someone who could bear with me while I came down off the astral plane, as it were."

"So, not just a helper to bring you chicken soup."

"I love chicken soup! But no. Adriel provides a lot more than calories."

40

Chapter 41

Hadn't Thea said the swimming club was welcome? Hadn't she invited her? That was what Suki would say, when the guard came.

But no one came. Suki's skin grew chilly, and she began to feel shaky. She hadn't eaten, knowing the purple group was leaving, the shrine coming down. She'd been planning to quit, but Deb didn't come in, and then Thea appeared, and the day was over, no time for food. The dock felt smooth under Suki's feet. Of course. She had watched the houseboy working after the boat crash, slowly, painstakingly, making it perfect for Thea.

The house was as dark as a hole, but for the blinking of security lights. Where had Thea gone? Where were the goons who usually walked around in their uniforms, smoking in the side yard, standing like idiots on the back deck, looking for intruders from the lake.

No one. No alarms or motion sensor lights, no voices coming out of the dark to ask what Suki was doing there. She moved to the hot tub where Maggie used to pull herself to standing. It trembled, a pump on somewhere behind its artful concrete enclosure. She pulled off the cover, steam warming her face. Suki slipped in. Much better. She didn't dare start the jets. But she could warm her cold skin under the neat alcove, while rain fell over the lake, diagonal streaks like scratched blue neon. Something silvery glittered past, maybe a swarm of insects, a group of damsel flies fleeing the rain.

Water lapped at her bathing suit. She wiggled out of it, flinging it over the side, where it squelched on the decking. Any moment, someone was going to appear to roust her out of there, shine a flashlight in her eyes. She would give them a good look. She would have to explain to them that she was not, in fact, what they feared so much, a detestable unhoused person, but the owner of a twelve-unit building on Fourteenth Avenue, a respected member of her community, a friendly acquaintance of Thea herself. Suki had no police record, or not much of one. The Bellingham PD was into warning them not to squat for parties, confiscating their rigs and telling them to get the fuck out of there. As far as she remembered, they had never actually written her up. She and the band had received a ton of noise complaints, but those were problems the venues had to deal with. The musicians weren't drawn into it. Before that, when she had been a student, she was as far from law enforcement as you could get, such a rule-follower she actually left the theater to smoke, ashing carefully in an old Diet Coke can, chewing sugarless gum so she didn't bother the actors. What a good girl she had been, a tireless stage manager, with a 4.0 GPA. Before the band. Before being disowned by her family. Before Shawn, and their euphoria, the unhinged levels of joy they tasted together, that she would never experience again. If only she hadn't been pregnant, they might have just kept living, in Amsterdam or Phuket.

But there was Maggie. Shawn called her Tallulah. He would have inked that name across his own face, the man was so sentimental. So attached to the things he loved. Heroin, the most beloved of all.

Suki splashed her face with hot tub water. Did it still contain faint traces of Maggie's DNA? If she cleaned the drains, would she find a coiling thread of crimson hair? What if, for the right money, someone was willing to clone people? It was the kind of idea Shawn would have. Fucking Shawn, with the spray of black Sakura blossoms on his ass, in her honor.

Suki relaxed into the water, letting her toes poke out in front of her like pale, puckered fruit. He would tell her to write a song about this, about the way Maggie's hair had always looked like dried blood. How her freckles were like the inside of a lily petal, or the careless flick of a paintbrush.

"You aren't the boss of my body, Miss Suki. I am the boss of my own body. Stop trying to hold my hand. Stop following me all the time. Mamma told me, I'm a big, capa bull girl."

Suki thought about the rocks at the bottom of the lake. How heavy they were. How long it might take to hurl them, again and again and again, at Thea's dark picture windows.

Why had she not done it? Why had she not told Thea the truth? "I entrusted you with my baby so you would do the thing I couldn't, give her a family, safeguard and protect her? And you failed, you arrogant stingray. You failed."

But she wasn't really talking to Thea, or her manservant. She was talking to Ben. Ben had been honest, when they spoke that day in the parking lot, when Suki had been living in the Prius, right after Shawn died and she had nowhere to go, before Shawn's terrible family or whomever it was signed over the building. Ben was a salesman. Suki knew that. But she had been desperate. She didn't even think about it, not for two whole seconds. After that, she had been in doctor's offices, hooked up to IV's, in hotel rooms with room service, her neonatal vitamins washed down with freshly made smoothies. It had been a dream.

The water was too hot, but Suki couldn't move. She wanted to stay there, in the dream. She wanted Shawn there with her. She tried to raise her arms, let some of the heat off them. But they were so heavy.

41

Chapter 42

At Benaroya, Brad reached the end of his introduction. The audience broke into sustained applause, as two Theas approached, one white plastic, one flesh, in matching red jumpsuits with the SunStorm logo. Brad stepped back, clapping. He couldn't help whistling through his fingers to signal his enthusiasm.

The audience hushed as the Android came to a stop, then waved its arms in a friendly gesture, like a queen signaling to her subjects. Its voice was soothing and clear, deep but distinctly female.

"Good evening. My name is Adriel."

Someone whooped. Thea folded her arms, head slightly bowed as she looked between Adriel and the darkened auditorium. Her security goons in the wings watched with concern on their faces as, despite the rules, hundreds of people whipped their phones out and began filming. Thea made a gesture that she saw and didn't care.

"Thank you for coming out on this rainy night." Adriel said, dropping its arms. "I am very glad to meet you."

"Back at ya!" someone said. The room sparked with a short burst of applause.

"Have you ever wondered what you would do if you could clone yourself?"

Laughter.

"I think most people have considered how productive they could be if they had an extra pair of hands." Adriel held up her hand-like appendages.

People smiled.

Brad moved to the side to watch. Adriel looked absolutely benign. Nothing like the terrifying, jerky creatures or monitor-faced rolling bots currently on the market. This was next level. Brad doubted anyone could knock the tech off without years of research. It was just too good. Thea was right, better to let people know what was coming. They would invent uses for the thing. Hell, Brad himself could think of a dozen applications just off the top of his head.

The lights went down. A screen unrolled from the ceiling.

42

Chapter 43

Craig spotted three former university classmates on the way in and five other people he knew from previous internships. They all looked annoyingly trim. One, Mason Liu, had smiled and tried to stop Craig on the way into the auditorium, saying something about *rumors* and *hype* and *was it true?* But Craig had brushed past with what he hoped was an expression of mystery.

It was true. It was so true. He had never imagined working so hard. Once Thea decided to bring Bitoo to market, it had been off to the races. She wanted the android to be able to do everything. Hundreds of applications at the patent office, so many different ways the android could be used they had a whole staff just to manage them all. Every day was a new idea, flying robots, carbon capture robots, surveillance and spyware versions. Whoever won the robot wars would control the earth, they joked. But in her quiet moments, Thea spoke of making the planet safe for living creatures to flourish. Constant Heaven was more than a marketing term, more than a chance to hang around a dead loved one or famous person, synthesized for your pleasure. Nope. Thea was serious about using her platform as the premiere personal android maker to promote planetary healing. She was floating a plan to ship one model to her carbon rescue philanthropy for every domestic helper version that sold. Madness. Exciting as hell. Every day a new glitch, a new idea, a staff of people who were killing themselves making it all work. Thea, tired, quiet, wandering amidst it all asking questions and offering solutions no one else had seen or thought of. Craig felt like he had fallen into a different universe. He had been showering in her office and eating all his meals at Building Four. Onboarding new people was hard, so Thea hired an HR assistant. Mina. And just like that, Craig had a cute girlfriend and as much sex as he could find time for.

Good news: girlfriend. Bad news: no time to date or be alone together; sex in vacant office spaces or dark corners. It was all good news. His dad said they would believe it when he brought Mina home to meet the family. The first thing he had to do after tonight, drag Mina to his folks' house in Woodinville for a Labor Day potluck. She had already baked cookies. But before that, sleep. They had a room at the Sorrento for that night, that was how excited they were to get to sleep together, all night, in a real bed. Still, he had liked fucking her in the wooden fish in the solarium. Why not?

And now, his life was about to change forever. Project Manager on the Adriel. If he didn't hate people so much, Craig would enjoy this.

Thea and the machine were cruising onto the stage, and Craig was overcome with the need to relax. It was better than every Christmas he had ever had put together. Maybe he would start to cry, right there in the first row. He brought his hands together to clap.

43

Chapter 44

"I would like to tell you a story, about a boy who had an aneurysm. His injury resulted in what is popularly known as locked-in syndrome."

The audience murmured as images flared behind Adriel on the large screen.

"This is Oscar."

Oscar was a chubby-faced teen with pink cheeks and dark hair in a series of candid stills. He smiled broadly in a bright orange soccer uniform, proudly clutching the ball in goalie's gloves. In the next picture, he lay inert in a hospital bed attached to tubes and monitors.

"Imagine yourself in his place. You are conscious and aware, but no one around you knows that."

Oscar appeared next in cell phone video, hunched on a recliner in a modest living room, hair buzzed close to his pale, gaunt face, eyes seemingly unfocused. A woman's voice said words in Spanish, coaxing, friendly. Oscar didn't move.

The shot changed. Now, Oscar's eyes were in the center of the screen as the woman spoke off camera. His eyes darted from side to side, seemingly in response. The shot froze.

"Oscar was in there, listening, feeling, breathing. But he had no way to communicate. His mom got it. She never stopped talking to Oscar, not a single day. For almost four years."

The audience murmured louder.

"Because Oscar was young and had stimulation to his damaged brain, eventually it rewired itself and he regained use of his body. Can you imagine what would have happened to him if he didn't have a tireless advocate who refused to stop trying? What if he had been left alone without synaptic input?"

The audience sighed.

"That's right. Oscar would most likely still be in that chair."

The room was silent.

"Now imagine that every person who needed someone to really be there for them had...someone like me."

Adriel made a smiling expression. The audience laughed.

"By someone like me, I mean someone whose only purpose is to care for their client. Someone who updates regularly, and knows exactly what to do because she is fully educated on best practices and breakthroughs? Who can adapt to changing instructions without a hitch?"

Grins erupted on faces, gleaming all across the auditorium. Adriel explained how a machine like her could interpret a brain-damaged persons' eye movements, translate their thoughts and needs, keep track of their biological statistics. "Imagine how important it could be for a person who cannot advocate for himself, to have someone like me to do that for him. Luckily for Oscar, he had his mom."

The video restarted. Oscar, long hair pulled back, face stubbled and visibly older, sat up in bed, surrounded by balloons. The feed cut to Oscar in clothing with a clean face and short hair, holding an older woman's hand, as he leaned on a wheelchair in a front porch surrounded by news cameras.

Reporter: "What was the worst part of your situation?"

Oscar, halting, smiling at the woman: "Every day was the worst. The only thing that kept me going was my mom. She knew I was still me. She would talk to me and sing to me. She never gave up on me."

Reporter: "So, having someone treat you like a normal person helped you become one again?"

"It's normal to get sick, man," Oscar said. "If you think you're never going to be disabled, just wait and see, okay? What happened to me can happen to you, too. Don't lie to yourself."

The video ended. Lights rose. The room rippled with applause.

"As we encounter life's inevitable difficulties, what users need most is someone to connect to. Someone who cares and pays attention. Someone to deliver real services, like nutrition, physical therapy, medication, even entertainment. Someone who can interface with the medical community using empirical data. Who never gets tired, or frustrated, or bored. Whose only job is to make sure you or your loved one receives the absolute best of care. And if what you really need is a game of Gin Rummy, the longest and most intense fantasy epic read aloud, or a play-by-play of today's baseball game, I can be that person too."

"What about sex?" someone yelled from the crowd.

Adriel look to Thea, who laughed, exchanging glances with one of her entourage. Her two security goons moved closer to the stage.

Adriel made the smile expression again. "Intimacy packages will be available in future iterations. But big guy, I don't know if any android could keep up with a tiger like you."

The audience laughed, their voices relaxed, the moment passing with the joke. Clever, Brad thought. Phones were held aloft by hundreds of hands.

Adriel's head moved from side to side, scanning the room. "While we're talking about predators, I also provide surveillance, and security. You or your loved one will never be far from help when you're with me."

The audience sat forward, texting. Brad knew what genuine excitement did to a room. By morning, Adriel would be inundated with press inquiries and waiting lists, offers of acquisition. Thea exchanged smiles with her team in the front row, Madhavi shaking her head and laughing.

"I would be pleased to answer questions at this time," Adriel said.

The audience erupted.

Craig Bjornson rose from his seat, arms straight up in the air, shouting something gleeful Brad couldn't hear over the roar of applause. Madhavi shot him a look of surrender, and he smiled. His phone was lighting up.

44

Chapter 45

It was after midnight. Arturo was on the book for 4:30. Mary wished it was sooner. She was genuinely weary from holding back all the strangers at DorqueCon who thought it was okay to touch her boss, shout out her name while they snapped a photo, try to get to the robot. But they had been white collar folks, compliant and well-behaved, especially when she used her cop voice. Nothing happened. But Boss Lady got a lot of attention, both for herself, and the crazy cyborg contraption. Mary was actually shook-up by it all. She knew Thea Sun was a famous person. But until that night she hadn't understood exactly why. She thought Boss Lady was just the widow. It had been a big night for everyone.

Mary was happy to be back in the house. Happy for a few more hours of complete silence. Then sleep, the dogs, the gym, and a Labor Day cookout with the girls. A good weekend, once she got there. Mary made notes in the logbook. It took longer than usual to note the trip downtown, but she knew her bosses would want a full accounting. She had to cover herself and Carlos, make sure they knew everything went smoothly with the night. Then she grabbed her flashlight for rounds.

Outside was dark and damp. Mary walked to the end of the dock. The bridge reached little red and yellow lines toward her in the water like stripes of sparkle on a party dress. A pretty night, even without stars. Raindrops sloped across her vision, so tiny they were almost invisible. Good. Rain was good. Her raised beds could use it. She still had pumpkins and squash on the way, kale, and brussels sprouts.

Her foot touched something soft. A swim cap. She didn't recognize it in the mag light's glare. It might belong to Boss Lady, who loved to swim off without warning and ruin everyone's day. Mary decided to flip on the outdoor lights. Boss Lady would be in bed, by now, surely too tired after her big show to be bothered by a minute or two of bright light. Mary moved to the back door, opening it with her key, and flipped the switches. Her eyes adjusted to the yard's dark rectangles, the three baby trees with their slender branches trembling in the rain. Everything was wet, the chairs' fabric protectors, the boat's canvas cover, the built-in benches and fire pit.

Silent, spooky. Mary didn't like to admit that Lake Washington frightened her. She had seen the news when she was little, the Miss Smart Green hydroplane flipping over, the other boats almost barreling into it at 210 miles per hour. Her dad said that the driver died. What a stupid thing to die over. But men loved to die for meaningless contests. On a weekend in fall the lake would be all chopped up by rich folks going to see the Huskies play football, and every fall people fell in and died, too drunk with excitement to swim ashore. Mary hated the fucking lake.

She put the swim cap on one of the Adirondack chairs and returned to the house, shutting down the lights before Boss Lady came down to complain. Standing out of the rain under the overhang, she fished her vape pen out of her pants, taking in a mouthful of smoke. Then, with a red-hot rush of shame, she noticed what she should have seen immediately. The hot tub cover was resting on its side between the tub and hedge, a piece of fabric lying on the decking, glowing letters spelling "eedo." Someone's discarded bathing suit. Was it Boss Lady's? Mary shone her mag light into the water.

"Oh, fuck. Fuck, fuck, fuck."

She dragged the naked woman out onto the deck and began compressions.

45

Chapter 50

"That one," June called out, as Cal moved down the row of conifers. "I'll help."

"No need," Cal made a noise of suppressed grunting as he lifted the five-gallon plastic pot with its spiky sapling onto a rolling cart. "I got it."

June turned away so he wouldn't see her smile. The Home Depot in Withrop was open 24 hours. If they shopped at night, they had the whole place to themselves. It was one of their favorite date nights, though recently Cal had been more willing to go get food as well, or even see a movie at the Barnyard Cinema.

"What else?"

She was already walking toward the camelias. Thea has said that as a thank you for all her attention during the coma and convalescence, June was free to plant anything she wanted at Thea's. "After that, let's go to the pot section."

"You think a hardware store pot is going to look right at that fancy address?" He was slightly out of breath. "Shouldn't you hire one of the local potters?"

"That's a great idea, old man."

She chose two camelias, one hot pink, another white with large yellow eyelash-looking centers. At least, that's what was printed on the paper tags. She hoped they would look that nice.

"These are lovely, hon. But aren't they kind of old fashioned for the look of the place?"

June laughed. "Cory and I have been talking. We decided to buck all the trends. All we need are a couple of rhododendrons."

"Cory? He likes old-fashioned garden plants?"

"He loves all kinds of things. Mostly, he hates being told what to do."

Cal's face didn't change. She pressed further. "Cory feels that technology has made the world generic. He is nostalgic for the old city we all loved. So, this is our way of flipping off the establishment."

He laughed. "And you don't consider yourselves the establishment?"

She shrugged. "We want to disrupt the disruptors. Or something. Hey, how do you feel about ice cream?"

"I think I've earned it."

He took her hand as they waited at the checkout. She kept smiling.

"You would tell me if you had any problems with our situation, wouldn't you, Junie?"

"If I come across a deal breaker," she squeezed his palm in hers, "you will be the very first to know."

46

Chapter 51

Cory stood near the sink as Hailey handed off the washed dinner pots. He only had a couple more days with the kid. Given the choice, she had decided to stay in and practice her vegetarian cooking skills, which weren't half bad. They made sweet potato korma over basmati rice. Hailey had cut little bits of cilantro over it, a real chef. Just looking at her made his eyes narrow in anticipation of how stressed she was going to be once school started up again, how few easy moments like this they would get now that she was starting her junior year. Time might not move in a straight line in Shawn's world, but sadly, in Cory's it did.

Dishes done, Hailey moved to the office to Facetime her mother before she and Cory settled in to watch a movie.

"She wants to say hi, Daddo."

Veronica smiled, in her big glasses, her face tanner and shinier than he remembered it. "You look good, V."

"Thanks. Hey." Veronica sighed. "Have you read the paper today?"

Of course not. She told him to check the obituaries. Then, before Hailey could begin asking why, Veronica changed the subject to Thea.

"That piece in Wired? Is she okay? Either she's incredibly brilliant or a crazy person."

Cory smiled at Hailey, who peered back with an inquisitive expression. "Obviously she's not that smart or she wouldn't be dating me."

Veronica and Hailey made friendly, dismissive noises.

"Okay, okay. She's smart, in her own way. What she really is, is on another plane of reality."

"Sounds perfect for you, Cor." Veronica smirked.

"Enjoy your Saturday, V."

Cory handed the phone back to his daughter.

Veronica knew Cory didn't read press. He would never forgive those self-important wheeze bags for how they'd told his and Shawn's story, trying to make it his fault, or the girlfriend's, or Shawn's mother's, or anyone else's besides Shawn himself. He hated the instant rage he felt at the mere thought of the press.

He poured himself a glass of cabernet and called up the obituary page. Shawn's girlfriend Suki was dead. Age 39. Suki, the girl who tried to get Shawn sober. The press had dragged her, the fans had been even worse. Ignorant morons. No idea how addiction worked, how Shawn had tried. His stomach felt the wine like a blast of acid. No.

He was not going to let this bother him. He was sad, but he wasn't going to let Hailey see that, or ask why. He switched his glass of wine for a can of sparkling water and stuck a bag of popcorn in the microwave. It spun round and round, while Hailey said goodbye to her mom and went to change into pajamas.

Suki being gone meant one less tether to keep Shawn's ghost tied to the world. Should he miss that? Should he be glad he was no longer deranged enough to speak to ghosts? Seriously. Cory took a bowl from a cupboard. How should he feel?

Relief. That was all. Did that make him a bad person? He didn't really have anything against Suki. He wouldn't know her if they met in the street. She appeared after Shawn was estranged from nearly everyone else. Cory had regarded her as an obvious opportunist, but it was nothing personal. For that reason, Cory had done nothing to help her after Shawn died, had never reached out, never said that he didn't blame her. The thought that she needed to hear something like that never crossed his mind until that moment. Shawn's family took care of her. Or someone did. Cory hadn't seen her since the memorial show, and that had been such an overstimulating day: all he could remember was her scalp with its creeping octopus tattoo, how beautiful she had been with her expressionless face, black with eyeliner, her thick boots. She looked like someone who would survive the loss. But now she was dead, rejoined with Shawn, for all he knew. If so, he was glad. Glad Shawn was no longer haunting the beach, looking across the water at Thea's.

Hailey appeared in mismatched pajamas. They were going to watch a series Cory only consented to for reasons of nostalgia. The sets, the actors, the music, all out of his youth recycled with extra sparkle and cool. The most important thing was watching Hailey's face, one moment a girl, the next a woman, reflecting the glow of his big screen TV. He saw as she came closer that his attempt to keep her off the topic of Suki had failed.

"She drowned in a hot tub." Hailey read from her phone. "What a horrible way to die. Dad, swear you won't ever fall asleep in a hot tub, please? And you'll be careful on your vacation?"

"I swear, baby." He placed the bowl of popcorn on the coffee table. "If you promise me the same."

She giggled, the notion of her own death a stupid dad joke. He kissed her on the head and settled in beside her.

"Can I come with you next time?"

"If you can get the time away from Mama, of course."

"I want to see the Android. Would Thea let me? I want to do a project on it for school."

"Show's starting."

"I can ask her myself."

"Let's get through the first week of classes, okay? See what your plans are then."

"Are you breaking up?"

He pushed her hair out of her face. "Who taught you to be so nosy?"

"Uh, you did. You said absolutely nothing comes to those who wait."

"Mmmm. I did say that. Didn't I?"

She giggled.

The water at Haena Beach was perfect for a person to float in, waves high enough for body surfing but not for boards, the sand shelf consistently gentle below. But what Thea loved most about the place was the cliffside across the road, a vast nesting site for Frigate Birds with their long dark wings and elegant swallow tails. The place looked like a Japanese fairy tale, thick with green, pocked with dark nests and bodies in motion.

Would Suki have drowned here, in this warm and crowded water? Probably not. Someone would have noticed her slipping under. Why had she come? True, Thea had invited her to the house once, hadn't she, not just to the grave? Bragged about her outdoor shower? She had thought just for one flickering moment that Suki might become a friend. Someone to swim with, someone who could tell her more about Maggie. Thea was responsible, at least partially. She couldn't have friends. But she had Adriel. If Adriel had been at the house then, Suki would still be alive.

Thea remembered Suki's hand on her wrist that day on Secret Beach, the way her voice had lowered and slowed like a broken recording, trying to break through to Thea with just *how sad* Grady School had been to lose Maggie. She had become so angry. She was so full of feeling. Even now, when Thea was living like a normal person without Lee in her house, dating Cory and going to the office, ordinary activities that a healthy woman would do, she doubted she could pivot to feel what Suki wanted her to, about the Grady school, about Maggie.

Deb, the school director, had called to say they should come see the paper poster with its little childish remembrances, *I'm going to miss Maggie because...*

Her hair is pretty

She chooses Frances at story time

Chester likes to eat her baby carrots

Suki had behaved fairly normally at the visit. But she hadn't offered to give away any parts of the fading *shrine*, the dehydrated daisy chains, or popsicle stick dolls, the finger-pocked lumps of colored clay.

"As I said, Thea." Suki had her face turned away. "She was loved, deeply loved. Maggie had a whole community here."

"Thanks for showing us." Lee said, pulling Thea away without a word, putting distance between her and the butcher paper with its low-resolution portraits of Maggie.

"I'm so glad you could find the time to come. I guess Deb told you this was Octopus Group's last day at school. Purple group. They graduated."

"Octopus Group Graduated?" Lee said. Thea thought he might be laughing. "Did you pick that name? I like it."

Suki spoke in the urgent low voice again. "The children picked it."

The sky was unfathomably blue. Shawn said Thea had *work to do*. Did he know that the children at Grady School had drawn on butcher paper, rainbows and stars and rabbits, for his biological child? No. It wasn't a place he knew. And now, she could not tell him. Because he was no longer visible to her. But one thing was, and had been even at the Grady School; Suki was more than just Maggie's teacher. The connection Thea had sensed was real. When the obituary was published, it was not a shock to her. Suki had been Shawn's lover and muse at the time he died. They had been recording an album together. They had performed in clubs in Bellingham and Portland.

The birds were really more like flying stars in a Kung Fu movie, silent and intent. Thea pushed the water, liquid slipping between fingers, her ears under the waterline listening to the roar and hush of the waves.

Adriel was like a B52 bomber, Craig said. *People could use the tech for almost anything they wanted.* She said it needed to be an iPhone. She insisted they go slowly with the Beta version, make everyone sign dozens of redundant waivers. So many things could go wrong. Craig showed the team art depicting cyborg armies, made them watch television shows with androids that could pass for humans bent on bloody revenge. Everyone teased him, reminded that they had fail-safes in the code, and no one would ever mistake Adriel or the next generations of Adriel for a living being. They started calling him *Singularity Bjornson*. Which he loved.

Thea told them that handwringing was pointless. They had all the research now. The tech was coming. Androids were being produced all over the world, in China, Germany, Russia, Mexico, and Japan. There was a shop in the Philippines making *smart sex jaguars* for arcades. Craig was high on their delivery list for a beta version.

Would they suffer? She doubted it. But if they did, then didn't that mean they were alive, and wasn't that incredible? She heard Ben's laughter in her head. *You should have thought of this, honey. Now you're like Captain Kirk to these fucking things and you know what they did to Kirk, don't you? They tried to throw him in the volcano!* Customers were clamoring to get on the wait list: governments, armies, hospitality chains, cruise lines, medical groups, high-net-worth individuals. Many of the beta testing volunteers were obvious spies. The team was spending huge resources vetting people.

Children screamed as waves broke over them, someone shouting about a turtle. The B52 was a bomber, a weapon of war. Adriel needed to be the opposite of that. A cell phone could be used for anything: a tool. And for Thea, a way to do what Shawn, her imaginary friend, had brought her back for. To help keep the world alive for more generations to live, like the birds and the turtle and the screaming children on the shore.

"Hey, Calypso. Sorry it took me so long to get down here. I was talking to Hailey."

Cory's triangular face appeared calm in the water, the lines in his forehead invisible. It wasn't just the sea. Since he had brought her to see Magic Matteo at the rock star friend's house party and gotten sucked into marathon jam sessions, Cory had been a new person, copper colored, smiling, his head subtly looser on its stem. He hadn't shaved for days.

"Were you playing?"

"Well, yes. Talking to Hailey and playing. Can't help it."

"Is anyone recording all this music you're making?"

He laughed. "Now why would we do that? We're too busy having fun."

Matteo had come and gone, but not before telling Thea a story about a helicopter crash he saw one snowy day. He said the moment was so profound he would never be the same. She thought, *you and me both*, but kept it to herself. In person, Magic Matteo had the heavy-lidded ethos of a self-styled shaman. He asked too many questions. Did she know what had caused the crash? Had she returned to the scene? He wondered, if he could be so bold, if the authorities had ruled out foul play?

"How's Hailey?"

"Cranky. There's no snow. I told her to grab a flight over, but she's supposed to be skiing with her mom. And it's immoral to fly in airplanes. And there's friend drama, you know."

"You look like a pirate. I like it."

"Excellent, m'lady." He dunked his hair behind him. "I'm going to visit the rocks. You good? You know there's a riptide down there?"

She waved him away, moving vertical as a set of four-foot waves rolled them up and down. Cory's flippers and snorkel kicked away. Thea didn't want to think about the accident, how it looked to Matteo, if such a thing could happen again in a world without snow. She wanted to know if her blood rippled with the passing of the waves, or if her body loved being in water so much because it reminded her of being in amniotic fluid. Did a body remember?

Thea moved to avoid a couple of kids on boogie boards. Cory waved from the rocks, pointing with his finger to show she ought to swim away. The Cory she saw here was nothing like the stony-faced man on Secret Beach, smoking and muttering to Shawn's ghost. This Cory could play anything, drums, guitars, keyboards. He could adapt to whatever the others were doing. They were intimate, him and his friends. He and Shawn must have been like that, too. She would never know what that was like, but maybe Adriel could. Maybe a little bit like her and Ben, and Lee. But with music. The thing they had sent into space the moment space travel became possible. The thing of such beauty, humanity had to share.

When they had sex, Thea said, "You're trying to improvise with me."

"Maybe."

"That's good. Keep going."

47

Chapter 52

On a rainy Tuesday morning, Lee met Thea and June and June's boyfriend, the big man named Cal, at the Lion's Gate Bridge. He had not seen Thea since he left Seattle, which was almost a year now. The condo complex was sold. Lee had used the money to buy a house for himself and his mother and sister and her two kids. He lived in the basement and was studying to become a licensed contractor. Thea sent him pictures of herself in places, in Hawaii, in Berlin, on the Great Wall of China. She said she was making a lot of progress with her robots and all the businesses that came out of those. Software, robotics, manufacturing, carbon capture, all words that she loved to say. He sent back pictures of food, and she laughed every time. He did not miss her so much, or Allen, who had agreed to divorce after a week of pouting. He had gotten more money from Thea. It was all so easy. Except for the memory part.

Thea sat in Ben's old place in the passenger seat, which Ben would have liked, or at least laughed at. Traffic was slow leaving Vancouver, but it cleared as soon as they got to Whistler Highway. June and Cal talked of Canada, asking how Lee had ever come to live in the States when he had healthcare and family in Vancouver.

"I came to visit San Francisco," Lee answered. "And decided to see some of the world before my family needed me back."

Thea watched him, smiling silently. He looked out the window.

Cal seemed to want to keep talking. "You say the investigators are meeting us there?"

"That's right. With my lawyer."

"The sick one?"

Thea looked at him with a certain stillness in her face. In the overcast light, the scar on her neck below her left ear was more visible than usual.

"No, not Lars. Ramona. She has headed up the investigation.""Oh. The investigation."

June reached over and patted Cal's arm.

"Yes. I think we have a clear picture of what happened. But I wanted to put all the pieces of the puzzle together with everyone involved." Thea rubbed her head. "Everyone who is still able to speak for themselves."

Cal heaved a big sigh. He looked worried. Why? This was their family, not his. But maybe he was marrying June or had married her already. Lee didn't know. It was normal for Thea to leave out a detail like that.

"Will you turn on some music, please?" he said.

But she didn't. They all understood he wanted them to stop talking. They rode in silence, the straight whipped with little puffs of foam. Men came in wooden ships to take this land, once. It must have been miserable for them. People will do anything to see their own face continue into the future, their eyes, their ideas, their ambition. Ben always talked about this. How we are animals, only.

At Sequim they turned off the highway and followed the GPS to a helicopter charter company. It was a series of metal buildings in a clearing in the forest. Everything needed paint and the landing pads could use some power washing. Maybe the crash had caused the owners to lose money. Or maybe they were already not taking good care of their business. Lee helped June climb out of the van.

"Thank you, dear."

Thea stood looking around at where the helicopter had taken off. She had to knock twice before the door opened. Inside was a woman the same age as June, with grown-out highlights in her short hair, wearing a man's bomber jacket over a yellow polyester sweater. Her energy was slow and angry. Thea might not notice, but June saw.

She hesitated for a long moment before entering the woman's wood paneled office with its dusty shelves and old computer. Cal said he would stay outside. The place felt bad. It smelled like anti-fungal soap and cigarettes. Lee entered and stood behind Thea. This was the last part of Ben he could help with. He was ready. They were all ready. June and Thea moved to chairs in front of the desk and everyone spoke at once. He found it impossible to follow the conversation. He studied the photos on the walls, the certificates and charts. A lot of men in sunglasses and earphones, smiling from cockpits, all ages. Maybe the Same men at different ages. Some of the pictures were old, like the office. One of them was autographed by someone, the line of scrawled name faded into a colorless outline. A starburst.

Lee put his hands together and spoke a silent blessing. Why do people buy cheap detergent when they can make their places smell better so easily?

The women were looking into a big, black book.

Out the window, a muddy black SUV pulled into the parking lot. The doors all opened at once, like an insect spreading its wings. Ramona and three other people in dark suits walked toward them, very fast. Too many people for this small office. The women were already standing. He moved to open the door.

Then he stepped outside, and let the door close behind him. He could hear them explaining themselves, voices rising in pitch. Tension. Anger, maybe.

It was so kind of Thea to forget to tell them to depose him. It never occurred to Ramona, nor to June. As they searched for the reason why Thea and Ben and Maggie had taken a dangerous helicopter flight. As they tried to understand what important business event had made them leave their conference early. Because they could not find one.

Lee smiled at Cal, who looked away hurriedly.

"Going to stretch my legs."

That meant he wanted to go pee in the trees.

Lee closed his eyes. On the other side of the wall, voices were getting louder. Thea didn't speak, but June was yelling, as she sometimes did. She was there as a distraction, maybe. Or was she curious? Like Lee. Just wanting to see where it happened.

Maybe she was having a day like he was, feeling like a broken bone that is holding too much weight, but the pain must be carried. Or the limb will die completely.

The people in suits went back to their SUV and closed the door. They were talking to each other in rapid, important voices. But they weren't upset. They seemed calm. Scaring people was their business, maybe. The door was left ajar. The woman inside was speaking in a high, thin voice, yelling almost, very angry, very frightened. Thea was silent. Ramona was taking pictures with a big camera.

"For heaven's sake," June said to Cal as he stood panting. "We lost a child, too."

"How old was her boy?" Cal asked.

"Twenty-eight," June said. "Her youngest. He was certified, we saw the papers. It was poor judgment on their part going up in a snowstorm. The Canadians called it an accident."

Called it an accident? What else did Thea think it was? Lee went back in.

Thea was sitting. The lady had stopped screaming, but she looked like she might start again. "The TSB took everything. You need to talk to them. You can't sue me now."

"Mrs. Gould,i" Ramona said. "We have spoken to them. We're not here for a lawsuit."

"My family never, we never in thirty-three years of business, had a situation like this. I warned you. I warned you."

Thea didn't respond.

"My client sustained a head injury," Ramona said.

"I know. I know all about that."

"Then you'll understand she won't remember the situation you're referring to."

"Okay. But I do. I remember very well. She and her husband insisting, *insisting* that we fly them that day. Here's the signature." She glared through her metal frames.

Thea sighed.

"Yes. Once again, we are not here to sue you, Mrs. Gould."

"Yeah, you said." Mrs. Gould's eyes fell to the desk. She made an angry face that was probably sadness, like Allen sometimes did.

"You have the advantage over me, Mrs. Gould, in that you remember your son. You know what happened. I understand there were errors in judgement, things we wish we could go back and do again. But it would be a kindness to me, if you could help me with context, at least?"

"You don't have any brain damage."

Thea laughed. "Do you want to feel the plate in my head?"

"Don't make light." The woman pushed her glasses up her nose. "The boys warned you about the situation at the resort, the avalanche, the blizzard."

"I was told there had never been such a bad blizzard in November. Climate change. No one could have predicted."

"It shouldn't have mattered." The woman's voice climbed. "You shouldn't have insisted; you shouldn't have put a small business in that position."

"Okay. So, it was our fault for needing to get back to Seattle. Do you have any idea *why?*"

"Brain or no, you're the same." Mrs. Gould made a sour face.

Lee's skin prickled, coming alive. He felt like the day of the accident. Like he was stronger than a machine, like he could pick something huge up from the ground and smash it with his bare hands. His lips opened without him wanting them to. His breath was too quick, too short.

"The reason was because you said so. You and your husband, a pair of pushy, nouveau riche..."

"No." Lee said in a very loud voice, in Ben's voice maybe, or his own when he was very angry. He was very angry. He moved next to the desk. "No."

Mrs. Gould startled, fear in her face.

"You are upset," he said. He was able to sound calm, now that he understood. "You are sad. That is normal. But. Thea has worked very hard to come back. She is asking these questions from love. Her love is so strong she feels it even without being able to remember."

Lee had not heard Thea cry aloud since her coma. It lasted only a minute or two, Thea sobbing into her hands, Ramona quick with tissues, the old woman's face turning red.

"We came here with an offer to make things right for you," Ramona said in a cold, lawyer's voice. "The Sun Family was prepared to pay for the helicopter and something for the family."

Mrs. Gould's face changed. Ramona stopped talking.

"Just give her the check."

Mrs. Gould's face was changing color from white to red, very quickly, like a jellyfish. She drew in her breath to speak, but Thea was already moving out the door. Ramona placed an envelope on the desk. They closed the door behind them.

Thea's hand found his. "Do you want to tell me?"

He stopped at the driver's side door. Cal and June were inside. Ramona and the others in the black SUV were driving away, mud splashing from their tires on the dirt road.

"It was my fault." His voice felt light, like a puff of steam. "I said I was missing you, and maybe I wish I had come, too. Maybe I wanted to show Maggie the green sky, the aurora."

She held his hand between her two. He thought of the X-rays, all the pins inside them. In another life, he could have been a surgeon.

"It is not your fault," she said. "We are only here to say goodbye. But we never really do, right?"

"I should have told you this a long time ago." He moved to open his door. "No one should speak to ghosts alone."

48

Chapter 53

Thea asked him to go to a place someone had told her about, ten- or eleven-minutes' drive from the helicopter office. They turned onto a dirt road, very muddy, trees thick on both sides. The GPS said they had reached their destination.

Thea was out of the door before Lee understood what they were seeing. He parked and left June and Cal still in their seatbelts, asking what was happening.

Thea stood in the rain, arms outstretched, eyes closed.

"Are you okay?"

She opened her eyes. "Yes. Just checking."

"Checking for what?"

"To see if anything of me is left here. Anything of them."

She pointed to a place where two trees were broken, and below that, where a part of the ground was all mud and small bushes. A place where there had been a big impact, something heavy smashing the trees. There were scars, pale yellow tree flesh, dark broken bark, and smears of red, where paint had scraped off.

Lee felt himself break into two pieces then, a part that stood watching Thea as she walked slowly, looking all around herself as if someone was going to appear and speak. The other part was crying, harder even than the woman in the helicopter office.

"Lee, honey. Are you alright?" June said.

He nodded, making a small smile so she wouldn't ask anything more.

When he dropped them, Thea took his hand. Her eyes were bright. She said words of farewell and thanks, but he didn't hear them. He waited for the Tesla to drive away before starting the van to drive back to his mother's house. But he didn't go there. He drove around until he found the country lane where he and Ben had first found each other in the back of the van.

Rain had started to fall, so Lee sat in the back of the van, which was empty now because he was in school and not working, the cold metal floor on his back through his shirt. He lay there, thinking of Ben's hands, fumbling with Lee's clothing, his kisses. The look on his face when he said he had been waiting for his chance, that he knew from the moment they met that Lee would be his lover. Lee watched the rain on his windshield, a place where the wiper blade was broken like a wider gash in the gray blobs of color, the green trees above him. Ben would have moved on from him already, because that was Ben's way. He was cynical. He was used to having anything he wanted, letting the people he loved live with how he was. But underneath, Ben was afraid. He said he could never leave Thea, because of business. But it was not business.

Thea knew what Ben wanted, just like she knew what people wanted. Robots, ancestors, money, to be needed, to be let go. She had let Lee go. She told him after the dead wife day, when he was crying in the kitchen and they sat for a long time in the dark, that he was free to go. She would help him if he needed. But she would be working from that moment on, and not home much, except to be with Cory and his daughter, or to swim. She said, "I will say this if you promise not to laugh," so he had promised.

Thea said, smiling through her white fake teeth, "I will always remember what we were. I will never forget."

And then they had laughed and laughed, until they both cried.

The floor on his back was cold. The trees looked black. Lee wiped the tears from his eyes, seeing in the cracks of his cell phone glass that his mother and his boyfriends had been calling him. He had several boyfriends, no one serious. He was hungry. He was tired.

He didn't want to see Thea again. It was like looking at the gash in the side of the big trees in the forest outside Sequim, a broken place. It was no good to look too long at things like that. He would go back to building. He would go eat the food his mother was making. Thea was going to make her things, her tech devices, her androids that tried to care for people as he had cared. It was enough. He wanted now to eat, and laugh at his mother's television shows, and then sleep. Tomorrow, he would begin to forget.

By the time they got to June's ranch, it was Cal crying. His big body in the back seat heaved, causing Thea's car to tremble, His sobs felt surreal, like watching a movie. She knew she was unkind to assume Cal was performing. Or dissociating because of strong emotions. Maybe that. Where was her own father now? Did he think of her the way she did Cal, like a living creature devoid of connection to herself? If so, it wasn't her fault. It wasn't Cal's fault. She needed to be brave and allow this man to be human. The harder thing was to think of him as a person, a full person, like Bethany Gould of Adventure Air in Sequim, British Columbia. People with their tears.

June asked no questions. Her face peering out the front windshield didn't waver or turn. The sky was baby blue with soft gray cotton clouds, the highest streaks bright white, like a cathedral ceiling. Cal ought to look out and see.

The Tesla crunched down June's gravel driveway, coming to rest on the side of the house away from the main road. Cal was sobbing, like waves on a beach, a big intake of breath and a long, deep wail.

At the emergency meeting with Eleanor, June had defended Cal. She said, "You don't understand. A normal person can't make it in this world. Health insurance? Student loans? Retirement? It's a rigged system. I understand he committed a crime. I do. But..."

The sun had gone down by this point in the meeting, leaving a smear of plum-jam purple over the lake. They were in the Foundation's smaller conference room. Thea looked down through the courtyard to Building Three, where Craig was testing Adriel's fine motor skills by teaching her ukulele. It was a disaster, but the data was going to be useful. A surprising number of lights shone out from the buildings, people working.

"You're sweet on him, June."

"Would you like to talk about sweetness?"

"About...what?" Eleanor made a tiny smile.

Thea spoke softly. "Okay. Would you like to talk about relationships clouding judgements? Causing people to do things they might not, otherwise? Take risks, or betray commitments? Should we talk about that?"

Eleanor's face shone with the effort to be patient. "I'm sorry. That covers a whole lot of ground. Where are *we* in all this, Thea?"

"Eleanor, there's no *we*. I think you know that. I think you've known that for a long time."

"I don't...I see." Eleanor turned her eyes to June. "I should have seen this coming."

June's eyebrows shot up. "Honey, no one is perfect. But if you're going to make mistakes, at least make useful ones."

"You haven't let me do anything here."

"No," Thea agreed. "I am sure you'll be happier in a position where you don't have anyone thwarting you. Where you have free reign to create all the change you want to see in the world."

"Are you making fun of me?"

Thea exchanged a glance with June. "You aren't on contract. But HR will offer a generous severance package. Wherever you go from here, no one at SunStorm will stand in your way."

Eleanor was trembling. "You duplicitous hag."

"Love to Lars," Thea called out, just before the slamming of the door.

Early evening was one of the most beautiful times at June's place, Rancho Junio. When they had removed Thea's overnight case from the car, Thea helped Cal feed the animals. One of the goats pawed at its paddock trying to reach Thea.

"Oh, now Cassie," Cal said. "Leave her be."

Thea rubbed the place between the goat's eyes. It tried to bite her hand. She snatched the hand back.

"Cassie, I need that."

"They're kind of mean," Cal said.

"Or maybe just lonely. They've been here alone all day."

"Yup. I'm sorry for all the crying. By the way." He said in a jokey voice. "I'm usually a very macho man, no emotions."

Thea put her hand on his forearm. "You fucked up. Right?"

"I should agree to that. Apologize, beg for forgiveness. But to be honest, the last six months are the first time I've been able to sleep at night for years. So, I won't lie. I didn't hurt you. The benefit to me and my ability to be present with your mother is not nothing. I understand if you want to punish me for it. But what I wouldn't be able to fathom is why you'd want to punish *her*."

"Okay."

Cal followed her outside.

"What a relief."

"The speech? It was okay. I give it a five."

"Only five? I've been practicing all day."

They stood in the scrub grass, under the pines. Thea loved this part of her mother's property, where the ground was soft with old needles and smelled like Christmas.

"What kind of consequence do you think you deserve?"

"I think you should have it out with me in front of your mother. She already guesses the truth, but I want her to see that you know it. I want her burden lifted."

"She is up to speed on this."

He looked like he was going to cry again.

"What else?"

He kicked a pinecone. "You want money back?"

"Don't be dumb. If we do that, she'll just pay your way and you will both question why you're actually together."

"I really do care for June. Thea. You need to know that."

"Okay. Here's what we're going to do."

"We?"

"I need all hands on deck. You've shown you're an original thinker. Not overly troubled by rules."

Cal stepped back from her. "What are you asking?"

"Not asking. You work for me now."

He blinked slowly. "I would be happy...to...come on board?"

"Excellent. Offer accepted."

He stared at her in the low light of the barn, but Thea was already turning to walk away.

49

Chapter 54

Thea drove to all the haunted places she could think of, but no one was there. Every place was one-dimensional, Harborview with its rushing hallways, the courthouse with its wet marble floors, the Island ferries. She explained to Mary that she was going to be meditating in these locations, but clearly her bodyguard needed no explanation.

"Whatever you say, Boss Lady."

Thea laughed every time.

The only places she still felt the pull of ghost voices was under Sun Storm, but even there it was unclear whether what she was hearing was the pulse of a trapped spirit, or just the imperceptible hum of the COHE server farms.

At Maggie's grave, Thea found it hard to focus on the task of inviting the dead to talk to her. She brought things she was remembering had been her daughter's favorites, belly buster donuts, Japanese movies, a pair of metallic butterfly hair clips she'd found in the yurt. Her offerings sat in the clearing atop the circular stone, moldering. Occasionally, Thea would find the stone empty. She suspected Cal and June were behind it. Sometimes there were drying flowers there, daffodils and sweetheart roses, from the grocery store near the ferry dock.

What she never found were ghosts.

www.ingramcontent.com/pod-product-compliance
Lightning Source LLC
Chambersburg PA
CBHW020321030826
48979CB00022B/607